PRAISE FOR
THE BROKEN MOON SERIES
F.T. LUKENS

"Lukens writes a satisfying balance of action and romance in a science fiction setting that will feel familiar to fans of the genre… Add this title to young adult sci-fi collections, and expect readers to eagerly anticipate the next book in the series."

—*School Library Journal* on *The Star Host*

"*The Star Host* by F.T. Lukens hooked me from the blurb. It still hasn't let me go, and I finished reading it hours ago. I want more… like right, the heck now. I need more Asher and Ren in my life. You need more Asher and Ren in your lives."

—*Prism Book Alliance* on *The Star Host*

"The short version is that this book is amazing, and I am hard-pressed to be more coherent than ASKLJFDAH and OMGFLAIL."

—D.E Atwood, author of *If We Shadows* on *The Star Host*

"Fans of queer sci-fi adventure, this is the series for you. Start at *The Star Host* and plow right on through *Ghosts & Ashes* in one go. Told in Lukens' no-nonsense prose, this story will draw you in and not let go."

—*Teen Vogue* on *Ghosts & Ashes*

"This is a rollicking adventure that blends elements from westerns, sci-fi, YA, and romance into a cohesive page-flipping thrill ride."

—*Foreword Reviews* on *Ghosts & Ashes*

ZENITH DREAM

DREAM

F.T. Lukens

interlude press • new york

interlude press • new york

"The history of liberty is a history of resistance."

—Woodrow Wilson

Some readers may find some of the scenes in this book difficult to read. We have compiled a list of content warnings, which you can access at www.interludepress.com/content-warnings

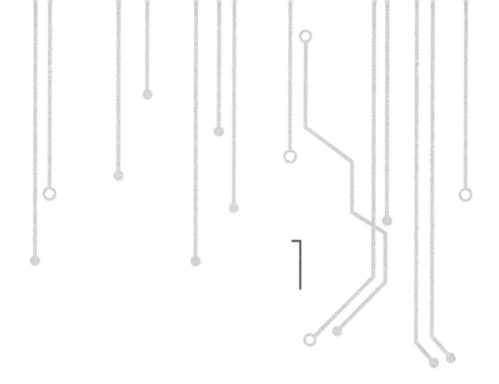

Wake up!

Ren snapped his eyes open and gasped. His back arched, and his body pulled taut, suspended in air by his shoulders and heels, before he flopped back to a hard surface. He gulped in oxygen. Wheezing, his lungs ached. His body shivered from the influx of adrenaline and from the frigid air; goosebumps bloomed over his skin. He weakly raised his head.

He was alone. The ship was dark, lit only by emergency lights. Ren pushed to a sitting position with trembling arms; his muscles were feeble. His chest heaved, his breath puffed out in clouds in front of his face, and the blanket that covered him fell and pooled into his lap. Bent forward, Ren grasped the bed railing next to him, and the cold metal burned against his palm.

Was this real? Or was it another dream with sense memories so stark they fooled him? Was he awake this time? Was he in the ship?

The bed beneath him was hard and unforgiving; a thin mattress was all that separated him from a flat slab of metal. He smelled of antiseptic and sweat. A thin tube, currently attached to nothing, stung in the crook of his arm. He rubbed his chest; the scratchy fabric of medical scrubs pulled across his stomach, caught on something, and tugged uncomfortably on his skin. Possibly not a dream—too many sensations.

Brow furrowed, Ren lifted the hem of his shirt. White tape and gauze crisscrossed a spot far left of his navel and above his hip. Tentatively, he pulled at the bandages to reveal a dark, bloody, and scabbed wound: a jagged circle of flesh, not quite healed, but not angry and new. Starbursts of yellow and green and brown spread outward from it and bled up his torso in a sickly, painful bruise.

Ren slammed his eyes shut and sat awash in memories that scrubbed him raw, caused bile to crawl up into his throat, and sent his heart pounding. Pain and smoke and rubble. Falling, the Corps, and Asher amid the chaos. Crei and Millicent and Vos and Asher trying to save him. Prophecies and blood and dreams of Liam and *Asher leaving.* He pushed his hand against the gunshot wound, smoothing the tape with unsteady fingers.

Don't look at it. Don't look at it. Don't look at it.

Hunched over, he reached out with his star, and the familiar signature of the ship welcomed him, calmed him, and staved off the impending panic. He didn't recognize this bed or this blanket or the room he was in, but he was on the *Star Stream.* He was safe on the ship, *in* the ship, but for now he resisted the urge to flee into the circuits.

He was awake: a state of being he hadn't thought he would achieve again.

He'd watched, of course. He'd been detached from it all, within the confines of circuits and switches and vid screens. He'd heard the messages on the comms, the disagreements about what to do, the times Rowan cried in her room, and when Ollie stalked the cargo bay. He'd seen Pen brush his dark hair from his forehead and Lucas pilot with bloodshot eyes. At other times, everything was black and muted, as if he was at the bottom of the lake and all his sensation was filtered through the water: sound and touch distorted by pressure and movement, sight blurred by currents and shadows. Still other times, he'd dreamed nightmares and visions so real he'd thought for certain he was awake, only to be plunged back into the depths of his body or sent scurrying for safety into the signals that sparked between relays.

Ren opened his eyes. He pressed the heel of his hand to his forehead and shook his head, trying to ease the fog in his brain. Everything was vague and strange. He had spent an indeterminate amount of time transferring between the ship and his comatose body, and his ability to perceive and process wasn't quite aligned.

"Hello?" his voice cracked in his throat. "Anyone there?" The words were clumsy in his mouth, and the raspy sound petered out into a breathy whisper.

Where was everyone? How long had he been asleep?

The *Star Stream* was powered down; reserve lights gave a gentle glow, and the core systems hummed softly, lazily, as they drew power, not from the engines, but from a power source beyond the shiny bulkhead. They were docked on a drift, but not one Ren recognized. The unfamiliar tech buzzed hazily in the back of his head. The noise was not nearly as loud as Mykonos or Delphi, indicating the drift was smaller.

Swinging his legs over the side of the bed, Ren gingerly stepped down and hissed as the pad of his foot touched the cold deck. Keeping his grip on the bedrails, he slid farther, pressed more weight against his feet. His atrophied legs clenched, and he hobbled like the newborn lambs on Erden. After a few tense moments, he steadied enough to fully straighten.

Ren grabbed the blanket and draped it over his shoulders. Unsure but determined, he lurched from the bed to the wall, stumbled, and clung to the doorframe. His body shook as he moved through the opening and found himself in the hallway through the crew quarters. Taking stock, Ren realized he'd been in Ollie's room, while his own was farther down the hall. But where was Ollie? Where was Rowan? Or Lucas? Or Penelope?

Stars, he was addled. Splaying his hand against the wall, he entered the ship and swept along the vid screens and the comm system. No one was onboard, not even Lucas who tended to stay with the ship. He scanned the ship's messages, and the last received was to Rowan, which stated a date and a time and a location. A coordinated exchange— Rowan was still doing business?

Ren flinched at the date. Six weeks had passed since Crei. He'd been asleep for six weeks. Asher had been gone for that whole time. Where was he? Why hadn't Rowan found him?

He disengaged from the ship and slid to the floor; the wound in his side twinged, reminding him of the reason he'd been asleep for so long. He gauged the small progress he'd made down the hall and sighed. Settling back into his body would be difficult, especially if being corporeal meant being trapped in flesh that didn't want to obey him and moved slowly. Already he was exhausted, and hunger gnawed his stomach. He touched the tube in his arm, and wondered if that was how Penelope had kept him alive.

Wrapping up in the blanket, Ren sent a blast of heat to his location, enough to warm the air and to stop the shivers that traveled up his body. Content to rest until his friends returned, he let his eyelids droop.

Would they be surprised to see him? Would they be happy that he was finally awake? Would they turn him away once he was stronger?

No. They wouldn't, and doubting them was an insult to the loyalty and kindness they'd shown him. He banished the thoughts, recognizing them for the poison they were. If only he'd recognized Asher's devotion when he'd had the chance.

Asher.

Ren's heart seized. He'd screwed up. He'd pushed Asher away and now he was gone. He could only wonder what he was doing now. Was he being punished for being AWOL? Was he being lauded for killing the star host who had attacked them on Erden? Did he think of Ren at all? Fondly? Indifferently? Ren swallowed around the lump in his throat. His only choice was to make it right. To fix it. And he would. If it cost him his last breath, he'd talk with Asher one more time and do what he could to make everything right between them. Whatever it took, he'd do it, because he needed Asher, because his feelings for Asher were deep and affectionate and like nothing he held for anyone else.

With that decided, Ren drifted, on the edge of sleep, cozy and gradually warmer wrapped in a blanket on the deck plate. He dreamed about an orange sun and a sandy shore and a clear blue lake. He dreamed about splashing in the froth and the green canopy of trees and a breeze that ruffled his hair.

As he slipped deeper into his doze, a disturbance shook him awake. He startled, eyes sliding open. Someone approached the ship from the drift, and their presence bristled over Ren's skin; his power alerted him to whoever was crossing the barrier he'd unconsciously created around the ship.

Ren merged with the *Star Stream*. Spying them from the security cameras, his hope that it was Rowan or one of the others fizzled when he saw the pair of youths huddled close to the bay door. Hats pulled low and dark scarfs over their features, they attempted to bypass the lock, inserting a chip and a code. Amused, Ren mustered a smile and blocked their inelegant attempt to open the door. They cursed when their override didn't work.

"Cogs! I thought you said the universal key would let us in," one hissed.

The other shrugged. "It does on most ships. Just not on this one."

"That confirms the theory then."

"How does that confirm the theory? It just means they have stronger locks than the other fools docked around here."

"They have stronger locks because they have something they want to hide."

Interest piqued, Ren focused in on the speaker—a girl with hair as black as his home's night sky save for streaks of nebula purple that peeked from beneath her cap and with dark eyes that darted between the door and her companion.

"Yeah, how do you know?"

She pulled down her scarf to reveal olive skin and a mouth she pressed into a thin, annoyed line. "It's my job to know. Okay? Trust me." She flashed an impish smile.

Her companion shook his head. "In case you haven't noticed, Darby, we live on the outermost drift in the cluster. Your information could be years old."

"Don't doubt me. I told you, there is something on this ship that the Phoenix Corps wants badly enough to chase it planet-side."

Ren physically recoiled, and pain flared up his torso. He snapped into his body; the back of his head smacked into the bulkhead. *The Corps.* Anxiety coursed through him, and he scrambled to his feet. He stumbled down the hallway, unsure where he was going, knowing only that he needed to move, escape. Breathing hard, he ducked into the common area, tumbled past the dining table, and fell to the deck in front of the worn couch.

Forehead pressed to the cool deck floor, Ren choked on fear. His breath went reedy and thin. He exhaled in choppy pants, and in his panic, his world narrowed to the thick dread pushing through his veins, and the sweat beading along the back of his neck, and the syrupy consistency of the air. The ship called to him, and he wanted to go to the systems, be embraced by wires and electricity, but he'd done that before and lost six weeks of his life.

He fought for breath and struggled against the impulse to give in to the warmth of his power. He couldn't run from his problems. And no one was around but him. No one was here to save him or protect the ship and that fact alone was his fault. He pressed his hands flat against the floor and counted in his head. He used the familiar rhythms of the ship to time his breathing and mindfully eased the tightness of each muscle until he relaxed, boneless, against the floor.

Once his body had calmed, he catalogued the facts he knew. The Phoenix Corps thought him to be dead. They'd seen him fall. Ren had watched Rowan report that they couldn't save them. This girl, Darby, had information, but it might be limited and old. And if they were after him, they wouldn't send a pair of thieves.

Clearheaded, Ren sat up and draped his body across the front of the couch. He found it funny how surviving didn't erase the scars of the past and how panic made it difficult to be rational. Not so funny was how, in his panic, he lost his attention on the door and he didn't block the override.

The sound of the bay door opening on creaky hinges echoed through the ship. *Weeds!* Ren crawled to the comm in the common room and flicked it on with a thought.

"Third time's the charm," Darby said, her voice crackling over the open line.

"Shh, you don't know if anyone is here."

"Oh yeah, I do. Crew manifest says four hands and all four of them are on the drift. The captain and her muscle are coordinating a merchant exchange and the medic and pilot were in the marketplace picking up supplies. And I know Rowan Morgan—she doesn't trust anyone enough to leave them on ship without trusting them enough to be on the list."

Ren frowned. He eased into the ship and into the monitoring systems and the security cameras. The intruders were already in the cargo bay, wandering around the large open area, inspecting the few boxes. She kicked a crate and muttered *junk* under her breath. It was the box Ollie had given him, full of broken tech, a way for Ren to channel his energy.

Irritated, Ren crackled in the comms.

"Did you hear that?" her partner asked. "I think someone is here."

"No one is here, okay! I scoped it out. The ship is empty. I promise."

"Not quite," Ren said. "And don't kick my things." His voice rang out, its rasp echoing down the corridors and into the empty spaces. He sounded like a ghost, like the specter of a dying ship.

Darby startled, and her companion turned and ran. He jumped through the open bay door and disappeared. Before she could run, Ren sped through the systems and engaged the airlock. It slammed shut just as Darby skidded to a stop in front of it. She grasped the handle, but it wouldn't turn, and she pounded her fist on the keypad, to no avail.

"Let me out!" She threw her body against the bulkhead, then gave it a kick and cursed when her boot collided with the thick metal.

"How do you know about the Phoenix Corps following this ship?"

Darby pushed away from the airlock and narrowed her eyes. "Let me go, and I'll tell you."

"I don't bargain with thieves."

She spun around, eyes narrowed, hair falling in her face. "It's not fair that you can see me, and I can't see you. Come on out. Let's talk." She scowled. Hands in her pockets, shoulders hunched. "Besides, I haven't stolen anything."

"Yet," Ren said, noting how the side of Darby's mouth tilted up at the addendum. He swallowed, his throat dry, and leaned heavily against the wall. "You're trespassing."

"And you sound horrible. Are you sick? Quarantined? Is that why you're not on the drift with the others?" She tapped her temple. "Ah, that would explain why you're not on the manifest. Don't want to alert drift authority to a potential duster contagion. Confined to the ship, but that also means you're probably confined on the ship as well." She hopped up a step onto the stairs that led to the interior of the *Star Stream*. "You wouldn't be able to stop me, would you?" She skipped up a few more, daring, teasing.

Ren frowned. A drop of sweat rolled down his spine. "Tell me what you know about the Corps and this ship, and I'll open the door. I won't tell the captain that you were ever here."

Darby spun on her heel and jumped down to the bay floor. "She doesn't scare me."

"Then you don't know her. And I'm fine with keeping you here until she returns."

Paling slightly in the dim light of the cargo bay, Darby held up her hands. Her fingernails sparkled with purple polish. "Fine. What was the question?"

"What do you know about the Phoenix Corps and the captain?"

"It's true, isn't it? Morgan has something valuable to them. So valuable they followed the crew planet-side *twice*. Rumors say it's a weapon. That they destroyed it and took one of your crew."

Ren bristled. "Where did you hear that?"

Darby brushed her knuckles on the fabric of her shirt and ambled around the cargo bay. Discovering the camera mounted high in the corner, she moved beneath it and stared. She winked and mouthed *hi there* then blew a kiss. "I hear things. I know things. Information is currency."

"If they destroyed the object, then why are you here?"

Darby shrugged. "I don't think they actually did. Morgan has been staying away from the main drifts for several weeks. Almost like she's hiding but still in plain sight. She's staying on the outskirts."

"And?"

"And that's what I would do if I had a weapon the Corps thought they'd destroyed but hadn't. I'd still look like I was functioning as normal, but I wouldn't waltz into their den." Darby shuffled through the cargo and peered into crevices. "Nice trick with the door, by the way," she continued. "Not many are wired to close like that with remote access. It makes them too easy to open that way as well, and that's dangerous, especially in space. Who are you?"

Ren rubbed his forehead with his thumb; a headache thumped over his right eye. He resisted responding with *the weapon*. "I'm the ship."

Darby laughed. "Yeah, right. I'm guessing you're some poor dust bunny who's hitched a ride with Morgan for a few stops but isn't doing so well in transit. Space sickness? Though that's not contagious and not limited to dusters. You sound a little like a duster. And they have been planet-side. Pick you up in a space port? Did you bat your eyelashes and tell them how you wanted to see what was beyond your dirty little world?"

"Not quite." Ren slumped against the wall. His strength was failing. He needed the crew to return. "You talk a lot."

"It's how I think."

Ren wasn't sure who was stalling whom now. Was she waiting for him to pass out? She wouldn't find the kind of weapon she thought she was looking for. Would she leave if he gave her an out or would she run to her friend and return?

"Last question," he said, voice grating. "Then I'll open the door, and you can leave and not return."

"Sounds fair."

"What do you know about the crew member that was taken?" He spoke around the lump in his throat. *Asher.* What happened to him? Was he all right? Grief sapped the rest of Ren's strength, and he sagged.

"Nothing, really. Some rumors say it was a member of Rowan's blood family, but if that was the case, wouldn't their mother intervene? She holds a bit of influence, right? My theory is that it was her lover. But Rowan isn't really known for lovers either."

Ren shuddered.

"But who knows? When the Corps wants someone gone, they're gone. They'll never see that person again."

Tears stung behind his eyes. He unlocked the door and it popped open. "Go."

He watched through the security screen as Darby hesitated at the threshold. "Hey, are you okay, ship? You sound... I don't know... sad? Can ships be sad?"

"Leave!" All the lights flared to life in one blinding moment. The ship filled with sound and energy and blue sparks gathered in the corners and the air went heavy with potential.

Darby ran.

Ren slammed the door behind her. Sluggish and empty and miserable, he pulled from the ship. His side throbbed, and his head ached, and, for a moment, he wished he hadn't woken up at all. He stretched out as best he could on the deck plate and used his arm as a makeshift pillow. His eyes fluttered shut, and he passed out.

⊣⊢

Blurry shapes spun around him. Outlines of shadows and bright light and indistinct globs of color swayed on the outskirts of his vision. Something darted in the corner of his eye, but Ren couldn't chase it, couldn't turn to figure out what was going on. A voice, distorted and slow, called to him, but Ren couldn't decipher what it was saying. Everything was nebulous and strange: streaks of color moved with no discernible patterns and sound bumped into sound, discordant and awful.

This was a dream. Ren had been here before, confused and disoriented, but the feeling was the same, the feeling of being watched, of being compelled, of sensing someone desperate to reach him.

Slowly, impressions solidified into shapes and became objects. Ren concentrated, and his surroundings sharpened, came into focus. It was like looking through an old telescope with someone turning the lens and the soft-yellow fuzzed circle becoming the broken moon he knew from his childhood. Except he wasn't on Erden, and he certainly wasn't looking through a telescope he and Liam had found in a trash heap.

Liam.

The space cleared suddenly, and Ren's stomach twisted with the quick change in clarity. He stood in a blinding white room.

"Ren? Is that you? You're alive?"

Ren raised his hand to block the harsh light and peered into a corner.

"Liam?"

Ren reached out—

-ɪɪ-

An ear-piercing shriek jolted Ren from his sleep. He pried his eyes open in time to watch a crate of supplies drop from Penelope's hands and scatter across the floor. A roll of gauze tumbled past his outstretched fingers.

"Ren?"

He jerked in surprise, then groaned when pain flared from his side. Pen was on her knees in an instant, her soft hands cradled his face, and her wide, brown eyes filled his vision. Her long curls caressed his cheeks and ears. Ren turned his head away and closed his eyes, searching for the white room and Liam, but that only earned him a slap across his cheek.

"Hey!"

"Don't 'hey' me, mister. Stay awake."

"What's going on?" Her boots banging on the deck plate, Rowan thundered into the common area. Ollie's rapid stomps followed, as well as Lucas's. "Pen, are you all right? What happened?"

Ren tilted his head back and caught Rowan's eye.

She squeaked; her hands flew to her open mouth. "What the stars? Ren? How did you get in here? What's going on?"

"Ren?" Ollie yelled as he and Lucas fought for position in the doorway.

Ren smiled weakly. "Hi."

"Help me get him to the couch," Penelope ordered.

Ren gritted his teeth as they lifted him and moved him the few feet to the old sofa. He protested being laid flat, and, despite Pen's scowl, they maneuvered his body into a sitting position. Rowan handed him a glass of water, and Ren drank it down. The cool liquid felt like rain on his desert-dry throat.

Penelope pulled up his shirt and poked at the bandage.

"Are you the reason it's a sauna in here?" Rowan asked, taking the glass from his trembling grip and setting it on the nearby table. She placed her hands on her hips. Her long blonde braid fell over her shoulder so the end tickled the indent of her waist. She wore her jacket open and a weapon strapped to her outer thigh.

Ren clutched at the blanket around his shoulders. "It's freezing."

"No," Penelope said, frowning at the wound. "That's only you. And luckily you didn't undo any of my work."

"You fixed me. How?"

"Cobbled together supplies. Medicine, medical glue, small antiseptic forcefields, nutrient tubes, and well, mending thread." Her touch light, she smoothed the bandage.

"And no small amount of skill," Lucas added.

Ren touched Penelope's hand. "Thank you."

Penelope's long lashes fanned her cheeks as she blushed. "You're lucky to be alive, Ren."

"Yeah, and most people think you're dead," Lucas added. He spun one of the dining chairs around and straddled it. "Though you look good for a dead person."

Pen cast her husband a withering glare, and Lucas grinned, cheeks dimpling.

"Thanks, I guess." Ren picked at a thread on the hem of his shirt. "I figured we weren't being followed or we wouldn't be docked at a drift."

Penelope settled next to him on the couch. Rowan stood in front of him. Lucas stared intently from his chair. His goggles sat atop his head, contorting his light brown hair in messy spikes. Ollie stayed on the outskirts of the group with his massive arms crossed over his chest and eyed Ren as if he was a ghost. Ren didn't mind, since he felt like one anyway.

The four of them were beautiful and Ren was lucky to know them and to be a part of their family. "What happened?" he asked.

Rowan quirked an eyebrow. "I was hoping you might be able to fill in some of the details we're missing. Asher gave us a quick and simple version—how things went to dirt on Crei, Millicent betrayed you, and then the Corps showed up and you were injured. You died right there," Rowan nodded to the table. "At least, that's what we told the Corps."

"I even showed them a vid of when you flatlined," Penelope said. "It fooled them enough."

Ren swallowed. He didn't think he'd be able to eat at that table ever again.

"What Ash said was true. Millicent betrayed us. The whole time on the ship, she could pull me in and push me out. Those times when I almost hurt all of you, that was her, luring me into the systems during my nightmares." Ren studied his hands. "She wanted me to embrace something I couldn't be and, when I fought her, when I kept myself from hurting you all, from allowing the power to consume me, she turned on me. On us. She sided with Vos, and they escaped."

Vos. The name was sour in Ren's mouth. Previously baron of a fief on Ren's home world, he was responsible for Ren's capture from his village. He was the catalyst for Ren discovering his powers. Ren had foiled Vos's plans of drift and planet domination once and helped make him number one on the Corps' most-wanted list. But when they'd met again, Vos had outmaneuvered him, and Ren had lost. Ren vowed he wouldn't lose again.

"How did the Corps find you?"

Ren blew out a harsh breath. "Asher called them when we realized Vos was on the planet. He thought he could trade—Vos for me. And that, once the Corps had him, they'd reinstate Asher and let me go."

Rowan's features softened. "And you were shot?"

"By Corporal Zag. He figured out on Erden at the citadel that the usual weapons wouldn't work on me. So he used an ancient projectile and… you know that part."

Penelope's mouth turned down at the corners. "Yes, we know that part."

"I remember a little from being in the ship and watching through the vid feeds. But… Asher?" he hazarded.

"Out of our reach," Rowan said with a disgusted noise. "The Corps swept him away, and we haven't heard from him since. He didn't get much of a chance to talk to us before he left. He only made it clear that we must look after you."

"We need to find him," Ren said. He clenched his fists on his knees. "I have to find him and save him, and maybe he'll forgive me."

"You're dead," Rowan said, bending down. "Do you get that? This is your chance to leave. You can disappear. Go home. I'll even pay your way. But if you go looking for Asher, all of his hard work, all of our deceptions, will have been for nothing."

Ren ran a hand down his face. His eyes stung. His lips were chapped and raw. Every movement took effort. His stomach growled with intense hunger. "I can't thank you enough for all that you've done for me," he said, voice soft. "And I understand if you're not going to follow me into this, but I'm going to find Asher. I'm going to free him from the Corps. I don't know what will happen after that, if they're going to chase me the rest of my life, or if I'll get to rest. But Asher did everything he could to save me, and I'm returning the favor. With or without you."

The group stared in silence and the declaration fatigued Ren further. He sank into the ratty cushions. Even though he'd slept for the last six weeks, the excitement of waking up, stopping a potential thief, and proposing espionage against a major military power had sapped the little strength he had.

Rowan dropped her hands from her hips. "Let's table this discussion. For now. You're tired and probably hungry. And we've planned to stay on this little drift for at least a day."

Ren nodded, the fight having bled out of him. "Oh, by the way, someone broke into the ship."

Rowan's features clouded. "What?"

Ren told them about the override and the conversation he'd had with Darby. The longer he spoke, the more upset Rowan became, and Ollie's eyebrows inched higher.

"You told her you were the ship?" he asked with a large smile.

Ren shrugged. "She didn't believe me, if that helps."

Rowan pinched the bridge of her nose, an action oddly reminiscent of Asher. Ren's heart ached. "No more leaving the ship unguarded. And no leaving the ship at all, Ren. We can't risk Phoenix Corps finding out you're alive. I don't like the fact that this Darby person interacted with you at all."

Ren perked up. "There's Corps on a drift this small?"

"There's Corps on every drift," Lucas said, propping his chin on his folded arms. "A small regiment at the very least. This one has the dubious privilege of also having a recruitment center."

Pointing in Ren's direction, Rowan frowned. "I recognize that expression, and whatever you're thinking, the answer is no."

"I'm not thinking anything," Ren lied.

Rowan crossed her arms. "Right. At least get your strength back before you go running headfirst into a reckless rescue attempt. For all our sakes."

"Yes, Captain."

At that, Rowan finally cracked a smile. "Glad to have you back, Ren. Eat something and rest, and we'll talk in a few hours." She gestured to Ollie and Lucas. "You two, I want to look at the vid loop and this Darby person. I don't like that she was on my ship and I want to know where she's getting her information."

The three filed out, but not before Ollie clapped a huge, dark hand on Ren's shoulder.

Pen shook her head. "Come on, let's change your bandages and get some food in you that's not liquid. And then you'll feel better, I'm sure of it."

Ren wasn't so sure himself, but he did know he needed his strength, especially if he planned to infiltrate the Corps and rescue Asher.

-‖-

Ren slept fitfully on the medical cot after Penelope changed his bandage and eased the tube from his arm. He'd eaten little, and the food sat heavy in his stomach. He'd learned that the crew had bargained and bartered for supplies to keep him alive—packets of liquid nutrients that spacers used for long trips, medicines, tubes, and gauze, even heated blankets. There was nothing on the books and nothing to alert the Corps, but he found it hard to believe that the military organization bought the ruse that he was gone, though Ollie said the crew had been convincing. Ren had seen the vid of his bloody body the crew showed General VanMeerten. Maybe Asher willingly leaving, combined with Pen's tears and Rowan's defeated demeanor had been enough.

After a tortured rest in which he didn't dream, didn't try to kill the crew, and had no contact with Liam, Ren hoisted himself to standing. His body responded strangely, and he didn't know if it was due to atrophy or living in the ship for the last weeks or a combination of both. Unfortunately, inhabiting a corporeal form that was weak and uncoordinated was cogging annoying, especially when he could traverse the length of the ship in a nanosecond using his technopathic abilities.

He washed, brushed his teeth, peeled off the medical scrubs, and dressed. Wearing his own clothes was a relief. The fabric felt familiar against his skin; the scent was comforting. Mindful of the bandages, he smoothed his shirt.

Leaning heavily on the bulkhead, he made it the short distance from his current quarters to the common area.

"Look, I want to find Asher as much as anyone," Lucas said, as Ren slumped against the door. "But what will happen after? Asher made his choice. Shouldn't we honor that?"

Ollie rose from his chair at the table and stood by Ren's side, offered his arm, and guided Ren to his spot.

"Thanks," Ren said, cheeks hot.

Ollie smiled.

"It was a stupid decision," Rowan said, plopping a helping of mashed tuber on her plate. She took the spoon and threw a helping onto Ren's as well and slid it toward him. Lucas added a piece of bread, and Ollie poured water into his glass. "I love my brother, but he's naïve. He waltzed back to the Corps thinking he could salvage his position with them, but those cogs don't take slights lightly."

Penelope sat beside Lucas and smoothed his hair away from his face. "Asher made a decision out of desperation and love. If it were me and you, I'd do the same thing."

Lucas took her hand and pressed a kiss to her knuckles. "I know, but I wouldn't want you to put yourself in danger."

"But you wouldn't have a say. Ash made a choice, and now we get to make ours."

Lucas acquiesced and took a bite of his food.

They ate in silence. Ren pushed his dinner around his plate with a bent fork. He sighed. "I can go alone. You don't need to follow me."

Ollie snorted. "Asher is my brother in everything but blood. I'll go with you."

"Not without me." Pen reached across the table and wrapped her hand around Ren's cold fingers. "It took a lot of work to fix you. I'm not letting you mess up my handiwork."

Rowan and Lucas exchanged a glance. Lucas straightened his goggles. "I go where my wife goes," Lucas said, pointing his fork in Ren's direction, flinging bits of food. "And anyway, I'm driving."

Rowan tugged on her blonde braid. "Well then, you have a crew at your disposal. But I'm warning you, little one, if you get yourself hurt again, Asher won't be the only one in line to kill you. Understand?"

"I think so?"

Rowan gave a sharp nod. "One problem, we don't know where he is."

Ren bit his lip. It was reckless, but it was the only lead they had. "I know a girl who knows things."

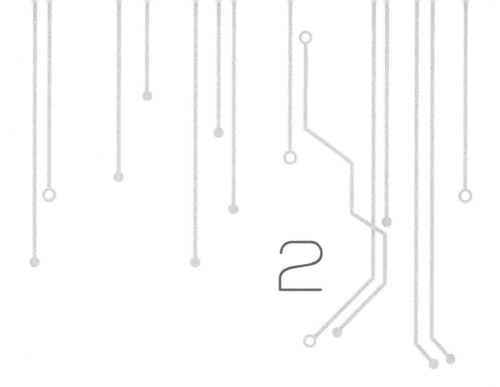

2

THE NEXT MORNING, AFTER BREAKFAST, Ren stretched on the couch in the common room. Drowsy, and full of food, he listened to the familiar conversations around him. The crew's voices blended into a low, comforting buzz, and Ren smiled, closing his eyes and resting his head on the cushions.

He woke a few hours later. Someone had repositioned him, which he appreciated since he didn't wake with a crick in his neck. The room was empty, the lights powered low, but Ren felt everyone on the ship. Fluttering his eyelids, Ren eased into the systems; the action was as simple as breathing.

Through the echo in the comms, Ren heard Ollie's heavy steps around the cargo bay. Propped in her captain's chair on the bridge, Rowan scrolled through newsfeeds. Lucas, hunched over his personal data screen in his and Penelope's quarters, reviewed routes and star charts. His fingers tapped restlessly, mapping paths to drifts and planets. Flipping through pages, Penelope read a novel, a fairy tale about a mermaid.

This was Ren's family—and he was relieved they were okay—but they all missed an important member. Asher's absence echoed everywhere.

Ren made his way to Asher's quarters, the ones that had been adjacent to his own. They were unlocked, though that wouldn't have stopped Ren.

He'd been in Asher's room, but that seemed like an age ago. It was much as he remembered—not an object out of place. Checking the drawers and closet, Ren found only a black drifter jacket with red accents. Ren slipped it on. He moved to the bathroom and picked through Asher's things with no real purpose in mind other than to be close to him through the objects and space he'd left behind.

Catching his reflection in the mirror, Ren eyed himself. Gone was the boy from Erden who had been captured by a despot. Gone was the shadow who'd walked around the ship pale and hollow-eyed, uncertain of his humanity, at war within himself. Staring at him was a man with a lean face, a slightly stubbled jaw, and a power that seeped into his bones, glowed from his eyes, nestled in the space beneath his ribs, had become a part of him. He wasn't afraid any longer, of himself or of others. His only fear was losing the family he'd built, and he was determined to fix the mistakes he'd made that had caused that family to be incomplete.

Beyond that was uncertainty: if he'd find his brother, if he could live a life on a drift or a planet without being chased, if normal was ever in the stars for him.

Ren's dark hair brushed his shoulders and fell into his eyes. It was a remnant of the time from his capture. He couldn't cut it at the citadel. Too caught up in his technopathic power, he hadn't cared about it when he lived on the ship, and he couldn't cut it while he was drifting between death and circuits. Spying a pair of scissors on the sink, Ren grabbed them and pulled a strand taut. He cut it, and the hair fell into the sink and curled onto the metal surface. The action was strangely freeing. With trembling hands, Ren continued to cut and cut and cut, and the hair in the sink mounted into a pile.

"Do you want help?"

Ren jumped and turned to find Rowan standing in the doorway. She leaned on the wall, her expression fond. She looked at the scissors Ren unintentionally but instinctively pointed at her and pursed her lips.

"I heard someone in here and figured it was you." She shrugged. "I knew it wasn't him, and the others wouldn't be interested in the things he left behind." She tugged at the collar of the jacket, and Ren's cheeks burned with a blush.

Cautiously, Rowan took the scissors.

"Here, it's all uneven. Actually, I think Asher has a pair of clippers somewhere."

Rowan slid Asher's chair from his desk into the small bathroom space and gestured for Ren to sit. He did and closed his eyes as Rowan ran her fingernails over his scalp. The snick-snick of the scissors was rhythmic and soothing.

She'd been suspicious of him once, wary and afraid of the unpredictability he brought aboard her ship. She'd softened, though, when she saw him for what he was—a scared duster far from home, thrust into an adventure he hadn't asked for. Despite her acceptance, he'd never imagined she'd be doing something like this for him.

"Thank you," he said, finally.

"I used to do this for Ash when he was younger, before the Corps. He had beautiful blond hair as a baby, and, when it grew long, my friends and I would braid it. He didn't care until he hit that pre-pubescent stage when everyone was stupid except for him."

Ren half-smiled. "Was he a brat?"

Rowan made an affirmative noise in her throat. "The worst. He was a moody little cog. But then he hit fifteen, shot up in height, grew muscles, and became handsome. And he knew it too. Then he was utterly unbearable."

With the heel of his hand, Ren wiped away the tears gathered in his lashes. "I bet he could've had anyone he wanted."

Rowan swung open the mirror and pulled out the hair clippers. She flipped the switch, and it sputtered before shutting off. Ren lightly touched the casing, allowed his power to flood into the wires, and it hummed to life. Rowan didn't bat an eye and ran the clippers along the shape of Ren's ear and up the side of his head.

"He could've, but he enlisted and disappeared. I hadn't seen him in so long when you brought him back to me, bedraggled, and awful-smelling, on that woman's ship at Nineveh. I would've paid any amount of credits for him right then."

"I'd pay any amount to have him here right now."

"I know." She gently pushed Ren's head forward and used the clippers on his neck. "You're young and stupid and inexperienced and you care too deeply. And you're exactly the person my brother needs."

He didn't know if he was the person Asher needed. He hoped he was the person Asher still wanted. But what really mattered was just having Asher back and the family whole.

"We'll get him back. I promise."

"Don't make promises you might not be able to keep. But," she said before Ren could respond, "I'm glad you're determined." She turned off the clippers. "There. All done. I think it suits you."

Ren stood and peered in the mirror. She'd done a good job: the sides and back short, but the top still slightly long and wild.

"Thank you."

She patted his shoulder. "You're welcome. Now, do you honestly think this girl will be able to help us?"

Ren ran his hand over the back of his neck. "I think it's a good place to start."

"Well, then, let's go find her."

-||-

Finding Darby wasn't difficult. Ren used his connection with the ship to link to the video feeds of the drift. Phoebus was a tiny drift, constructed of a few levels and the docks. After a couple of minutes of flicking through the feeds, Ren found Darby outside a storefront. He almost missed her, since her outfit blended in with the moving populace and the walls of the drift, but a strand of her nebula hair peeking out beneath her slouch hat caught his eye.

Darby moved with a grace that Ren hadn't seen before. Her movements were quick and fluid. Ren almost missed it when Darby pickpocketed a woman leaning over a display of bracelets. The glint of a credit chip was the only reason he caught the movement; that and the slight sway of the woman's purse. The sleight of hand was practiced and easy. Then, for good measure, Darby took a few bracelets before ambling away.

She went to the elevator, and Ren lost track of her until she emerged on the floor below.

"Third floor," Ren said into the comm to Ollie, as Darby meandered to a bench positioned to look out at the stars. "Near the observation window. The one with the hat and the rainbow socks."

"That little thing?" Ollie said a few minutes later. "Are you sure? She doesn't look like much."

"Yes, that's her. Be careful."

Ollie sighed over the line. "Okay, I'm on it."

Ren eased from the drift and contracted to the ship. He opened his eyes and found Penelope staring at him.

"Hi," he said with a wave. "Everything okay?"

Brow furrowed, Penelope stared at him. "It seems easier than before." She made a gesture at her eyes. "You're not as… unpredictable."

"I have better control." He pressed his hand to the bulkhead with fingers spread, leaving smudges on the shiny surface. "It was harder when I didn't know what I was doing. And then Millicent manipulated me. And then… well after spending so many weeks in the ship…" he trailed off and shrugged. "It's instinctive now."

"Do you think you'll need to worry about being overwhelmed again? 'Go all glowy' as they say. Should I carry a list of impossible questions to ask you, just in case? To force you back to being human?"

Ren frowned. "I think I'll always have to worry about losing myself, unfortunately. It's part of being what I am. But that doesn't mean I can't balance it, that I can't be both human and star host. I don't have to be one or the other." Ren flexed his fingers. "I can choose to be both."

That was something Millicent hadn't understood when she'd tried to force him to choose. She could only see a constant struggle between one or the other, so she'd abandoned a part of herself. Ren couldn't do that.

"That's good." Penelope gave him a warm smile. "Well, let's get you ready to broker your first deal. It's exciting, I think. You're becoming a true drifter."

"I wonder what Jakob would say to that."

Penelope laughed. "He'd say something along the lines of, *what have you weeds done to my best friend?*"

Ren chuckled at her impression.

Penelope helped him to his feet, then smoothed the lapels of Asher's jacket. If she noticed he'd pilfered it from Asher's closet, she didn't say anything. Ren looped his arm around her shoulders and together they made their way to the cargo bay.

⊣⊢

Ren reclined on the stairs in the cargo bay with his elbows propped behind him and his booted feet on a lower step. He was still becoming used to his body again, and this pose allowed him to appear relaxed but not weak. It killed his elbows and shoulders, though, strained his joints, and put pressure on tender places.

As soon as Ollie neared the dock, Ren perked up, feeling him cross the barrier Ren had erected around the ship. He alerted Rowan and

Lucas to their impending visitor. They all turned toward the airlock door and waited.

They didn't wait long.

Darby's string of expletives was both impressive and creative. While she wasn't physically fighting Ollie, she was making the job of escorting her difficult by playing dead weight, dragging her feet, and generally being a nuisance.

Lucas's eyebrows shot up. "We're kidnapping now?" he asked, as Ollie hauled an uncooperative Darby through the cargo airlock with his thick brown arms wrapped around her waist. "I thought we were asking politely?"

"I did ask politely," Ollie said. "She refused rudely."

Once inside the cargo bay, and with Ollie distracted, Darby kicked out, catching him in the knee with her thick heel. He dropped her with a grunt, and she took off for the door. From his spot on the stairs, Ren thrust out his hand, pushed his star outward, and the door swung closed before she could reach it. He locked it for good measure.

She slid to a halt and scowled. "I hate that trick."

Lucas shook his head and waved his hand over his shoulder as he left the cargo bay. "I'd love to stay, but I don't want to be an accessory." He stepped past Ren on the stairs and rubbed his head. "Nice jacket."

Ren swatted his hand away.

"You're already an accessory," Darby yelled. "You all are. I'll turn every last one of you in to the Corps."

Ollie, an imposing figure with his height and bulk, stood near the airlock, and Rowan scowled from the other side of the stairs. A pulse gun was strapped to her outer thigh. She sighed, put upon, and brushed her golden braid from her shoulder and pulled on the hem of her black shirt. "Seriously? You are in no position to threaten us with the Corps. Especially since you're carrying stolen merchandise on your person right now."

Darby let a slow grin spread over her face. Her hair, a mixture of black and purple, was cut short at her chin. She wore dark clothes and next to Ollie she appeared tiny. Ren couldn't judge her age, but he guessed it wasn't much different from his own. She snapped her fingers. "You must be Captain Rowan Morgan. Your reputation proceeds you."

"Unfortunately, so does yours, Darby."

Darby brushed off the sleeves of her jacket and spread her arms wide. "I have no reputation. I'm totally 'what you see is what you get.'"

"And I've seen vid of you pickpocketing, shoplifting, and trespassing."

"Oh, busted," Darby said with a wink. "So, I know you. You know me. But I don't know…" She pointed at Ren and Ollie. "…these two lovely boys."

Ollie didn't say anything.

"We've met," Ren said.

"I would've remembered if we'd met." Darby put her hands on her hips and batted her eyelashes. "I don't forget a pretty face."

Ren snorted. "Yesterday. Remember? *Don't kick my things.*"

Realization dawned. Her mouth dropped open, and she wagged her finger in his direction. "You don't look like a ship," she said, her gaze running from Ren's toes to his head. "You look like another fine mark though."

"Enough of this." Rowan dropped her crossed arms and stalked across the short distance between her and Darby. Her hand rested on her holstered weapon. "You violated the sanctity of my ship. You're lucky we don't turn you over to the drift authorities."

Darby placed a hand over her heart and gasped. "Oh no, an empty threat. Whatever shall I do?"

Ollie coughed into his fist. Rowan's glare intensified. Ren inwardly groaned; a clash of personalities wasn't what he needed. This wouldn't get them anywhere, and Darby was the only lead they had to Asher's whereabouts.

"If you had wanted to turn me in, you would've when you had the vids on me. So, what's the deal? Or the con?"

Ren gritted his teeth. Darby's attitude was wearing thin. "You're right. We're not turning you over to the authorities, but don't think for a second you're not in any danger here, or don't you remember when I told you to leave." Ren leveled Darby with a look and engaged the star in his chest. The lights in the cargo hold flickered. His eyes went blue. He lifted his hand, and sparks danced between his fingers.

Darby paled and stepped away, her defensive posture melting into fear. "What are you? How are you doing that?"

Ren closed his fingers and pulled himself from the systems. He ignored her question. "We need you to do us a favor."

Her eyebrows raised. "A favor?" False bravado back in place, she tilted her chin. "Favors can be expensive. And I'm not cheap."

Rowan narrowed her eyes. "How much?"

"Depends on the favor." Darby flashed a cheeky grin. "I'm guessing the great Captain Morgan doesn't want her to get her hands dirty. Don't want to sully your name with questionable activity?"

"From what you told Ren, my name is already sullied."

Darby shrugged. "Not so much. Just my own theories, that I was obviously wrong about." She cast a glance at Ren. "Or not so wrong. Maybe, they weren't after an object. Maybe, they chased you because of a person. Tell me, Ren. Have you ever been to Crei?"

That was too close for comfort, and Ren waved his hand, brushing off her theories like cobwebs. "Look, we need information. You're good at information. But this isn't going to be as easy as an override on a ship. We have a very specific target."

"What? Are we talking a little information, or are you talking outright theft? Because I can do both. And what's the target? No one on this drift is too difficult. Cogs, this ship was the toughest I've sneaked on in months."

Ren shifted on the stairs. His back was too tense, and the blunt metal edges of the steps dug into his legs. He would have bruises. But he shrugged, pretending nonchalance while his pulse thrummed. "The Corps," he said, as if had described the basic function of air recyclers.

Darby laughed. She tossed her head back and clutched her sides and *laughed*. "That's hilarious." She slid her fingers beneath her eyes to wipe away non-existent tears. "Oh, my stars, that was funny. I haven't heard a good joke in a while."

Rowan frowned. "We're wasting time. She can't help us."

"Wait?" She looked at the three of them and scrunched her nose. "You're serious? You want me to steal information from the Corps? No way, the only way you can get information out of those guys is to hack their database. And sorry, unless you are amazing and can get into their private and secure systems, you're DOL."

"DOL?" Ren asked.

"Dirt out of luck." Darby held up a hand and wiggled her fingers that poked out of her fingerless gloves. "One, you're not going to be able to get close enough, and, even if you do, the encryption is beyond what anyone on this drift can break. Second, the last guy who tried was thrown onto some dust ball and never heard from again. No amount of credits or favors or whatever is worth that."

She turned on her heel and stalked toward the door.

"Wait!" Ren pushed his body to standing, but hunched over. His legs trembled, and he crumpled forward. Ollie caught him before he tumbled off the stairs. Grasping Ren's arm, Ollie steadied him. "Wait. You weren't wrong. There is something on this ship that the Corps chased and thought they destroyed but didn't."

Darby stopped in her tracks. "I was right," Darby said, looking over her shoulder. "You're sick, aren't you?"

"Not sick. Recovering from almost being destroyed."

Darby's eyebrows shot up. "Rumors said it was a weapon. You don't look like much of a weapon."

"This is too dangerous." Rowan stepped between Ren and Darby. "Don't tell her another word. We'll figure it out without her."

"You'll be pegged in an instant," Darby crossed her arms. "I had your number before you finished docking. You won't be able to get near the Corps, and your friend, the ship over there, is wanted, right? One scan and he's done for. You'll never get your missing crewman back."

Her words were a slap. A pang shot through Ren and sank to his core at the thought of not finding Asher. He saw the same reaction in Rowan and felt it in Ollie's tightened grip.

Ren touched Rowan's elbow.

"We knew there would be risks. I'm okay with them as long as we can get the information we need."

"Fine," Rowan's response was immediate.

Stepping from Ollie's hold, Ren faced Darby. "You won't have to worry about any of the hacking," Ren said, shoving his hands into his pockets. "That's my job. I'm a technopath."

Darby blinked.

Ren waited for the fallout.

She scrunched her nose again. "Huh. That explains a few things." She shrugged. "All right. That's great. What's your plan?"

"You're not afraid or curious?"

"I'm more curious about what my role is. If you can do science-magic, then why do you need me?"

Rowan tapped Darby on the forehead. "You are the distraction."

"I don't get it."

Rowan leaned closer with a slight curl to her lips. "For someone so smart, you're not thinking outside of the box. This is a recruitment center, which means turnover and fresh meat. We just need you to distract the right green newb and get his data pad close enough to our good friend here. That's it. One little data pad, and you don't even have to lift it, just creatively maneuver."

Darby licked her lips. "Doesn't sound like too much of a challenge. But this is a big favor for the measly exchange of not turning me in. I mean, a little shoplifting is time in the pokey here. A little espionage and I'm planet-side or in Perilous Space."

"Consequences didn't seem to keep you from *breaking into my ship.*"

Darby polished her glittery nails on her shirt. "Consequences matter now. Compensate me, or I walk out of here and blab all about the alive-and-well, mythical being on your boat."

Rowan bit her lip so hard blood welled up in a perfect red bead. She wiped it away with the back of her hand, smearing red across her mouth. "What do you want?"

"Credits. I want a lot of credits. And passage off this spinning heap. There's only so much trouble you can get into on a drift this small without people beginning to notice."

Rowan narrowed her eyes. Hands on her hips, she regarded Darby. "We can spare a few credits and we have room for one more. But not for long. We're not dragging you around the cluster."

"No problem. I want off at the next drift."

Rowan held out her hand. "It seems we have a deal."

Darby spit in hers, and slapped her palm against Rowan's. Rowan made a horrified face and quickly wiped her hand on her trouser leg.

Laughing, Darby punched Ren in the shoulder, which almost sent him toppling. He massaged the sore spot.

"Great." She rubbed her hands together. "Let's do this."

⊣⊢

Phoebus drift was indeed tiny. While Mykonos was stacked with floors upon floors of businesses, residences, gardens, and government offices, Phoebus had only six stories and was sparsely populated. Located on the bottom level was the docking platform, and the five floors above contained a smattering of businesses, a few apartment blocks, and the recruitment office.

"I feel claustrophobic," Ren muttered as he and Ollie went up in the lift. He scuffed his boots against the floor. "We're going to get spotted."

"We're fine," Ollie responded, voice low. "Merchants like us come and go from here all the time. It's just like other drifts where it's not out of the ordinary for new faces. Why do you think it has a recruitment office? The outer drifts are where people go to hide, to get away. Desperate people make desperate decisions."

"Like joining the Corps?"

"Yeah, sometimes."

Ren tugged his hood lower over his forehead. Asher's jacket wasn't hooded, and Ren had switched it for one that belonged to Penelope. It hid his face, but it lacked warmth, and Ren missed the smell and the weight of Asher's. "Was Asher desperate when he joined?"

"That's a question for Ash."

Ren huffed. They exited the lift, which dumped them at the end of a corridor. And at the other end was the recruitment center. The Phoenix Corps logo blazed above the entrance, daunting and brilliant and terrible. Ren turned his head away, closed his eyes, and shut down every camera on the level. He doubted anyone would notice.

"We're here," he said softly over the comm.

Rowan's voice came back. "So am I."

"Me too," Darby chimed.

Ollie and Ren moved, stopping every few feet to browse goods from vendors and for Ren to catch his breath. About halfway down the corridor, with the center looming at its end, Ren spotted the recruiter standing in the middle of the crowd. He wore a pressed uniform: the Phoenix Corps symbol spotless on his upper arm, the mythical bird rising from flames. His hair was close cut, his back ramrod straight, and his expression one of sheer boredom. The drifters of Phoebus ignored him. They streamed around him as he stood like a rock in the middle of a creek.

"Join the Corps today. Protect the Drift Alliance. Serve the people," he said in a flat monotone.

Ren had seen Asher fight and survive. He'd seen Asher run until he couldn't run any farther across an unfamiliar and treacherous landscape. He'd seen him battle through a snowstorm. He'd seen him command a group and bark orders while rescuing a drift and, at another time, organizing a retreat. He'd seen Asher stand in the face of impossible odds. Watching this soldier, Ren didn't see any evidence of similar experiences.

Darby appeared from within the crowd and bumped into Ren's shoulder. "He's our mark."

"Yes," Ren said.

She kept walking fast but nodded and again merged with the flood of people.

Ollie and Ren spotted a restaurant and shuffled to a booth near the window.

"Is this close enough?"

"Yes." Ren relaxed. He reached out, touched the energy of the data pad. "I've got it." Over the comm, Ren spoke to the team. "Darby, you're up."

"Right."

Ren ducked his head so the fabric of his hood cast his face in shadow, as Ollie interacted with the waitress. With his energy spread out and his vision tinted blue, keeping his focus on the data pad, he tracked the movement around their location. Ollie touched the back of Ren's hand.

"Okay?"

"Yeah, I'm good."

Amid the busy intersection, Darby materialized, walking backward, pretending to talk over comm to a friend. She knocked into the recruiter, her elbow went into his stomach, and together they stumbled.

"Oh!" she cried out.

The recruiter steadied them with one hand on Darby's arm, the other still gripping his data pad.

"I'm so sorry," Darby said, not stepping away, keeping her body close to his. She gently rested her hand on his forearm and tilted her face up. "Thanks for catching me."

His expression didn't change. "You should watch where you're going."

"Yes, of course. Sorry. Did I hurt you?"

The recruiter, his features stern, disengaged from Darby and took a step back. He clutched the data pad closer to his chest. "No."

Darby smiled, brightly and cheerfully, and tucked a strand of her hair behind her ear. "Right. You're big, strong Phoenix Corps. Little me couldn't hurt you."

"I think you need to move along, miss."

Ren winced. This wasn't going well.

"Maybe I want to talk a little longer."

"Unless you're interested in enlisting, no."

Darby bit her lip and fluttered her eyelashes. "I am interested. I want to enlist."

The recruiter looked Darby up and down. He shifted to cradle the data pad in his arm. "You want to enlist?" he asked, eyebrow raised.

"Yeah," Darby said. She pulled her shoulders back. "What? Do I not meet criteria?" Puffing out her chest, she frowned. "I may be small, but I would be an amazing asset."

He sighed and tapped on his screen. "I guess. At least I'll make my quota."

Darby twirled a strand of hair. "Do we have to do this right here? I mean…" She tossed her head to the side. "…that restaurant has nice booths."

"Look, this isn't a social club. This is a military organization."

"Oh, well, I wanted to talk to you about…" Darby trailed off. She floundered and caught sight of the standard-issue pulse gun at his side. "Your pulse gun."

The recruiter's stern façade slipped. "My gun?"

"Oh, yeah." Darby nodded enthusiastically. "I want to know all about your gun."

His face lit up. "You like weapons?" His fingers grazed his holster.

"Weapons? I love weapons. Guns, knives, electric batons, even explosives. I love them all, but I don't know much about them." She pouted. "Would I learn that in the Corps?"

"Oh, yes. We teach you everything, from the history of the old laser guns to the new kinds of stunners and electric blades. I heard a story about how one of our corporals recently used an ancient projectile to take down a star host."

Ren winced.

"Wow. That's amazing. I want to hear everything."

The recruiter looked around. "Okay, I have a few minutes until my shift replacement gets here. As long as you don't blab…" He jerked his chin toward the restaurant. "…we can sit for a minute."

Darby smiled coyly and crossed her heart. "I won't tell a soul."

He smiled, his cheeks dimpling. "Okay, come on."

A smidgeon of guilt at taking advantage of the kid's sincerity wormed into Ren's middle, but it was short-lived. He ducked his head and closed his eyes. He tracked the data pad's movement. He heard a shuffle of feet, a sound of metal sliding along a table top, and Ren stilled, waiting for Ollie's sign.

"He put it down. Go."

Ren focused on the data pad and delved into the system. With Ollie next to him, Ren didn't need to split his concentration. He wholly devoted his power to the device, speeding past passwords, burning through a firewall, and hurtling into the Phoenix Corps system itself.

This was different than disabling ships through a sensor grid. This was different than racing through circuits in the walls of the citadel. This was different than hovering in the electricity and relays of the ship. This was different than making weapons spark or beacons stop or cuffs fall from his hands. This wasn't mechanics, but information. This operation required finesse, not strength.

Ren poured his star into the system. He searched for any hint of Asher's name or whereabouts and flooded into every nook and cranny of the digital layout. He clenched his eyes, gritted his teeth, and allowed the star to consume him. He brimmed with power. Overwhelmed by static, sparks lit on his tongue, and white noise hummed in his ears.

Sliding through the torrent, Ren searched and searched and… found nothing.

He needed to go farther. Surging, Ren dug deeper, traveled from the surface information into hidden files. He found classified documents and bypassed the security levels. Desperate for Asher's name, he rifled through warrants and disciplinary actions.

He paused when he found a file on known star hosts. He spotted his own name, and his death certificate, signed by VanMeerten herself. He flipped through it and found names of people he knew—Abiathar, Nadie, Millicent—and names he *didn't* know. As interesting as it was, he couldn't get caught up in it. Unless…

Flipping back to his own file, he perused the information. Asher's name wasn't stated, but there was a mention about a companion to the star host: a Corps soldier who acted as a handler; a soldier who had gone AWOL and was pursued on Erden and Crei; a soldier who was disciplined, knocked down the ranks, and now stationed on the planet Bara.

Bara. Asher was on Bara. Asher was planet-side. What was the Corps doing there?

Ren went back to the star host file, elated he'd found Asher's location, and worried about what he was doing on a planet, especially after what Asher had suffered on Erden. Focused on Asher, Ren almost missed the name on one of the other files.

Liam.

Ren halted. It couldn't be. He slammed into the document and—

"Ren! Ren, come on. Let go. We have to go."

Snapping back into his body, Ren gasped. His teeth clacked together as Ollie shook him. His frame was limp and exhausted. Disoriented, Ren could only focus on one fact.

"Bara. He's on Bara. Asher is at an outpost on Bara."

But Liam. He'd lost Liam. He had to go back. He had to—

His resolve caught in his throat. The lights were off, even the emergency lights. Media boards and info screens and even the mood lights by the observation windows were out, pitching the whole drift into darkness. The background whine of the systems sputtered out.

Ollie cupped Ren's face in his large hands. "Ren? Ren, was this you? Did you do this?"

The citizens of the drift were afraid, and murmurs escalated into talk, then cries and shouts, as unease set in when the systems remained off. A tide of fear rose and crested and the populace of Phoebus drift burst into panic.

The recruiter Darby had distracted stared with wide eyes at his data pad, undoubtedly seeing the codes Ren had cracked and the firewalls he'd bypassed. *Or was he afraid? Stunned? Reading orders from his command as the drift sat dead in space?* The glow from the data screen, the only source of light, lit his features casting him in eerie shadows. He jumped to his feet, his chair skittered away behind him, and he ran.

Ren stood, but his legs collapsed beneath him, and only Ollie grabbing him kept him on his feet. The stars outside the window no longer spun idly by. The air recyclers shut off. The only system Ren detected was the grav, and even that quaked in his chest, dared to fail, and send the populace floating. The airlocks held, but docking had shut down. Sensors went dark. Communications silenced.

Ollie shook him again. His large hands were like iron on Ren's biceps. "Ren!"

"This wasn't me. This isn't me." A shiver crept down Ren's spine.

Rowan, having abandoned her lookout post, appeared. "Run." Rowan pulled Ren by the wrist. "Ren, we have to leave. We have to leave now before this place is torn apart!"

Ren froze. A recognizable star signature pinged his senses, echoed his own power, and pulsed under his skin.

"She's here." He swallowed. "Millicent is here."

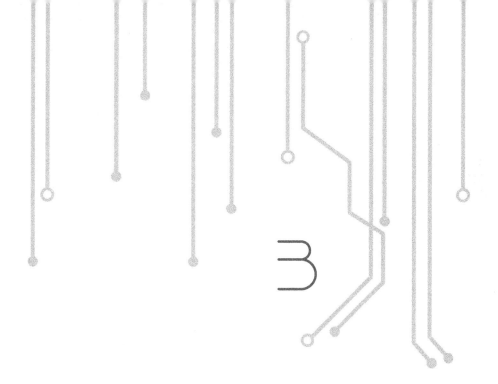

3

Phoebus descended into chaos.

Ollie lifted Ren and slung him over his shoulder, despite Ren's protests.

"I can face her!"

"No," Ollie said. He grabbed Darby's hand and hauled her out of her seat. Frozen with fear, her face pale, her limbs locked, it took both Ollie's and Rowan's physical urging to get her to move.

"What's going on?" Darby asked, voice small and terrified. She clutched Rowan's arm and stumbled as the four of them moved through the crowd. "What's happening? It's not a blip. It's too long to be a blip."

"This drift is under attack," Rowan said. "And we're not staying around to find out by whom."

"It's her," Ren said. He hung over Ollie's broad back. Ollie's shoulder dug into his stomach, aggravating his wound. He didn't appreciate being carried around like a sack of parts, but he didn't trust his ability to stay with them amid the frenzied crowds. Using so much power and exercising the amount of control needed to finesse the data had drained his atrophied body. Someone slammed into Ollie; pain sliced down Ren's torso and robbed him of his breath.

People ran and screamed. They pounded on locked doors. They yelled for others in the dark. They bumped into each other, pushed through crowds, and ran from the lifts to the stairs and back attempting to find an exit.

Through it all, Ollie and Rowan strode with a purpose, heading to the access stairs that led to the docks.

"Put me down," Ren said, tears gathering in his eyes at the sheer terror of the citizens. "I can fight her."

"No," Ollie said again.

Ren struggled in his grip, and Ollie's grasp went tighter until it was painful.

"I can help these people. Please, let me help."

Rowan paused long enough to turn and grab Ren's face in one hand. Her thumb and fingers dug into his cheeks as she lifted his head. Her green eyes blazed.

"Do I need to remind you what happened? What she can do? She manipulated you. She made you a ghost. She betrayed you, and you almost *died*. The only people you'll be helping is us to get off this drift before Millicent vents it."

Rowan let go, and Ren sagged.

They maneuvered through the crowd. Rowan dragged Darby by the wrist as though she was a disobedient child. Ollie's imposing figure cut a path through the masses, but the crowd became denser as they neared the exit that led to the docking platform.

A crowd had formed around the door to the access stairs. The mass swelled; the poor souls in the front were squished into the metal walls. The banged their hands and fought to pry the door open.

"Ren," Rowan said.

"If I do it, she'll know I'm here. She'll know I'm alive. She won't let me go."

Rowan made a frustrated noise. "What do we do?"

"Get to the front and put me down, and I'll tell you how to do it manually."

Ollie shouldered through, shouting for people to move. Gently, he set Ren on his feet, and Ren leaned heavily against the wall with Darby tight to his side. If he fell, he'd be trampled, and the information about Asher and about his brother would be lost.

"The problem is a lack of energy source. Open the access panel," Ren said.

Ollie gripped the metal and peeled it back to reveal the innards of the mechanism.

"Rowan, pull your pulse gun."

"Are you serious?"

Someone jostled close, and Ren grunted. "Yes," he said through gritted teeth.

Muttering under her breath, Rowan pulled her gun from the holster. "Now what?"

Ren had fixed weapons in the citadel's courtyard long ago. He'd made Asher's weapon fall to pieces in the snowstorm, and he'd disabled the weapons from the Corps. Rowan's would have much the same layout.

"Pop open the handle and find the energy source. Ollie, there should be a clump of wires that lead into the wall. Pull them out."

They worked quickly, and, after a moment, Rowan held a gleaming cube in her palm, and Ollie had several wires in his fist. Ren took the power source and found the connector he needed.

"Okay, so it's not going to be enough power for the door to open all the way, but it should pop it free for us to squeeze through."

Ren jammed the connector into the source. Sparks flew, and a shock sped through Ren's hands into his skin and up through his body to his chest. His hair stood on end, and a hint of ozone wafted into the air. His heart stuttered, but the door opened wide enough for Ollie to slide through. Back against the frame, hands on the door itself, Ollie pushed. His muscles strained, and his face flushed, and his features twisted up in exertion, but, with a screech of metal, the door skated into the wall socket.

The crowd surged forward, and Ren was lucky that Ollie grabbed him and pulled him through with Darby following, her hands clasped tightly around Ren's forearm. Rowan shoved herself through, then turned to face the swelling crowd.

"Get to the ships. Get your friends and family and get on a ship and hurry. Understand? You saw how we opened this door. Do the same for the others and clear the drift. That's how you're going to survive."

"We should help them open other doors," Darby said, breathless.

"We've done our good deed," Rowan stalked by them. "We're leaving."

Clinging to Ollie's strong arms, Ren didn't argue. He focused on how they were going to get off the dock itself, especially since all systems were down. He'd have to use his power, and then Millicent would know he was there and so would whoever was with her, presumably Vos. They wouldn't let him go. She'd never let him go if she thought she could convince him to join her and if she couldn't, she'd see him dead. She'd tried to manipulate him for months and when she couldn't, she'd left him to the nonexistent mercy of the Corps.

They made it to the *Star Stream*'s dock just as an announcement came over the drift-wide comm system.

"No need to be alarmed, citizens of Phoebus. Systems will all be restored once all Phoenix Corps soldiers and the local government have turned themselves over to the new regime."

Ren's eyebrows shot up. That wasn't Vos's voice. It wasn't Abiathar's either. Someone new? Someone else seduced by Vos's schemes?

"We suggest that all the populace find a safe space to wait. And we suggest that any holdouts to our demands recognize that their resistance will only lend to the destruction of their own people. We'd like this to be as painless a process as possible, but we are prepared to take drastic measures if necessary. Thank you."

"Friendly and threatening. Sounds like a politician." Rowan threw open the door to the cargo bay and shoved Darby through.

Ren frowned. He looked over his shoulder to see the surge of people in the docking area running for ships. He didn't know the voice on the comm, but that *was* Millicent in the systems. He couldn't mistake the sickly caress of her signature in his mind and over his skin. He ached with betrayal and burned with revenge. His stomach turned at the thought of how she'd pulled him into the circuits on the ship and pushed him out of the communication tower on Crei, how she could control his star in a way he couldn't.

She may be able to manipulate him, but he was more powerful. He didn't have to touch an object to exert his will over it. She did. Which meant she had to be on the drift. She had to be there, among the crowd.

He could find her. He could find her and….

"Whatever you're thinking, don't." Rowan jostled Ren into the *Star Stream* and closed the door after Ollie. "I know that look. It's the 'I have a stupid idea' look."

Ren's legs gave out and he sank to the deck plate. Splayed on the cool surface, he rolled his head to stare at the other three. "Millicent has to touch whatever she's controlling. That means she is on the drift. She's there. Among the crowd. With whoever that is with her. We could find her. We could stop her. *I* could stop her."

"No. And it doesn't matter." Rowan crouched and poked his cheek. Her hard stare pierced him. "Did you get the information about Asher? Do you know where he is?"

"He's on Bara."

"Then that's where we are going. We're not interfering here. We've learned our lesson about dealing with Vos and Millicent and becoming embroiled in their feud with the Corps." Ren placed a hand protectively on the side of his stomach; his fingers spread over the fabric of his shirt. Her sharp gaze drifted to the wound. "Are you okay?"

"I'm fine." His side throbbed, but the stiches held, despite the unceremonious way Ollie had hauled him around.

"What about me?" Darby asked. She hovered by the airlock door, one hand on the locking mechanism as if she was going to flee to the drift. Face pale, obviously terrified, she looked from one of them to the other.

Rowan straightened. She put her hands on her hips. "Do you want to stay on Phoebus? Or do you want to come with us to Bara?"

Darby narrowed her eyes. "Neither. The deal was for you to take me to another drift."

"And we will. After we've found my brother."

"You're kidnapping me?" Her voice went high, breaking on the last word.

Rowan rolled her eyes. "Hardly. We're saving you. Or did you forget the power outage and the mass panic going on right outside the door? And the threat announced? Do you want to be here when a new regime takes over?" Rowan swept her hand toward the exit. "You're more than welcome to leave."

Eyes wide, Darby shook her head.

"Besides, we can't really kidnap anyone." Lucas appeared at the top of the stairs with Penelope close behind. "Docking is completely dark, and we can't leave until someone lets us out." Lucas crossed his arms and leaned on the railing. His goggles mussed his hair. "We're stuck unless Ren here can do anything about it."

"What's going on out there?" Penelope asked. She looped her arm through Lucas's.

"Millicent," Ren said.

Penelope gasped, her hand flew to her mouth, and Lucas made a face. "Great." Lucas scuffed his boot against the deck. "Return of the creepy lady with questionable understanding of personal space."

Darby's eyebrows raised. "You guys really have a problem with this person."

"Understatement," Ren muttered.

"We have to leave." Penelope tugged Lucas closer. "She'll recognize the ship. She'll know we're here, that Ren's here. She could hurt him again."

Ren pushed his body to sitting and grimaced at the pull on his injury and the weakness of his limbs. "We could fight."

"No," Rowan and Ollie said immediately in unison.

Ren sighed, but they were right. He was too weak. "We could wait it out. Hope that Millicent doesn't realize we're here and wait for systems to resume once the Corps and the government turn themselves over. If whoever that was on the comm system keeps their promise."

Rowan cocked her hip to the side. "Or?"

"Or you let me open the docking bay, and we leave."

Rowan shook her head so her braid swung behind her. "It's too dangerous. We know what she can do to you, and, if she realizes you're here, she'll waste no time in trying to keep you here or kill you. No, we need a better option."

Being reminded of his own inability began to wear on his nerves. Ren listed to the side. "There are no other options! Unless we try to pop the dock like we did the door!"

"That would mean we would have to manually access the docking system, which is more than likely housed in the control center, which would be in the middle of the drift." Ollie stepped forward. He crossed his bulging arms. "I could do it. If Ren could talk me through it over the comms."

"No!" This time it was Penelope and Rowan speaking together.

Rowan touched his arm. "We've lost Asher. We're not losing you too."

"Great, just great!" Darby threw up her hands. "We're stuck here. *I'm* stuck here, apparently, since you are *kidnapping* me! Again, I might add! And there's no way out unless we can magically transport out of this bay without being noticed by a creepy lady and her handler. Right? Am I right?"

Lucas's head snapped up. "Say that again."

"Kidnapping!"

"No! Magical transport." Lucas whipped his head around to stare at Ren. "Can you do it? Would she feel it?"

"It wouldn't matter if she felt it. We'd be long gone. Right?" Rowan asked, leaning on the stair railing.

"I can do it." He wasn't sure, but it was their only option. "She'd know I am alive. I think she'd feel the disturbance, but she might not, especially if she's occupied with other things."

"We don't know if she knows you were dead in the first place. She had left before the…" Penelope waved her hands. "Shooting, right?"

"This is our chance. We're taking it." Ollie held out his hand. "Come on. Let's get you to the bridge." Hauling Ren to his feet, Ollie guided him to the stairs.

Ren gripped the railing and shook off Ollie's help. "Everyone stay here. I'll do it. I don't want to… accidentally hurt anyone."

"Better hurry." Rowan jerked her head toward the airlock. "We have no idea what's going on out there."

Nodding, Ren climbed the stairs and, leaning hard against the bulkhead, stumbled to the bridge. His pulse raced. Sweat beaded along his hairline. The last time he'd done this, he'd been under extreme duress, pressed into the corner of the bridge, shaking and afraid. Abiathar's tow lines had thunked into the hull, and he'd threatened Ren's newfound friends. He'd wanted Ren as a weapon, and the terror of being captured again, of having whatever this power was used against innocent people, had been enough to push Ren over the edge. Panicking, Ren had tapped into *something*.

He'd once thought of his star as akin to water. He could navigate a stream, but not the river that raged inside him. His control was a dam and it had broken with his fear, and he'd flooded and transported the entire ship across the cluster.

He could do that again.

Ren's body trembled just as last time, but not from fear. He slid to the floor, propped himself against the navigation controls, and closed his eyes.

It was never easy. There was always the anxiety of burning too brightly, filling up with too much, becoming something other than

Ren. He didn't have Asher to pull him back, to ground him in his humanity. But he was intimately connected to the ship now: her systems, her personality, her capabilities. He'd spent the last six weeks inhabiting the wires and switches, surviving in the circuits and systems, thriving in the ether between potential and kinetic energies. He could do this.

Palms pressed to the hull, Ren gritted his teeth and focused.

"Not to interrupt," Lucas said, hopping into his pilot chair. It creaked beneath him. Ren startled and opened one eye to squint at Lucas. "But I've pulled up a chart for you on the navigation console. Bara is the green glob in the northeast quadrant. If you could get us close, there would be less time between now and Asher's rescue." He cleared his throat. "No pressure or anything."

"No pressure." No pressure but the possibility of another capture. No pressure except the fate of this crew, his family. No pressure except that Asher's rescue lay beyond his reach unless he could save them first. No pressure. Ren's anxiety ticked up. His heart beat in his ears.

Ren clenched his eyes shut and listened for Lucas's retreating footsteps. Once they'd faded, he dove into the ship's systems and pulled the stopper that held back the full force of his power. His star flooded through him, filled him with warmth and light, and electricity crackled through his veins, played over his skin, dripped from his fingers in torrents of white and blue light. Energy flowed from him to the ship and from the ship into him. He poured into the nav system and followed the directions Lucas had left behind.

Ren's hair stood on end. The air sizzled. Blue frizzles of power gathered in the corners of the bridge. Ren pushed and pushed. He grunted and gritted his teeth. Willing the coordinates, he overwhelmed the system, bent the physics of travel and space and time. The star pulsed under his skin and slammed into the ship, into the circuits. Ren's bones creaked. His muscles burned. His throat scorched on a yell.

A blast of light and sound rocketed from the *Star Stream*, and everything dissolved into blinding white.

⊣⊦

Ren woke to the sound of water lapping gently at the shore. Water tickled the bottom of his feet and dampened the cuffs of his trousers. Cracking his eyes open, Ren turned his head and was greeted by the sight of waves bleeding up the smooth bank of the beach. His fingers curled into the wet sand; particles dug under his fingernails. His clothes stuck uncomfortably to his skin in the humidity.

Ren sat up. The low-slung sun cast sparkles on the water, and he squinted against the riotous orange and pink hemorrhaging across the horizon. His head pounded. His mouth was dry. His body ached. He pulled his knees to his chest and hunched forward, dug his toes into the beach, and sighed as cold foam washed over them.

"What the weeds happened to you?"

Ren straightened and craned his neck. "Liam?"

A boy stood next to Ren's shoulder. It sounded like Liam, but it didn't look like him. The Liam he knew had a full face and red hair and freckles. This person who sat down next to him had hollow cheeks free of baby fat, and was pale, as if he had never seen the sun. His red hair sat limply on his forehead, and the once-vibrant fire color had faded to resemble a dying leaf. He wore a beige outfit, like the medical scrubs Ren had awakened in, and they swallowed his frame.

Ren inhaled sharply, then coughed. "Liam?"

Knees bent to his chest, arms loosely wrapped around them in a mirror of Ren's pose, the person beside him turned his head and blinked.

"Who else would it be?"

Ren moved quickly, and his head spun, but that didn't stop him from tackling Liam to the sand. He hugged his brother as they tumbled over each other and laughed. Liam thumped him on the back and chuckled in Ren's ear; his voice was lower than Ren remembered.

They stopped rolling, and Ren shoved Liam off. He pulled away and held Liam by the shoulders at arm's length. His grin split his face; his cheeks hurt. "You look so different."

"So do you." Liam grinned. He ran his hand over Ren's head. "I like it."

Ren pushed Liam's shoulder, and Liam playfully smacked his hand away.

Settling next to his brother so their shoulders touched, Ren stared out over the water. "Is this a dream?"

Liam snorted. "Obviously."

"Good, I wasn't sure."

Eyebrows raised, Liam frowned. "Why?"

"I think I may have just done something stupid. I can't really remember what happened but… I don't remember falling asleep."

"Well, you are. If you were anything else, you couldn't be here."

Ren pushed his fingers into the sand. The grains, warm from the sun, rubbed over his skin. "I always dream about this lake." Ren frowned, remembering his visit to Erden. "I hate this lake."

Chuckling, Liam knocked shoulders. "I'm doing this. Not you. And stop it. You love this lake."

"I did. Not now."

"Ah, too good for us dusters now that you're on a spaceship? Have you become a full spacer?"

Ren huffed a laugh. "Not quite."

"Good." Liam slung his arm over Ren's shoulders. "Just because you've changed doesn't mean you can't look back at your past with a little fondness."

That sounded parroted. Not like Liam at all. Unease pricked at Ren's nape. "How mature."

"I talked with Mom," Liam said, expression sheepish. "She told me about your visit and how things ended."

Ren stiffened. "You can enter her dreams?"

"It's easier with other star hosts. And I get it. You're mad because she didn't tell us. Especially you. They set you up for a life you didn't want. I'm sorry about that."

Rubbing his brow, Ren relaxed under Liam's arm. "I would've told you I saw them, but I didn't think you'd understand."

"I'm your brother. I've known you my whole life. Of course, I understand. It weeding sucks."

"Then you understand why I'm never going back, right?"

Liam's mouth tightened. "Yeah."

Ren hid his wince. Liam wanted to go back. He had never wanted to leave. Was he thinking about how he might not step on soil again? Was he thinking about how he might not hug his parents? Or dunk his brother in the lake again? Even if Ren could find him, he might not be able to rescue him.

Liam cleared his throat. He unwound his arm from Ren's shoulders and picked up a stray shell. He shook off the clinging sand. "I've been trying to reach you for weeks. I thought… well…" He furrowed his brow, and his throat bobbed. "It doesn't matter what I thought. I guess I was wrong."

Ren grimaced. "I was… incapacitated." He squinted against the bright sun and noticed how it had stalled on the horizon. "I was injured."

"Understatement. Was it her? That other one?"

"Yes. You warned me about her. I should've known."

Liam shrugged. "I wasn't sure. This power thing is still new. I'm learning the nuances. But your dreams always seemed… off… when she was near you."

"She was influencing me. I didn't know. I didn't know she could do that."

Liam nodded. "I don't know the depths of what I am capable of. Do you?"

That was a sobering question. "No. I don't. And I don't know if I want to." Ren met Liam's gaze. "Do you know where you are? Are they still monitoring you?"

Liam's mouth twitched into a smile. "I don't know where I am. And no, they can't monitor me. They never could." He sighed; his gaze dropped to his hands where he played with the shell. "When I woke up here, I was scared. I was scared they would kill me if I wasn't useful. They heavily implied it. So, I did what they told me to. I went into people's dreams and drew out information and fed it to the guys that brought me food. I thought they would know if I lied or if I couldn't reach the people they wanted. But after being here a while, I've realized, they can't follow me here." He swept his hand toward the lake. "If those weeds knew how to dream-walk, then they wouldn't need me. They're not going to kill me. They don't know if what I tell them is true or not. I keep it vague and give them kernels of truth, but never the whole." He squinted, his green eyes narrowing against the suspended setting sun. "I don't know who they are, but I know I'm not helping them anymore." He threw the shell into the lake. It skipped once, twice, three times, but instead of plunging into the water, it kept bobbing across the surface, disappearing into the infinite.

Ren swallowed. "It's the Phoenix Corps. I saw your name in their files."

Liam's eyebrows ticked up. "Do you know where I am?"

"No." Ren shook his head. "I didn't get a chance to find out. But I won't stop looking. I promise."

Liam smiled fully. "I have to go." Liam stood and wiped the sand from his pants. "You're going to wake up soon."

Ren hopped to his feet. The lake wavered. The sky thinned. The trees flicked out of existence one by one. Sand disappeared from his fingers. "I'll see you again?"

"Yeah. Of course."

They hugged, and Ren squeezed Liam tightly. "I miss you."

"I miss you, too, big brother." Liam pulled away. And it was his turn to hold Ren at arm's length and look him over. "Promise me, Ren. If you have a chance to run away, to be safe, to live a life. Take it. Don't put yourself in danger for me."

"I can't promise that."

Liam shook his head. "It was worth a try." He punched Ren in the arm before walking away. "Don't be a weed," he called over his shoulder. His body slowly became transparent.

"Take care," Ren called back.

Liam waved, and the dream fizzled out.

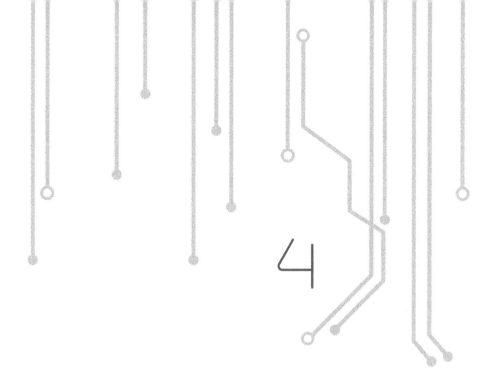

4

REN STARTLED TO WAKEFULNESS. SPRAWLED on the deck near the nav system, he lifted his head. The crew stood around him. They stared at him with varying degrees of concern or, in Darby's case, open wonder. They seemed unharmed, which filled Ren with relief.

"Did I do it?"

Ollie's dark eyebrows drew together. "Are you okay?"

"You passed out." Penelope knelt by his side and took his hand in hers. She pushed two fingers against his wrist, where Ren's pulse thudded hard under the thin skin. "It's a disturbing trend."

Eyes squinted, Darby peered at him as if he was a bug under glass. Rowan pushed her back. "Give him room and a minute. Are you okay, Ren?"

Ren opened his mouth, then shut it. He wasn't sure, but that wasn't what he was worried about. "Did I do it? Did I transport us?"

"Yeah," Lucas rubbed a hand through his hair, knocking his goggles askew. "You did it. But uh… when I said to shoot for Bara, I meant the general vicinity."

Pushing up onto his elbows, Ren squirmed away from Penelope. Ollie grabbed his arm, helped Ren to his feet, and held him steady.

His head spun. Pushing the heel of his palm to his forehead, he looked through the vid screen. But he could see nothing but a blanket of black. "How badly did I mess up? I didn't hurt the ship, did I?"

Lucas laughed nervously. "Of course not. You didn't hurt the ship. I don't think you are capable of damaging it. You're like best friends."

"Then what did—"

"You put us on the planet!" Darby's eyes were wide. Her fists clenched at her sides. "Your terrifying science-magic transported us and now we're on a planet, you freak!"

Ren winced. "Oh."

"How is that possible?" She waved her arms. "You shouldn't be able to do that. No one should be able to do that. How did you bend physics? How did we jump in time and space? Why are the rest of you not freaking out?"

Rowan crossed her arms. Lucas shrugged. Penelope pursed her lips.

Ollie chuckled, the sound low and deep. "You get used to it."

"You get used to it?" Darby's voice went shrill.

"I put us in a forest?"

"If that's a cluster of green things, then yes. That's where you put us." Lucas patted Ren's shoulder. "Good job."

"On Bara?"

"Yeah."

Ren's gaze flitted back to the screen.

"It's the planet's night time," Rowan said by way of explanation. "It doesn't help that there is a canopy of green things above us that's blocking out the light. We had to open the aft airlock to sneak a peek while you were passed out. Not only did you drop us on the planet, you made sure we are well hidden."

Ren rubbed his hands over his face. "I guess that's good."

"It's amazing, considering our hopeful expectations were that we wouldn't blow up." Lucas grinned. Penelope smacked him in the arm.

"Why don't we have a bite to eat and rest. And we'll figure out our next move once it's morning on this planet. Whenever that might be."

The group agreed with Penelope, and, with Ollie lending a shoulder, Ren followed the crew to the common room.

—⊩—

"I talked to my brother," Ren said, when only he, Ollie, and Rowan were left in the common room. Rowan stopped drying a dish, and Ollie looked up from the box of broken tech. He handed Ren a burned-out part to an air-recycling system.

"When?" Rowan asked. She placed the dish on a stack. It clinked against the others with more force than she'd been using.

"When I was asleep. He came to me in a dream."

She nodded. "Did he tell you anything?"

Ren turned the tech over in his hands, frowning at the blackened wires and broken relays. He prodded it with his star and realized the energy to fix it wouldn't be worth it.

"He doesn't know where he is, but I saw his name when I looked through the files on Phoebus. There was a list of people like me. My name was there, which is how I found Asher's location. There was also a death certificate." Ren's voice dropped on the last part. He ghosted his hand over his wound. Pain and fire danced along the edges of his senses, the report of the shot echoed in his ears, and the memory of metal on his tongue filled his mouth.

"I guess you didn't get a look at your brother's location?" Ollie took the part from Ren's lax grip and switched it for a salvageable one.

Ren shook his head; the memories fell away. "No. I didn't. But the Corps has him. That I know for certain."

Rowan rinsed out a cup. "He wasn't on Crei with Vos. He wasn't on Erden at your village or the refugee location."

"Vos never had him."

"The Corps could have him stashed anywhere." Ollie dug around in the box. "They were on Erden. They were on Crei. They're here on Bara. Who knows what other planets they've set up on? Or what they're doing here."

"We'll ask Asher that question when we get him back." Rowan finished with the dishes and dropped the towel on the counter near the sink. She leaned back against it, facing them, her elbows behind her. "I'm sure he's been doing his own reconnaissance, that selfless cog."

Ren's vision went blue as he repaired the mobile comm system Ollie handed him. His stomach twisted at the mention of Asher's self-sacrifice. "I'm sure he has."

"Liam could be in Perilous Space." Ollie shrugged. "Isn't that where they took that general?"

Rowan scoffed. "They wouldn't put a child in Perilous Space."

"He's sixteen now. Not so much a child anymore. And they would if they thought he was a danger to them," Ren said, frowning at the thought. It's what they had threatened him with after all. Ren had perceived their threats to ship him off to prison as having to do with Ren's potential for misconduct because of his technopathic ability. It was the technopaths they had gone to war with so long ago. Now, Ren knew they thought all star hosts had equal potential for uprising and treason.

Perilous Space made startling sense. Ferret out the star hosts living on the planets and shuttle them off to a place where they would be isolated and, in theory, wouldn't be able to start trouble. Abiathar was already there, and he was dangerous around other star hosts since he could coerce them to do things against their will. Unless... he'd been subdued.

Liam wasn't subdued because the Corps needed him to gather intelligence.

"He has to be there."

Rowan pushed off from the sink. "You thought he was on Erden, and he wasn't. Then you thought he was on Crei, and he wasn't. I don't think we're going to risk going to Perilous Space to find out he's not there either."

"I wouldn't ask you to," Ren said. He drew his eyebrows together. "Not there."

"We'll find Ash first. And then we'll decide what we're doing from there. Ren, we can't fight every battle. We're not equipped to save the cluster."

Ren half-smiled. "I know."

"Good. And even if we could, is it really our place? What obligation do we hold to these people?"

Ren shrugged. "I don't know."

"Neither do I. I only know how to take care of my family, and that's what I'm going to do. Idiot dusters included." She rubbed a hand over his head. "I miss ruffling your hair."

Ren ducked his head and blushed. He accepted another piece of tech from Ollie and focused on the circuits and the mechanisms as Rowan left the common area.

Rowan was right. The *Star Stream* and her crew were not equipped to save the cluster. Stars, they were barely equipped to save themselves. But he was. He was power and light, and he would fight until Asher was safe, he would fight until his brother was safe, and he wouldn't stop until Vos and the Phoenix Corps couldn't tear any more families apart, couldn't use the people of the cluster and the planets for their own gain ever again.

⊣⊢

When the sun came up after a few hours, the light barely filtered through the thick foliage that surrounded them. Ren thought he'd dropped the ship in the middle of a forest. He was wrong. These weren't the trees he was used to on Erden: tall, thin evergreens filled with needles, and deciduous trees with leaves that would turn bright red and gold in the autumn. These weren't the smooth laurels of the refugee camp where his family had fled.

These trees were clumped together, breaking out of the ground, then twisting toward the light, tangling with the canopy overhead. Thick, green vines wrapped and climbed the trees and hung, webbing them together, while large spiky fronds sieved the light between their spindles. Roots bubbled up from the ground in intricate networks, and moss clung to every surface of rock and bark. The canopy spread above, a barrier between them and the sky. In the spaces where light reached the ground, dense vegetation grew, filled with thorns and leaves bigger than a full-grown human. Wild birds called to each other with shrill voices and fluttered with vibrant plumage from perch to perch. Small animals scampered in the brush.

Ren stood at the open airlock. Sweat prickled at the back of his neck and rolled over his skin. The humidity was an oppressive blanket and it settled in his lungs with every breath. He craned his neck to look up. "We're not flying out of here."

Rowan stood at his shoulder. "No, we're not." She flinched away when a loud caw echoed close by. "This is too much nature."

"What is this place?" Lucas asked, standing on his toes, peering out over Rowan's shoulder. "And what is that?"

Ren shifted his gaze to where Lucas pointed to find the largest snake he'd ever seen. He yelped as it slithered close to the ship with its the smooth scales shining brown and black. Ren jumped back. He slammed the door, eyes blazing blue, arms tucked close to his chest.

Rowan raised an eyebrow. "I've seen one of those in a drift zoo. It's a snake. Right?"

"I don't like snakes." Ren shuddered. "And that thing was big enough to eat us."

"They eat humans? Unreal." Lucas adjusted his goggles. "So, no wandering around without a buddy then. Not that I would. Too much... fresh air and dirt and danger."

Ren rolled his eyes. "We need to find the Phoenix Corps base where Asher is being held. I doubt it's around here though."

"Use the sensors. See if you can pick up a settlement." Lucas leaned on the bulkhead. "You know what Corps tech feels like, right?"

Ren nodded. "Yeah, I do."

"But even if we're close, I don't know about traversing this..." she waved her hand.

"Jungle," Ren said.

"Jungle." Rowan pursed her lips. "It's thick and there are *things* out there."

Lucas snorted. "Never thought I'd see my captain afraid of a little dust."

Tugging on her braid, Rowan narrowed her eyes. "Oh, really? You think I'm afraid?"

Lucas held up his hands. "I think everyone should have a healthy fear of planets. Seriously. Who likes dust and dirt and… fauna."

"You know you're coming with us now, right?" Lucas sputtered out a protest, but Rowan raised her hand. "Save it. We've determined we don't need a pilot, but we will need someone proficient with maps."

Lucas wilted. "You're not joking."

"No."

"Aw, stars."

Ren snickered. Lucas punched Ren in the shoulder, and Ren stumbled into the wall. He leaned on it heavily and rubbed the sore spot.

"If we're done acting like children," Rowan said, glaring, "we need to prepare. Ren, use the sensors and see what you can find. Lucas, get ready."

Grumbling, Lucas headed for the bridge. Rowan patted Ren on the shoulder. "Are you going to be able to hike through a jungle? You're still weak."

"I'm better. I can do it."

Rowan sighed. "I'm not going to argue."

She read in his expression that he was not going to be left behind. He was going to rectify his mistakes. He was going to find Asher even if it took hiking through a thousand jungles and encountering a thousand snakes.

"Find him." She headed for the stairs. "Find him, then we'll plan."

Ren left the cargo bay and ended up in the common room. He slumped onto the couch, closed his eyes, and relaxed into the worn cushions. Maybe after everything was over Ren could convince Rowan to get a new couch.

Ren tapped into the comms. "Lucas, watch the vid screen. I'll put what I find on there."

Lucas responded with a mutter of acquiescence.

Flooding into the ship's sensors, using them to boost his power, Ren reached out in a circle from the ship and gradually expanded the perimeter. He didn't have to travel far until he was overwhelmed with feedback from tech. A cluster of ships, a comm tower, and a docking platform were nearby, they were merely... up. Beyond the canopy, almost directly above them. It was promising, but not what he was looking for.

Brows knit together, Ren pushed out farther until he encountered more signatures. A small town, maybe? Not Phoenix Corps—Ren didn't recognize the tech.

He didn't know how much farther he could go, but he ballooned outward, ignoring the transports that flew from the ground to the spaceport and the kitchen appliances that whirred on the edge of his consciousness and the messages that hovered in the air. Frowning, he scanned and spread and *there*! A ping of a Corps weapon! Ren pulled his circle in, then focused on that direction, and shot out in a line. Corps tech flooded him. Weapons and generators and forcefields bled into him. Communications buzzed beneath his eyes, and vehicles hummed in his chest, and data pads tickled over his skin.

Ren threw the information on the vid screen of the bridge and listened over the comm to the rest of the crew's reactions.

"I've got it, Ren," Lucas said. "You can pull back."

Ren snapped into his body like a rubber band and tipped sideways onto the couch.

"That is cogging weird," Darby said from her perch on the table. "Your eyes glow and your face goes totally blank." She waved a hand in front of her nose. "Like you're not there at all."

"You're calmer now," Ren said.

Darby waved her hand. "I needed my moment of escalation, but I'm good now. I think. I'm more curious. If I had punched you, would you have felt it?"

Ren blinked. "Uh... yes?"

"You don't sound very sure."

"It's hard to explain."

"Try. How does the freaky science-magic work? And why do they..." She lifted her chin in the direction of the hallway that led to the bridge. "...get all jittery when you do it?"

"They do?"

"Are you kidding me? They're like a rare-meteorite peddler in a room full of thieves. You know... skittish."

"I understood the metaphor."

Chin in her hand, knees bent, she shrugged. "Well, I don't know. You're a duster. You have different frames of reference."

Ren didn't want to have this conversation lying down and grudgingly pushed to a sitting position. "There is always a price to... freaky science-magic. I need to have an anchor, or I might forget that I'm human."

Darby's mouth thinned into a line. "Okay. And I'm guessing someone on this ship is your anchor."

Grimacing, Ren looked away. "I lost my anchor. But I'm going to get him back."

"Ah. That explains a few things. I think. Maybe. Okay, not really."

Ren sighed. He rubbed his temples. "I haven't been well, and my perceptions of some situations were wrong. Part of that was someone manipulating me. The other part was me and how I panic sometimes. And I scared the crew. I scared myself."

Darby wrinkled her nose. "But they trust you."

"I think so."

"That wasn't a question." Darby brushed a lock of her dark hair behind her ear and leaned in. "They may get skittish, but they trust you. They trusted you to get the information from that data pad. They trusted you to get us through that locked door on the drift. And then they trusted you to transport us across the cluster. And now, they trust you to find the missing crewman."

"How do you know that?"

She waved her hand. "Gaining trust is kind of my specialty. I learned how to recognize it young and how to exploit it. Don't worry," she amended hastily. "I'm not trying to pull anything on your crew. I'm not addled."

"Thanks," Ren said drily.

She pulled back. "I don't get it, though. Why do they put so much faith in someone who scared them? How can they believe in you?"

"Because they're good people. They're my friends, my family."

She threaded her fingers and rested her chin on them with her elbows planted on her knees. "Huh."

"Yeah."

They sat in companionable silence. Darby dropped into a chair and bounced her leg on the deck plate. Her gaze was far away. Ren saw someone different from the cocky thief with the big mouth who had stolen aboard their ship looking for a quick credit. He saw a vulnerable young woman who readily left a drift with a bunch of strangers because there wasn't someone for her to run back for and save from the chaos. He saw a girl who questioned kindness and didn't quite grasp forgiveness. He saw someone who was as lost as he sometimes felt.

He was glad of the quiet and leaned back into the cushions of the couch. He was scared of what he'd find or wouldn't find beyond the thick crush of nature that surrounded the ship. Was Asher really here? Would they be able to find him? Would they be able to free him? Would he want to be freed? Was he even trapped?

Before the doubts could completely creep in, Ollie's voice boomed over the comm.

"All crew meet in the cargo bay. We're going exploring!"

⊣⊢

"I can't believe I'm doing this," Lucas said as he followed Ollie. For once, his goggles weren't tangled in his brown hair, but were pulled down onto his face. In his hand he held a data pad that guided them. Their path to the village was a winding red line, and they were a blinking blue dot. "If I die, take my body to space and eject me into the nearest star. Please ensure my constituent atoms are able to roam the cluster freely and aren't trapped on this dirt hole."

"Stars, Lucas, I didn't know you could be so dramatic." Rowan walked behind him and picked her way through the overgrowth. "Does Pen know this side of you?"

"Of course she does."

"I guess what they say is true then."

"What's that?" Lucas asked as he swatted away a large bug. He ducked and shrieked when it swooped at his head and then took off for a higher branch.

Rowan's lips lifted in a small smile. "That love makes fools of us all."

"Hey!"

Ollie snorted.

Ren rolled his eyes but couldn't argue. Asher had done things for him that couldn't be classified as rational, and he was tromping through a teeming rain forest on a hunch that Asher may be nearby.

Using a modified welder and a large knife they found in the cargo bay, Ollie cut a trail. In some parts of the rain forest, the canopy blocked all light and thus the growth on the floor wasn't too difficult to maneuver through. Other than the trunks of skinny trees, there weren't many obstacles. In other areas, where light did filter through gaps, the group encountered thick undergrowth that snagged their clothes and grew higher than their knees, sometimes their waists.

Ren, certain he'd disturbed some animal's nest, grimaced as he trudged through the small opening Ollie had made. They'd seen the huge snake, and Ren had added colorful frogs, birds with magnificent plumage and loud caws, and something that had growled at them from a perch. He hadn't caught of glimpse of it other than patterned fur, but Lucas had dropped the data pad and almost jumped into Rowan's arms at the sound. Ren's skin had prickled, and he'd wished he hadn't turned down Rowan's offer of a pulse gun.

It was difficult to determine the passage of time, since the sky wasn't visible and the light seemed filtered, so, when the trees became sparse and the edge of the jungle was discernible, Ren was surprised to find it was twilight.

Rowan frowned. "Bara has short days." Thunder rumbled above them, and rain smattered the leaves. "And frequent rain storms."

"Great," Lucas mumbled. He clutched the data pad to his chest. "We're close. Finally. That village is ahead; the Corps camp is a little farther. There should be a road."

Ren huddled into Asher's jacket and tugged the collar higher around his ears. They trudged forward, breaking out of the jungle into a clearing.

Before them, the metal of buildings rose from the landscape and gleamed in the last of the sun's rays. Houses made of wood and stone dotted the perimeter. It wasn't a town, but a city, and it was certainly bigger than Ren's village had been. It nestled between the rain forest on one side and a ridge of mountains on the other. Roads and buildings sprawled outward following the contours of the land. Craning his neck, Ren spied the towering space port; transports floated to land somewhere in the middle of a cluster of buildings. Along the ridges of the mountains, the sunlight reflected from structures, and Ren followed the line of development which connected the main part of the town in the basin with the buildings on the ridges all the way up to a bridge built out of the side of the mountain connecting to the spaceport. This gave access by both air and land to the platforms. It was genius.

"Wow," Rowan said, shielding her eyes, as she also stared at the construction. "Who knew dusters could be so…" she waved her hand, looking for the word.

"Smart is the word you're looking for," Lucas said.

"Necessity is the mother of invention," Ollie said.

Ren huffed. "You're all so arrogant." He pushed past the others and headed into the town. "Come on."

They passed a line of clothes becoming damp in the drizzle. Rowan tugged a dark cloak off the line. She tossed it to Ren.

"You and Ollie are going to go check out the Corps encampment. Lucas and I are going to stay here. I want to talk to a few locals."

Furrowing his brow, Ren wrapped the cloak around him. He pulled up the hood. "Won't you be noticed?"

Thumbs hooked into her pockets, she shook her head. "A town next to a spaceport with the Corps nearby, they'll be used to travelers." She scanned the city's outskirts. "We'll maintain comm silence until you contact us. We'll meet back here." She leveled a hard gaze at Ren. "Don't do anything stupid."

Ren bit back a frown and nodded. "Yes, Captain."

"Good."

Lucas smacked the data pad into Ollie's chest. "Don't break it. It's precious to me."

"You're ridiculous."

Rowan sighed and rolled her eyes. She pointed her finger at Ren then at Ollie. "Nothing stupid."

Ollie and Ren skirted the city, which took longer than either of them would have guessed. The sky darkened, and clouds and thunder rolled ahead. Three sister moons glowed in the sky. Despite the descent of the sun, the heat didn't abate, and sweat rolled down Ren's skin, followed the curve of his spine, and gathered at his temples.

Transports whizzed past them, and they walked around carts pulled by small work animals, but the farther they went, the more the population thinned. Once they were the only ones on the road, Ollie tilted his head and Ren joined him to dart into a patch of trees.

"It's just up ahead."

"I know." Ren tugged on his hood and concealed his face, except the burning blue of his eyes. The power generators from the camp thrummed under his skin. The warning beacons surrounding it pulsed in his ears, and forcefields hummed in his chest. The ping-back from weapons threatened to overwhelm him, but he centered his power with thoughts of seeing Asher again. He swallowed hard. "I can feel everything."

Ollie flashed him a concerned look, and rested his hand on Ren's shoulder. "We'll be all right."

"What if he's not here?"

Ollie lifted an eyebrow. "Then we'll look somewhere else." His fingers squeezed. "We won't stop searching for him."

Fear clogged Ren's throat. His muscles tingled with fatigue. He felt pinched and drawn, and his senses were drowned in tech.

"Let's go."

Ollie and Ren approached the Phoenix Corps camp—a bustling makeshift city of temporary housing—under the cover of the surrounding trees.

Ren sweated beneath his clothes; the rain only made the atmosphere muggy. Insects as big as Ren's palm flew between the thick towering trees. Occasional howls and calls from local fauna cut through the silence of the night and sent chills down Ren's spine.

Ren's body tensed beneath his borrowed cloak. Clouds swept across the sky and obscured the stars, but one of the moons hung low and reflected the nearest star through breaks in the canopy to illuminate their path.

They skirted the perimeter, scouting the area, taking stock of the encampment. It wasn't large like the citadel on Erden, rather the size of a village, but the power it generated was overwhelming. Ren did his best to catalogue the buildings and the tech signatures, feeding the information into the data pad. They'd decipher it later and form a plan.

Ollie and Ren picked a path in the brush that ran to the muddy earthen road connecting the city to the Corps encampment. Following it, they came around a sharp bend and stopped short.

In front of them sat a small cargo ship with the symbol of the Phoenix Corps emblazoned on the side and several Corps members. Ren hadn't picked up the signatures from the transport or their weapons because his senses were flooded by the generators and the forcefields of the main camp.

Scrambling, Ollie and Ren ducked into a large pile of brush. Mud clung to Ren's pants, and thorns caught on his cloak, but he didn't dare move, almost didn't dare to breathe as he peeked through the dense crush of foliage. He fervently hoped he hadn't bothered any of the local wildlife, especially any snakes. Ollie crouched, his large body bent double as he clutched his pulse gun. Ollie held a finger to his lips, and Ren nodded.

Squinting, Ren made out four individuals in Corps uniforms around a small shuttle and a hovercraft that reminded Ren of the floaters back home. Pulling his power from the main area, Ren focused on the shuttle. It was old and damaged and had lost power. The smaller hovercraft hummed with low power, enough to float, but not near enough to make it to the spaceport towering over them a few miles away. Three of the four guards carried weapons, and all four wore comms.

"Did you hear that?" one of the Corps members asked, turning around to survey the area with weapon drawn.

"How could I hear anything over your complaining?" another one said. "You haven't shut up since we left the main base."

The original soldier huffed. "Well, I hate this place." His voice rang out clear over the buzz of insects. He slapped his palm against his neck and grimaced. "Cogging bugs. They're everywhere." He shook out his hand.

"And the heat," another one said. She tugged at her high collar. "It's nighttime. Isn't it supposed to let off? I feel like I'm going to suffocate. Where are the environmental controls?"

"This is a planet, cog. There aren't environmental controls." The second one wiped his brow. "Besides, if you didn't whine so much then you wouldn't waste the air."

The fourth member, who lugged boxes between the shuttle and the hovercraft, let out a snort. The leader, a thick tall man, whipped out a baton and smacked it against the box he carried.

"Have something to say, Private?"

"No, *sir.*"

Ren stiffened. It couldn't be. But Ren knew that voice. He'd heard it every night lying in a cell in a stone citadel. He'd heard it calling him back when he was immersed in the ship. He'd heard it whisper his name as he lay dying on a table.

Asher.

"You better not. And keep moving. Those supplies aren't going to unload themselves. Cogging supply transport busted like it is. I don't know how they expect us to get a job done with cheap equipment." He kicked the ship. The solid thunk of sound echoed loud in the night, followed by a curse and laughter from the others.

Asher sidestepped him and grunted as he hefted the box higher, then trudged between the two vehicles. The leader glared at him.

Ollie clamped his hand over Ren's shoulder, and that's when Ren realized he'd pulled his body into a crouch and had inched closer.

A break in the cloud cover allowed the three moons and stars to light the whole clearing. And Ren could distinctly make out the small group. Yes, four of them, including Asher, who was unmistakable in the moonlight—his light hair and his muscular frame and the way he moved and the sound of his voice were all achingly familiar. His uniform was torn and disheveled, and his boots were caked with mud.

Asher carried another box and slid it into the bed of the hovercraft. "I'm done."

"Took you long enough, grunt. Stars, my grandmother could've done it faster. Is that why you were busted? For being a lazy cog?"

Asher remained silent.

"I heard it was because he went AWOL. Ran away from his post and hid," the woman said. She sneered at him. "Job get too hard for the pampered little drifter prince?"

The third scoffed and joined the others in a semicircle around Asher. Rain fell heavier. Thunder rumbled.

"I heard he's a traitor. Consorted with the enemy."

"Oh yeah?" the leader asked. He prowled around Asher, moving closer. "Explains why leadership has been close-lipped about you. That true, grunt? Are you a traitor?"

Asher turned his head.

"I asked you a question. Are you a traitor?"

Asher tipped his head, looking to the sky.

"I think he's refusing a direct order."

"Sure looks that way."

The leader laughed, low and menacing. "You know what happens to traitors, right?" The punch to Asher's gut doubled him over. The shove had him on his hands and knees.

Asher coughed once, but otherwise didn't make a sound. He shifted to stand in the mud, but slipped while the other Corps members around him laughed. Rivulets of rain ran down his face, and he wiped them away with his sleeve, smearing mud across the sharp jut of his cheekbones. He attempted to stand again, but was pushed back to the ground with a weapon that reminded Ren of the prods the soldiers' used during his own captivity.

"How's the dirt down there, Private? Does it taste good?"

The biggest of the three kicked Asher's leg from under him and Asher fell all the way to the ground, landing on his bad shoulder. He grunted, features twisting in pain.

Ren *burned*. He moved to stand, but Ollie grabbed his arm, pulled him down, and shook his head.

Don't do anything stupid. Stick to the plan. Ren needed to stick to the plan. But for that to happen, he needed to look away, and he couldn't do that either.

"I asked you a question, Private!"

Asher laid in the mud, breathing hard. He stayed silent, expression hard, jaw clenched as he watched the three standing above him.

His silence seemed to anger them.

"Well, come on. On your feet."

Asher rolled to his stomach and pushed up on his elbows. He was rewarded with a kick to his ribs which sent him sprawling. His chest heaved. His head splashed in a puddle. The three above him guffawed.

"He gave you an order. Get up."

Asher grimaced. "Yes, sir."

"I'm sorry, what was that, *nub*?"

Ren didn't know what the word meant. It wasn't a term he'd heard, but it meant something to Asher, because his entire demeanor changed. Asher staggered to his feet. He wiped his thumb over his bottom lip; blood smeared his chin. He looked at his thumb, then looked at the three that surrounded him.

"Don't touch me again."

"I don't think I like your tone, nub." The leader grabbed the weapon from his friend; the end of it sparked in the rain. He raised it, the energy hummed, the tip glowed blue and hovered close to Asher's face.

Ren reached out, submerged himself in the power source and the mechanisms, and *yanked*. The weapon sputtered out, but he didn't relinquish his hold, daring them to touch Asher again. He'd light it up, burn the safeties out of it, until it fizzed and popped, until it turned on the person wielding it. He'd done it before, at the citadel on Erden to Corporal Zag's unit. He'd scorched them for daring to threaten his friends. He'd do more than that to these cogs, to these men who dared *touch* Asher, who dared to make Asher grovel in the wet earth.

The big man narrowed his eyes and cursed. He jimmied the handle, checked the power source, and cursed again when the tip wouldn't light.

"Must be your lucky day," he snarled at Asher.

Asher tossed a glance over his shoulder, scanning the tree line. "Must be," he said, voice flat.

Ren shuddered as Asher's hot gaze passed over his hiding place. Could he see Ren? Could he feel his presence?

"Shut up!" The big man gave Asher a shove. "Back to the cell with you."

"Traitors get their own special private rooms." The group laughed.

Asher turned away, but not without one last, longing look at the tree line. He hopped in the back with the cargo while the others piled in the front. They sped off in a puff of smoke and a spray of dirt.

Ren and Ollie emerged from their hiding place.

"We're rescuing him. Tonight."

Ollie nodded. "Agreed."

"Let's go."

Ren turned, stride determined, expression grim, star throbbing in his middle, and stalked back the way they'd come. He burned with anger and with strength. He'd save Asher as Asher had saved him. No one would stop him. Then they'd scorch a brilliant contrail through the planet's dense sky and leave the Phoenix Corps behind in a pile of ash.

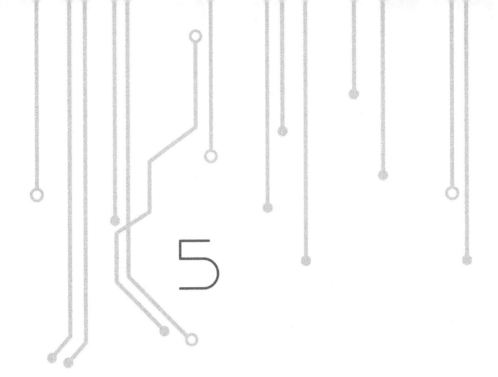

5

Ren sank into the captain's chair despite the look he received from Rowan. He had to. His atrophied legs and torso, exhausted from the trek to and from the Phoenix Corps encampment, couldn't hold him up much longer.

On the screen in front of them flashed the information he'd secured from the scouting mission. Asher could be housed anywhere in the camp, but he was there. Ren had seen him, muddied and bleeding, but beautiful all the same. Based on the camp layout and the strong forcefield signature emanating from a small building toward the center, they'd guessed that was Asher's probable whereabouts.

Darby sauntered onto the bridge as she bit into a piece of fruit she'd snagged from the bowl in the common area. She chewed loudly as she peered over Lucas's shoulder at the map of the encampment on the vid screen. Her knee bumped Ren's leg. He grimaced from the flash of pain and inched away.

"We need a diversion," Rowan said, pointing to the map. "To draw everyone away from the cell."

"I'm good at diversions," Darby said, taking another bite.

Ren tilted his head. "This isn't the kind of diversion we used to get the data pad."

"Nah, that won't work." She pointed to the power generator. "You need to take that out."

Rowan arched an eyebrow. "Take it out?"

Crunching, Darby nodded. "Yeah. Blow it up. Boom!" She made a motion with her hands that Ren guessed was supposed to be an explosion.

"Can you do that?"

She glanced at Ren. "Yes, and so can you. You can do it with your science-magic."

"Ren will have other concerns than blowing things up. He'll need his strength to disable the perimeter alarms and lower the forcefields and then to transport us since we won't be able to fly out." Rowan leveled a stare at Darby. "So, are you willing?"

Darby took another bite. "Oh, yeah. I love blowing things up."

"Now," Rowan tapped her lips, "how to get in."

"Capture," Ren said.

Rowan's eyes widened. The group shifted their attention to him. Rowan caught on first.

"*No.*"

"Yes. They'll take me to the cell, and I can power down the forcefields while Darby creates a diversion."

"No, Ren. No. You can't guarantee they'll take you to the right building. They may kill you on the spot."

"They can't."

"They *have*. Stars, Ren, are you addled?"

"I can do it." In defiance, Ren straightened from his sprawl. His joints protested, and he bit his lip to keep from grimacing. "I need to do it. It's the best way to guarantee Asher's location. And I'd rather risk myself than any of you."

"You're still recovering," Penelope said gently. "Maybe you should stay on the outskirts and do what you need to from afar."

"I can't," Ren said. "I need to be close to—"

"That's a coggin' lie." Rowan crossed her arms. "We all know you don't have to be in the vicinity to do what you need to."

Ren gritted his teeth. "I do this time."

Ollie and Lucas exchanged a glance and backed away.

Rowan huffed, her green eyes narrowed, and her lips thinned. "Don't think you have a monopoly on wanting to free Ash. He's my brother. He's been a friend to this crew for years. You aren't the only one who cares about what happens here. You aren't the only one who loves him."

Ren shot to his feet. "But I'm the one who put him there!" His legs quivered; his muscles strained to keep him upright. "It was my stupid decisions. My altered perceptions. My *mistakes* that forced Asher to give himself up to save *me*." Ren's eyes watered, and he scrubbed the tears away with the heel of his palm. Exhaustion pulled at him, and pain throbbed from his side to combine with the swirling emotions he struggled to keep in check. His chest heaved; his breathing hitched. "I need to save him."

"Ren," Rowan said softly, "after everything that's happened, I can't ask you to be taken captive."

"I'm volunteering." Ren's voice wavered.

"What if it triggers a panic attack? What if they beat you? You couldn't take that right now. What if they use iron shackles instead of a forcefield?"

All color drained from Ren's face, and he fell back into the chair. He opened his mouth, but he had no response, much less any air.

"Then we'll intervene," Ollie said. "We'll have a solid plan B in our pocket. But Ren is right. He can disable weapons and tech and has a better chance than any of us. This is the best way."

Rowan slammed her fist on the console. The image of the camp wavered. "I know it's probably the best way, but I will not give up one crew member for another, no matter who they are. I'm not losing anyone else. I *can't* lose anyone else!" Her composure fractured. Her expression crumpled; her bottom lip trembled. Strands of hair escaped from her braid. Silence descended on the deck, and the only sound was Rowan's harsh breathing. She turned away from them and bowed her head.

"Rowan," Penelope said softly, but Rowan held up her hand and stopped her.

She shuddered, then turned, eyes red, but seeming collected, to address them. "I apologize for my outburst." She rested her hands on her hips. "And if you are bent on following this course of action, I advise that we at least rest for a day. And then we'll go. Ren can barely stand."

Ren shook his head. "No," he said cautiously, twisting his fingers, "we go tonight. We can't let Asher stay there any longer. Not after what Ollie and I saw."

Ollie sighed, then clenched his fists. "Captain, I agree with Ren."

Lucas shrugged. "Well, you won't have me complaining about getting off this humid, frightening rock."

Rowan frowned and threw up her hands. "I guess it was my mistake to think I had any control over this crew anymore."

"If it's any consolation," Darby said, crunching a mouthful of fruit, "I don't think you had control to begin with."

Rowan turned a murderous glare on Darby, and Darby shrank back to hide behind Ren.

"Anyway," Lucas said, bringing the conversation back to topic, "the sooner we leave the better. The populace here aren't keen on the Corps, and there are grumblings."

Ren perked up. "What do you mean?"

"When Rowan and I were in the city, we hit up a bar and listened. The citizens aren't happy the Corps is here, and there have already been a few scuffles between soldiers and townsfolk."

Rowan cleared her throat. "We'll use it to our advantage. Maybe the Corps will think our diversion was caused by the locals. It doesn't hurt that they'll capture a duster lurking around." She pinned Ren with an intense stare.

Ren's throat went dry, and he squirmed. The full implication of their plan was settling in, and with it, all the things that could potentially go wrong. But what choice did they have? He wouldn't leave Asher there any longer.

"I'll be fine," he said to the unasked question. He hoped he wasn't lying.

-||-

Ren approached the camp with his cloak pulled tight around his body and the hood pulled up to cover his face. The night had darkened considerably. The moons had moved, and only a few stars were visible behind wispy clouds. The air sat heavy and humid in Ren's lungs. As he walked the road, his boots sank in the clinging mud and panic swelled in his chest. His throat tightened, and his breath whistled as if he sucked through a straw.

"You okay, Ren?" Rowan's voice came over the comm clipped to the hood of his cloak.

He wasn't. Everything hurt. Every joint creaked and protested as he moved. Every thump of his heart echoed in his temple. Every second out in the open made his skin crawl. Every pulse of electricity scorched through his veins.

"I'm fine," he rasped.

"Are you sure?"

Ren closed his eyes and sought out the nearest perimeter alarm. He found it a few feet away and set it off. Then he shut down all the others for Ollie and Darby. No turning back now. He stopped at the edge and waited.

"Yes. Alarms are down."

"Remain calm." Ollie's voice was a comfort in his ear. "Darby and I are nearby."

"I know."

Ren stilled and waited. Soon the thump of approaching boots sounded, and the chatter of voices filled his ears. He crossed the perimeter line and ducked his head.

"Who are you?" Ren peeked from below the hood. The voice came from the large soldier who had kicked Asher. Ren bit his lip and fought the urge to latch on to the pulse gun in the soldier's holster and exact revenge. Instead he held his body still. A beating like Asher had taken earlier would crush Ren in his still-healing state, and then they would need to enact their plan B. That plan was haphazard at best and put Ollie at risk—something Ren wouldn't allow.

The soldier neared and slowed. He squinted at Ren and stopped a few feet away. Another soldier flanked him, and his comm crackled on his chest.

"What is it? Another animal? Or did it short out with the rain?"

"Some duster," he responded. He lifted his chin. "Are you going to answer me? Who are you? What are doing around here?"

Ren unclenched his hands. "No one and nothing."

"Yeah, right. Are you selling something? Or are you snooping? Because we're not buying. And if you're snooping, well…" He pulled out his weapon and hefted it in his hand. "We've already had some problems with you backward mud dwellers."

When Ren didn't respond, the guard pushed him hard in the arm with the tip of the pulse gun. Ren wobbled and took a step back. "*Don't.*"

"Or what?" He huffed. "You going to fight me, little duster? You're obviously too foolish to stay away from where you're not wanted."

Ren didn't speak. His throat closed at the unwanted touch. His pulse sped beneath his skin. His chest tightened.

"Go away and don't snoop unless you want trouble."

Ren's comm crackled. "You have to do something for him to take you," Ollie's voice was muffled, but even and sure. "Insult him."

"What was that?" The guard stepped forward and grabbed Ren's upper arm in his meaty grip. "Do you have a comm? What is this?"

He ripped Ren's hood back and snatched the device clipped to the fabric. "What are you up to?"

Ren swallowed. "I... I don't...."

"Do you think we're addled? That we don't know about your little duster resistance?"

Ren's focus zeroed down to where the guard's hand grabbed him. His senses fuzzed. Static filled his head. His vision grayed at the edges. He closed his eyes and reached out for tech. He latched onto their data pads. He took comfort in the circuits and bled into them, surging through and burning out the wires.

The guard shoved Ren toward his subordinate. "Take him to the cells. I'll go report."

Ren tripped and landed on his hands and knees. The charge of a baton reverberated in his veins as the tip pushed hard against his ribs. He opened his eyes. His fingers curled in the sticky earth.

"Get up."

Staggering to his feet, Ren complied. Head ducked, his hood hanging in his eyes, Ren meekly followed. Moving farther into the camp, Ren noted the pole lights in various areas. Finding one near the main generator, Ren reached out and cut it off.

"Cheap lights," his captor muttered. "Always shorting in the cogging rain."

Ren took that as permission to cut out a few more.

The soldier led Ren to the building in the middle of the camp and scanned his silver tags in the reader. The door swung open. He grabbed Ren by the back of the neck and pushed him over the threshold.

"Dim duster," he spat as he manhandled him into the building. He pushed him down a few corridors and into a room with two forcefield cells. Ren stifled the hysterical laughter that bubbled in his throat at the irony and kept his head down as they pushed him into the electric cage.

He tripped and landed hard on the wood floor, and dust from the hay wafted into his face. Ren sneezed, and the soldier laughed.

"You've got a roommate for the night, Private. We'll figure out what to do with witless dusters who snoop in the morning."

The forcefield went up around him; the hum buzzed in his chest, under his skin. Once the soldier left, Ren sat up and rubbed his sleeve over his face while keeping his back turned to the other occupant of the room.

Asher sighed. "Sorry for them. They're not exactly the pinnacle of Phoenix Corps decorum."

Ren closed his eyes and allowed Asher's voice to soothe him. The anxiety that had swelled in him during the encounter gradually bled away, like the tide receding from the beach, a slow ebb and flow, until he calmed. He had made it. Asher was next to him. Anything else could transpire and it would be fine because Asher would be by his side.

Asher cleared his throat. "Hey, are you okay? Don't be afraid. They'll release you in the morning."

Ren stood and turned, wearing a smile so wide his cheeks hurt. A tear spilled down his cheek. His body filled with warmth and happiness, and he was going to burst. "We won't be here in the morning."

The gasp was immediate, and Asher stumbled away from their shared wall. "Ren?"

Asher's face was smudged with dirt, but his green eyes were bright despite the mud smeared in his hair. Dark circles spread like bruises beneath his eyes, and the sharp cut of cheekbones spoke of harsh weeks.

Ren moved forward and pulled his hood away. With a thought, he powered down the forcefields, leaving nothing between them except the musty air and the thick memories from the last time they parted. He reached out a trembling hand. His star instinctively sought out the mechanism in Asher's shoulder and tingled through it, inspecting the joint; a blueprint of the metal fused with bone lit behind Ren's eyes. Nothing appeared damaged despite the beating Asher had endured.

Ren's fingertips grazed Asher's jawline, then across the line of his cheek, until they caressed the soft skin of Asher's ear and his palm cradled Asher's face.

"Ash." Ren said his name on a sigh. "Oh, Ash, I've missed—"

Ren's words were cut off by Asher's mouth on his. His hand cupping Ren's face was gentle, but his arm wrapped around Ren's waist in an iron grip and pulled him tight enough to bruise. Ren kissed back. His loneliness and grief and relief at finally finding Asher manifested in every rough pass of his lips. He brimmed with emotion—good and bad, light and dark—his body and spirit were bursting and overcome. Power crackled in the air, and goosebumps bloomed over his skin despite the stifling heat and the tight grasp of Asher's hands. They kissed, needy and frantic, as if they were each other's air and life and everything good in the world. Ren didn't pull away despite the need to talk, to plan their getaway. Instead he allowed Asher to back him against the wall and devour his mouth with the same intensity he did everything else.

Asher finally broke the kiss but didn't move away. He buried his face in Ren's neck; his breath was a hot, rhythmic brush on Ren's skin. He trembled when Ren clutched his body in a desperate embrace.

"You're alive," Asher said, voice breaking. He cradled the back of Ren's neck with his hand; his fingers scratched through the short hair at Ren's nape. "You're alive. You're alive and you're here."

Ren's stomach swooped, and his throat clogged with tears. "I thought you knew that."

"You were when I left, but I didn't know. I didn't know if Pen was going to be able to save you. If you were going to wake up."

"I'm alive," Ren said. He patted Asher's hair. "And you're found. And we're getting out of here."

Asher pulled back and placed his hands on Ren's shoulders. "What the cogs are you doing here?" he said, eyes narrowed, jaw clenched. "You're risking yourself. You could be anywhere. You had your freedom."

Ren took Asher's hand and threaded their fingers. "What's freedom without you?"

The blush spilling over Asher's cheeks in the dim light was the most beautiful sight Ren had ever seen. Erden's sunsets paled in comparison. The view of stars rotating outside a drift window was breathtaking, but nothing in the face of the shy lift of Asher's mouth.

"When we get out of here, we are going to have a fight about this—a loud fight—but right now, I'm so happy to see you."

Ren smiled, his eyes crinkling. "As I was saying, I've missed you. Every bit of you, even the surly part. Now, are you ready to run?"

"They'll know it was you. Or they'll blame Rowan. I can't leave."

Ren shrugged. "Actually, the soldiers didn't log me in because suddenly their data pads wouldn't work. And you're not escaping. You're going to go missing in all the confusion."

Asher raised an eyebrow. "Confusion?"

Ren smiled. "You don't think I was stupid enough to come alone, do you?"

Asher's brow furrowed. He shook his head; his lips were pulled down at the corners. "Who did you—"

The explosion cut Asher off with a tremendous boom. The sound deafened them, swallowed the words Asher shouted, and left the world muffled for agonizing seconds. The ground shook violently, tossing Ren to his knees; the packed earthen floor of the prison scraped through the fabric of his trousers. The makeshift building shuddered. The walls threatened collapse from the force of the shockwave. The remaining forcefield wavered, then fell, as the lights cut out.

Pitched into darkness, Ren had the breath knocked out of his lungs when Asher stumbled and collided with him. Knowing the explosion was imminent didn't keep Ren from being rattled. His ears hurt and rang. His head pounded as he fell forward on his palms.

"What the cogs was that?" Asher's voice sounded squeezed, as if his breath had been surprised out of him.

"Our cue," Ren said, overly loud. He shook his head, hoping the fuzz would clear. "Let's go." Ren held out his hand in the darkness to what looked like Asher's outline, and Asher grabbed it with a strong grip. He threaded his fingers through Ren's and tugged Ren to standing.

"Follow me." Asher stepped out of the cell and pulled.

Together, they ran. Bursting from the building, they found the night sky lit with flames almost as bright as the planet's sun. Thick smoke plumed and curled and blocked the scant light from the stars and the moon. The combination of flickering flames and smoke bathed the camp in moving and twisting shadows; frightening omen-like shapes danced around them, chased them as they ran, but provided reassuring cover for their escape. Asher skidded to a stop, mouth open, orange fire reflecting in his eyes. Around them, soldiers scrambled to put out the burning generator, trampled over the grass and dirt, yelled orders in panicked voices.

Ren flipped up his hood and hid his mouth with the back of his sleeve to keep from choking on the smoke and the ash which fell like snow.

"What did you do?" Asher coughed, mirroring Ren's pose.

Ren shrugged. "It wasn't me. It was a friend. Come on, we need to leave, quickly, and use the diversion they created for us."

Asher gave the camp one last, lingering glance: the mayhem as soldiers poured from buildings, officers yelling orders as the flames climbed higher and leapt to another building. The wood framing caught quickly despite the rain as it crackled and warped with the heat.

Ren didn't know what Asher saw, other than chaos, but something in his expression told Ren, despite the urgency and their need to run, to allow Asher to have this moment, to allow him to say goodbye.

"Okay," Asher said with a nod. "Okay."

They ran from the camp to the road. The second explosion hit the generator on the far side of the camp. The concussive force was not as devastating, but Ren staggered as they crossed the road and hid in the ditch beside it.

Ren's muscles trembled. He wheezed in the hot air. "We need to get to the rendezvous."

"Please don't tell me you've docked the ship here. The Corps logs everything at that spaceport. The *Star Stream* is too recognizable."

"The ship isn't there. It's in the jungle. Come on."

Ren stood and took Asher's hand. His palm was damp against Ren's skin.

"How did it get there?"

Ren tugged and stumbled to his knees. The trek through the rain forest and the spent adrenaline from being captured again made him quake with exhaustion. His legs didn't have the strength to hold him, and his hands shook like leaves in a wind.

"Ren?"

"I'm fine. Help me up."

Asher pulled Ren to standing, then looped Ren's arm over his shoulder. "You'll tell me what's wrong."

"Later. This way."

Ren and Asher took a few steps before Ren's power pinged with the burst of a pulse gun. The hair on his arms stood on end. The electric charge fizzled behind his eyes. "Drop!"

They fell to their knees, and the blast flew over their heads and smashed into a tree. Splinters rained on them. Ren lurched to his feet and spun to find the guard, who leveled his weapon at Ren.

"You! Cogging duster. I should've known there was something wrong with you! You did this!"

"I did."

Asher stood up behind Ren, and the soldier's face went nearly purple with rage. He swung his gun arm to focus on Asher. "You are a traitor."

The sky opened on a crack of thunder, and a torrent of water unleashed. The rain pounded on their heads and shoulders and turned the ground into treacherous swift-moving puddles. Ren's boots filled; the muddy runoff from the road was suddenly up to his ankles. In the dark and the heavy rain, only the pulse of electricity from his weapon and the shadowy outline cast from the riot of fire yards away gave Ren an idea of where the soldier stood.

Asher disengaged from Ren and raised his hands. "Let us go."

The soldier laughed, body shaking; the sound bled into the chaos of the camp and the roar of the fire. Ren focused on the weapon; its signature was within his grasp. Ren could stop him if he shot again, but he wasn't going to risk it.

"No," he called out. "You're both going back. The only question is alive or dead."

The weapon charged with a whine, and Ren's eyes flashed.

Asher took a step forward, positioning himself between the soldier and Ren. His boots made indents in the mud. The rain flattened his blond hair. His hands were steady, and his voice was low and even when he spoke.

"It's not going to hurt anyone if we escape. Let us walk away and disappear. That's all we want."

The guard sneered. "If you think I'm going to let a duster and traitor escape after burning down half the camp then you're out of your cogging mind. Now, up on the road."

They didn't move. Asher tried again. "Please, understand. This is bigger than this moment. This is bigger than this camp."

"I'm not interested in your cause. Quit stalling. There might not be a cell to throw you in, but I'll find something." His finger twitched against the trigger, and Ren shuddered with gathering potential.

They had to leave. And if they left the soldier alive, he'd tell his superiors that Asher ran away with a duster. It wouldn't take much for the Phoenix Corps to put it together. They'd know Ren was alive. They'd come after the crew. They'd never be free.

Narrowing his eyes, Ren raised his hand. "I can't let you stop me. And I can't let you tell anyone else."

Asher whipped his head around, eyes wide. "Ren, no—"

"What are playing at? You can't do anything to me."

Ren allowed his eyes to go blue. "Corps tech tends to short in the rain."

Lines of blue lashed and arced from the pulse gun up the soldier's arm in a tangle of power. The comm on this uniform burst into flame and sizzled. The soldier fell to the wet earth, like a puppet with strings cut; twitched once, twice; and then lay still. Smoke wreathed around the body and mingled with the plumes rising from the camp.

Ren pulled back and settled his star in the center of his chest. He dropped his arm, boneless and weary. Ren hunched forward and slapped his palm over his mouth so his fingertips dug into his skin and hooked against the bones of his jaw. He bit back a scream and a sob, swallowing it into the depths of his self.

Asher clutched his other hand with force so bruising the bones of Ren's fingers mashed and ground together.

"Ren, we should go."

Ren nodded, shaky and unsure, and straightened. The edge of his hood lay sodden on his forehead. Rivulets of water ran down Asher's face. Ren swiped his thumb over Asher's cheekbone so it smeared mud, and his hand trembled. "Yes, but I…." Ren trailed off. He swallowed the lump in his throat. "I had to."

"I know."

Asher didn't offer a platitude. Ren didn't want one. He'd made a choice. He'd make the same choice again.

"This way."

They loped to the thick edge of the rain forest. Ren's pace was spurred by adrenaline and fear. His actions ran on loop in his head, and he was terrified of running into another Corpsman. He didn't think he could be responsible for anything else tonight.

Finally, they pushed into the cover of the jungle along the path Ollie and Lucas had created. Once under the cover of the dense foliage, the scant light created by the fires and explosions dimmed until all Ren could see through the branches was an occasional streak of orange.

They stopped and rested. Ren leaned against the slender trunk of a young tree and hoped that nothing crawled or slithered nearby in the impenetrable dark. Only by keeping close and allowing his eyes to adjust to the darkness, was Ren able to see Asher. The furrow of his brow was unmistakable, as was the set of his shoulders.

"We're okay," Ren said. "We're okay. We're okay."

"We're okay." Asher squeezed Ren's hand. He didn't let go. "How did you find me?"

"It's a long story."

"You didn't put yourself at risk, did you? You didn't reveal yourself to anyone."

Ren sucked down the thick soupy air and pressed a hand to his side. "No. I'm dead."

"Good."

"Wow, and I thought my relationships were twisted."

Ren jumped and whirled on his heel. Darby emerged from a cluster of brush with Ollie right behind her holding a small light.

Darby pointed at Asher. "Is this him?"

Asher's fingers curled tighter around Ren's hand. Ren brushed his thumb over Asher's knuckles to soothe him. "Yes, this is him."

Darby grinned. "Awesome. Glad you found him."

Ren smiled. "Good job with the blowing things up. Were you seen?"

Darby smiled wider; her teeth flashed white. "It was fun. And no. We set the charges and ran. But I don't want to stand out here with critters. That big flying thing I saw earlier was terrifying."

Shuddering, Ren agreed.

Ollie snorted. "Rowan should be a little way in with another light." He brushed past them and grabbed Asher in a fierce one-harmed hug as he passed. "Good to see you, brother."

Asher slapped Ollie hard on the back before letting him go.

Darby followed close on Ollie's heels. She gave Asher an appraising glance, then knocked her fist into Ren's shoulder. "Come on. We're going to need freaky science-magic to get us out of here before those soldier folks figure out where we've gone."

Asher raised an eyebrow and mouthed "freaky science-magic." Ren shrugged.

A bright orb bobbed in the dark where Rowan waited. They followed Ollie and Darby down the trail.

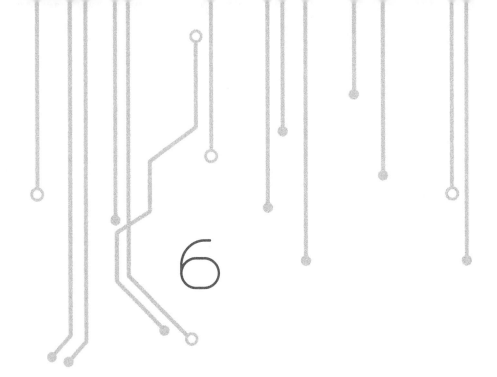

6

ROWAN GRABBED ASHER IN A hug, and Ren stepped back from the reunion. It only lasted a moment, but the intensity was not lost on the group. Holding a small light to illuminate the path, Rowan ushered the others the rest of the way. The ship waited for them, silent and dark, save for the low hum of the background systems.

Ren stepped through the bay door, and the ship welcomed him with a warm, familiar sensation. It enveloped him and soothed his frayed nerves. Touching the bulkhead, he closed his eyes and embraced the comfort of the *Star Stream's* systems. His clothes dripped onto the deck plate in small puddles, and he shrugged off the sodden cloak. It fell with a plop, and Ren squelched toward the bridge with his toes swimming in his boots.

Ducking under the arch, Ren entered.

"Ren," Lucas said, spinning in his chair. "We got him back?"

"We got him back," Ren replied.

Lucas grinned then turned. He typed in coordinates. "I don't want to rush you, but there is chatter over all the comm channels. We've got locals and Corps and the docking tower all talking. They're searching for the culprits, you know, *us*, and it won't be long before they head into the jungle."

"What's going on?" Asher stepped through the archway, flanked by Rowan and Ollie.

Lucas stood and leapt at Asher. He wrapped his arms around Asher's shoulders and patted him on the back. "Oh, it's so good to see you. But you smell awful. And you're drenched."

Asher smiled, but it didn't reach his eyes. "Thanks. But what's happening? How are we getting out of here?"

Rowan brushed passed him and settled in the captain's chair. "Ren? Are you ready?"

Ren blew out a breath. He spread his hand on the navigation console. "Catch me when I fall."

"Wait, what—"

Closing his eyes, Ren gathered his power. It bled from him into the ship, and the ship crawled up into his veins. A push-pull of power like a second heartbeat pulsed through him. Static filled his mouth, and sound played behind his eyes, and white and blue and red sounded in his ears. Sparks popped and crackled over his body, and his hair stood on end. Energy amassed in a whirlwind. He willed the ship to bend to the coordinates. His star throbbed under his skin and into the circuits. His body screamed in protest and his knees locked, but it was a secondary concern to the thrumming of the *Star Stream* and the creak of its engines and the shudder of its hull.

Time stalled and stretched and stretched until it snapped in one forceful second.

Ren blinked. He fell backward but was saved from a meeting with the deck by a strong grip. He craned his neck and stared out at a blanket of stars.

"Did I do it?"

Lucas checked the coordinates. "Close enough."

"Good. I'm… *tired*."

He leaned back into the embrace, and Asher grunted in his ear. "Stay awake," he said. "At least until I get you to the common room."

Ren didn't remember much of the short journey to the couch. He roused when he heard low voices and found himself laid out with a pillow under his head and a blanket over his body. His boots and socks were a sodden pile on the floor. He wiggled his pruney toes and squinted at the two figures at the table.

"Are you okay?" Rowan asked, taking Asher's hand in hers.

Asher lifted a steaming cup to his mouth and sipped. "I'm fine."

"You look like you've been hollowed out. And you're bruised. What happened?"

"Nothing important."

Rowan lifted an eyebrow. "What was the Corps doing on Bara anyway?"

Asher tapped his fingers along the rim of the cup. "Making inroads. Looking for things. I wasn't privy to specifics, but I know it has to do with Vos."

"Everything has to do with him. Everything goes back to his feud with the Corps."

"It's larger than that, Rowan. It started long before Vos and it's spread across all the planets. It's planets versus drifts now."

Rowan looked away. "I know. We were on Phoebus, and Millicent attacked."

Asher's cup shook. "You made it out."

"We ran. We had to. Ren wanted to fight, but I wouldn't let him."

"Good. What's happened here?"

Rowan sighed. "We've picked up another stray. Though this one isn't staying long. We're taking her to the nearest drift and dropping her off."

"She seems… nice."

Rowan snorted. "She's a handful, but that's no different than anyone else on this ship." She smiled softly. "I missed you. I worried for you. I… I won't let anything happen to you again."

Asher's lips lifted in a smile. "Don't make promises you can't keep. Rowan, we're going to have to face this. We're going to be a part of this battle. In one way or another. We can't hide. We can't flee. I just hope we end up on the right side."

She looked away and tugged her braid. She didn't respond, indecision was clear in her expression and posture. "What's the right side, Ash?"

Asher sipped his drink. "The winning side. That's the side we'll be on."

⊣⊢

Once Ren regained his strength, he dressed in the dry shirt and trousers left for him, then went straight to Asher's quarters. Asher had left shortly after his conversation with Rowan, claiming the need for a shower, fresh clothes, and a nap. Ren needed the same, but he needed to speak with Asher more.

He rapped his knuckles against Asher's doorframe. The door stood slightly open, but Ren didn't assume he was welcome or wanted. His skin tingled with residual power, and his hair smelled of smoke from the explosions. Humidity and panic sat heavy in his chest, pressing on his lungs. His skin was tacky. He needed a shower and a nap, but the urge to see Asher, to touch him, to breathe the same air, to feel the heat of his body, overrode everything else. The wet fabric brushing against his ankles and the dirt under his fingernails were minor irritants compared to the sudden rending joy of Asher's presence on the other side of the bulkhead.

"Ash," Ren said, his voice a rasp. He waited, his heart pounding with anticipation, as if he hung over a precipice and peered down, down, down into a crevasse.

The door creaked open. Ren stepped through and closed it behind him, locking it with a spark of his star.

Asher stood across from him. His blond hair hung in wet strands, limp on his forehead and around his temples, brushing over the curve of his ears. He needed a haircut. The vibrant liquid green of his eyes stood out from the thin skin and dark circles beneath. His cheekbones cut edges into his skin. His jaw, though set, trembled, and his bruised lip puffed out. The shirt he wore hung from his shoulders, and Ren imagined the blue and purple bruises which undoubtedly mottled Asher's skin underneath. He'd changed so much in such a short time.

"Ren," Asher said.

"Are you okay?" Asher looked away, and Ren closed his eyes. "I meant, are you injured? Does your shoulder hurt?"

"It's fine. It's not like before."

Ren swallowed the lump in his throat. "Good."

He opened his eyes and stepped forward. The void between them was expansive if only a few feet, and Ren couldn't handle the space any longer. Drawn toward him, Ren closed the distance and curled his arms around Asher's body. He drew Asher's head to his shoulder and held on.

Asher's body pulled taut, resistant for a strained moment, before he shuddered and melted into Ren's arms. He clutched at Ren, his fists clenched into the fabric of Ren's shirt, and pulled him in. He smelled of soap and warm skin, and the heat of him burned into Ren's middle and eased into his bones and sinew, and the tension that had set in his spine since he'd woken by himself on a cold metal slab, sloughed away. Ren had never felt at peace: always looking to the stars when on Erden, always looking for control when consumed by his star, always looking for family when lonely, always looking for calm when panic gripped him in its suffocating embrace. But this, Asher in his arms, and Asher's breath on his neck, and Asher's hands molded on his back, was as close as Ren had ever come. This was a kind of tranquility of the soul that he hadn't known was possible for him. Now that he had it, he would never relinquish it.

"I've got you," Ren said. He tucked his face against Asher's neck. "I've got you. And I'm not letting you go again."

Crushing Ren close, with their bodies cradled against one another, Asher held on.

"Don't. Don't let me go."

"Never." And he wouldn't. He wouldn't. And it was a dangerous thing, an exquisite ache that resided in his soul, a promise and a responsibility he'd never leave unfulfilled. "I killed him," Ren whispered. "I'd do it again. I'd do anything for you."

Asher shivered. "I know. I know, but I don't want that. I don't want you to do things you don't want to, Ren. I want you to be free."

"I told you. There is no point to freedom without you." Ren's cheeks heated with a fierce blush.

Asher shook his head against Ren's shoulder. He mumbled into Ren's collarbone while Ren petted his head.

"What was that?"

"I said, you smell," he mumbled.

Ren froze. Giddiness bubbled up from his chest to his throat. His body shivered, and he chuckled. Asher shook with him as he muffled his laughter into Ren's shirt. They laughed, holding each other as all the pent-up adrenaline and grief washed out of them in gales and chuckles, snorts and watery gasps. Ren pulled back, swiped his fingers along the corners of his eyes, then cupped Asher's jaw, and ran his thumbs over the stubbled and flushed skin, wiping the streams of tears away.

Asher caught his fingers. He turned his head and kissed the center of Ren's palm.

Ren's breath stuttered, and Asher pressed his soft smile into Ren's hand.

"I should go shower," Ren's voice was thick.

"Stay." Asher's response was clipped and quick with an undercurrent of fear. He closed his eyes, relaxed his shoulders, and ducked his head. "Stay with me."

"Okay."

"After you shower."

Ren swallowed. "After I shower."

"Yes, shower," Asher said. He guided Ren to the adjoining bathroom, his fingers curled around the indent of Ren's waist. "And then come back."

Ren raised an eyebrow. "Are you sure?"

"Yes."

"I've been sleeping in Ollie's room on a medical cot. Or on the common room couch. Or where I just…" he waved his hands, "wherever I pass out."

"Is that what you'd like to do tonight?"

"No," Ren breathed.

Asher's lips ticked up into a smirk. "Then come back."

Nervousness of a different kind flooded Ren's veins, and he welcomed it. He smiled back at Asher, helplessly, before closing the door behind him.

⊣⊢

Ren emerged from the en suite bathroom in a cloud of steam. His skin was pink from the warm water and from scrubbing away the stench of their ordeal on the planet. He smelled of soap and shampoo instead of sweat and ash, and that lifted his mood. Any reservations he'd held about returning to Asher's room to sleep had melted away. Now his nerves were from blooming excitement and thick anticipation rather than fear and panic.

The little hair he had left dripped, and beads of water rolled down his neck and over his collarbone. He rubbed a towel over his head, then tossed it in the corner.

Asher sat on the edge of the bed. He looked up from a data pad. He started, his gaze sliding over Ren's bare torso and landing on the stitched angry wound on Ren's side. Self-conscious, Ren covered it with his hand. "Sorry," he rasped. "I need to bandage it. I forgot the supplies. They're in Ollie's room."

Asher didn't say anything, merely beckoned Ren closer. He lifted a roll of medical tape and a sterile pad. "Pen brought them by when she didn't find you in the common room."

Ren swallowed. "Oh."

"Do you want me to?"

"I…" Ren's throat went dry. He swallowed, then nodded his head.

Ren cautiously padded across the room to the bed. The hem of his threadbare sleep pants brushed the tops of his feet. The bare skin of his chest prickled; the environmental controls were set a little cooler than usual. Rowan and Lucas were recovering from the hours spent planet-side in the heat and kept the ship nearly frigid.

His muscles jumped as Asher lightly ran his fingertips over the skin near his navel and drifted slowly to the stitches. Ren bit his lip. The air charged.

"Hold this."

Ren held the bandage in place as Asher tore strips of the medical tape, then smoothed them over Ren's skin. The process only took a few minutes, but, by the end, Ren was alight with anticipation.

"Are you tired?" Asher asked, as Ren stood and trembled before him.

"Exhausted despite the small nap."

Asher nodded. "Me too." He swallowed and met Ren's eyes, seemingly making a decision. "Well, come on then." He patted the bed.

Ren's pulse ticked up. His heart hammering, he sat on the edge. "Do you want near the wall?"

"Stars, no," Asher said with a shake of his head. "I just spent several weeks trapped and sleeping in a cell. I don't like the feeling."

"Okay. I like the wall. I can feel the ship. It's… safe."

"Okay."

Ren scrambled onto the bed and slid under the sheets. Asher followed and lay beside him. Flat on his back and stiff as a board, Ren stared up at the ceiling. His and Asher's arms brushed. Gone was the ease of the times they'd slept next to each other in a cell or in a hollow tree or on a ship with people they didn't trust. A dense potential energy lay between them now, and Ren didn't know what to do, how to act on the feelings that stirred in his gut. He clenched his fists at his side.

The bed was not big, and Asher had to be uncomfortable so near the edge. Ren squeezed as close as he could to the wall while Asher fidgeted next to him.

"This isn't what I imagined."

Ren was suddenly breathless. He cleared his throat. "What did you imagine?"

Asher chuckled ruefully. "Well for one, it wouldn't be freezing. And for two, you wouldn't be injured."

"I'm fine."

Asher rolled to his side and propped up on his elbow. The collar of his sleep shirt slipped and revealed the wide, ridged scar on his shoulder. He pushed away the sheet, and the goosebumps on Ren's skin betrayed him. He shivered, and Asher raised an eyebrow, silently questioning. Tentatively, Asher rested his hand across Ren's stomach so his fingers spread over the covered wound.

Ren flinched. "I'm sorry." Tears came unbidden. "I'm sorry."

Asher trailed his fingers over Ren's torso, away from the bandage, then leaned over and bracketed Ren so his body curled over Ren's shaking form. "Ren—"

"I'm sorry." Ren surged upward, wrapped his arms around Asher's shoulders, twisted his fingers in Asher's hair, and tugged him close. He squeezed his eyes shut. "I'm... so sorry. I should've trusted you. I should've listened to you. I should've never questioned your loyalty to me or to Rowan or—"

Asher brushed his thumb over Ren's mouth, and held it there. The pressure was gentle but grounding. "I could've been more transparent with my plans. I thought if I kept everyone in the dark, even you, that it would be better. That I could fool VanMeerten on my own. But I made you doubt me, and I'm sorry for that." He ran his thumb over the blush of Ren's cheek and slid his palm over the curve of Ren's jaw.

"Don't apologize." Ren swallowed, throat bobbing. "Please."

"It was all to protect you."

"I know. I realized in the tunnel on Crei that everything you did was for my benefit. You gave yourself up for me. You've done nothing but protect me since we met in that cell at the citadel." Ren opened his eyes. "Why?"

Asher smiled, a wry lift of his lips. "I'd still be in that cell if it wasn't for your fierce single-minded duster idiocy. You were so certain you could escape. And it was maddening and endearing. And I…" Asher laughed. "I couldn't help but think that if anyone on that planet could get out of that mess and save the cluster, it would be the cog with the glowing blue eyes."

"You never told me that," Ren said.

"I'm not good with words." Asher dipped his head and rested his forehead against Ren's. He continued the maddening caress of his fingers along the line of Ren's jaw. "I'm better with actions."

Asher's body was a wall of heat above him. Ren's stomach was a tight coil, and his muscles went taut with eagerness. Ren *wanted*.

"I'm not good with words either," he stammered.

Asher's laugh was a gust of air over Ren's lips. "We'll practice."

"I've never—"

Asher kissed him, tender and unafraid. Ren melted into it; his eyes fluttered shut; the tension eased out of him. He relaxed into the mattress, and all the scattered thoughts and the remnants of fear evaporated once he was wrapped in Asher's arms. He gave in, allowed his actions to speak for him, and trusted Asher to lead the way.

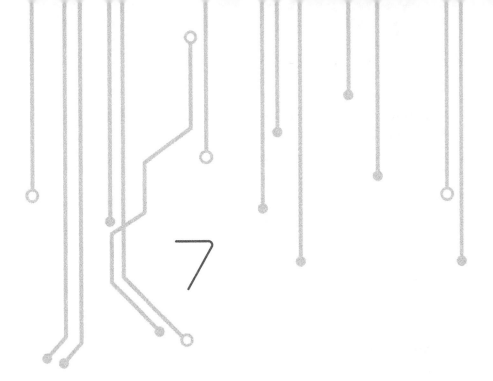

7

THE AIR AROUND REN SHIMMERED. Splotches of color appeared, then solidified and coalesced into a room Ren didn't recognize. He squinted as the bright lights dimmed and twisted, and shadows deepened, providing contour and depth. There was a low bunk with a thin mattress and four close metal walls. The door in one wall was short but thick with a forcefield around a small window. Ren pressed his fingertips against the field and found it solid and cool to the touch. Nothing stirred under his skin. No hum reverberated in his flesh. Brow furrowed, hands in his pockets, he turned and let out a squawk when he spotted Asher in a corner.

"Ash?"

Asher looked around, face pale. He wore his Phoenix Corps uniform and glossy boots, though the insignias weren't quite correct—the details were off because they were in a dream. Eyebrows raised in a look of confusion, Asher examined his uniform. Ren peered down at himself and saw the outfit he'd last worn on Erden.

"Where are we?"

"Liam?" Ren called. "Are you here?"

A blurry mass of color on the bed slowly came into focus. It morphed from a blob to the shape of a person. The figure developed features and red hair. Liam appeared, dressed in a simple, white outfit, stretched out on the bed's stiff white sheets. He propped himself up on an elbow. The square pillow dimpled beneath him. Metal clamps hung beneath the bedframe and they swayed as Liam sat up. He squinted at Ren, and then his eyebrows shot up when he saw Asher standing in the corner.

"You're both here. Are you two… near each other right now? Touching while asleep?"

Ren blushed. The tips of his ears burned. "Yeah, we are."

Liam's mouth quirked up. "So, this is the guy? The soldier?" He swung his legs over the side of the bed and stood. Approaching Asher cautiously, Liam eyed him up and down. "You're shorter than I imagined."

"You must be the brother," Asher said. He crossed his arms over his chest. He lifted his chin. "Is this a dream?"

"Yeah, it is."

Ren ignored the stare-off on the other side of the small room and rapped his knuckles on the wall. "Is this where they are keeping you?"

"Yes."

"You've hidden it from me."

"I've tried to project nicer environments. I didn't want you to worry."

Ren frowned. "I'll always worry about you." He cast a glance at Liam, and his frown deepened. Liam had dark circles under his eyes like bruises, and his face was pale. His cheeks were hollow, his lips chapped, and he had an abrasion and a collage of purple and green around his jaw. "It's the older brother's job to worry."

"You're not much older than me."

"Why did you bring us here?" Asher pressed his hand to the wall, fingers spread. He furrowed his brow, as if trying to figure out how their dream environment could appear so real.

Liam's shoulders drooped. "I think they're moving us. There are whispers about insurgencies and rebellions. They've made me dream constantly these last few days, going into people's thoughts, searching for information, manipulating things, and I..." Liam's throat bobbed as he swallowed. "I'm so *tired*. I just want to sleep."

"Liam—"

"I know I said to live your life, Ren, but I... I want to go home. I want to go home."

Ren rushed forward and caught Liam in a hug, wrapping his arms around his brother, trying to erase the image of Liam looking worn and lost. Liam rested his head on Ren's shoulder and clutched at Ren's back.

"It's okay. I'm working on it. I promise."

Liam shivered. His shoulders shook, and he sobbed. Ren's shoulder gradually grew damp, but he didn't pull away. Hot with shame and worry, Ren held on, upset with himself that he hadn't yet found Liam, had doomed him to a life in a cell, similar to what Ren had escaped from with Asher's help. He cast a glance to Asher, whose stoic expression had softened.

"Do you know where you are?" Asher moved from his spot by the wall. "Any idea at all?"

Liam shook his head, which was buried in Ren's shirt. "No." His voice came out thickly. He took a breath and composed himself before stepping out of Ren's embrace. "I've been trying to figure it out, but they're keeping me in this cell now. I'm not even leaving for sessions anymore. They come in here and..." Liam trailed off. Ren's gaze zeroed in on the clamps in the bed. Disgust rose in his throat.

"Do you have any idea of a timeline?"

"I don't... a few days, maybe? It's been the past week that everything has suddenly increased."

Asher ran his hand over his jaw. "Whose dreams have you walked in? Maybe there is a clue in there. Are they Corps members? Drifters? Dusters? Have you spoken to Vos?"

Liam wiped his eyes with the sleeve of his scrubs. He shook his head. "I just… there is a guy here who can make you do things with his voice. It doesn't work on the staff, only on others like us. He makes me go into the dreams, and then I forget after I report."

Ren jolted. Shock and fear and a vivid memory of Abiathar's voice compelling him to unlock his cuffs washed over him. He felt sick to his stomach and he staggered away from the bed toward the wall. He leaned against it.

"Ren?" Liam asked. "Are you okay?"

Ren nodded, but pressed a hand to his chest to focus on his breathing.

"We've met him before," Asher said. He moved next to Ren and threaded their fingers; the pressure from both their hands on his sternum grounded Ren. "He's the one who figured out Ren was a technopath. He was the one who wanted to weaponize your brother."

Liam's eyes went wide. "Oh, weeds, I didn't know."

"It's okay. He needs a minute and—"

Footsteps sounded outside the door. Liam's brow creased and he grabbed Asher's arm.

"They're coming to wake me up."

"Can you fight them?"

Liam shook his head; his green eyes were wild. "No. I can't. I *can't*."

Ren shook off the flood of memories and grabbed Liam's hand, forming a triangle between the three of them.

"Hold on! Don't let go!"

Ren reached for his power and grasped nothing. He looked to Asher, pleading for an idea. Asher's expression gave nothing away, but his grip on Ren tightened.

"I can't do anything," Ren breathed. "I have no power here. And if I try any more, I might access the ship we're on and—"

The door swung inward, violently banging against the wall. Shadows moved into the room, silhouettes of figures, their details indiscernible. One raised a hand and the impression of a baton folded out.

Liam's face twisted.

"I'll find you," Ren gasped. He gripped his brother's hand; his knuckles were white, and his palm was slick. "I promise, Liam. I will find you and—"

The figure brought the baton down.

Liam screamed. His back bowed, he clawed at Ren's arms, he choked on air, and then he disappeared.

⊣⊢

Ren rocketed out of sleep. Scrabbling through the thick fog of the dream, vision awash in blue, he fought against the arms around him. He cried out when they clamped against his wound, and he twisted and thrashed. The strong grip pinned his arms to his sides and he couldn't move. He couldn't *breathe*. He had to get to Liam. He had to free Liam. They had him. They had him and… He kicked and bent, until he could slip his fingers beneath the hands that clutched him. He pried them off, nails biting into the flesh until they released him. Legs tangled, he lunged to get away and fell to the hard deck plating. Fresh waves of pain rent him; agony lit his nerves. Adrenaline thudded frenzied and fast in his middle, and he scrambled along the floor, kicking out with his heel when fingers wrapped around his ankle.

"Ren!"

The voice shocked him into the present, and Ren blinked.

Asher's room.

He turned to find Asher half-hanging out of the bed, one hand clinging to the frame, the other holding Ren's ankle. The blanket and sheets stretched between them. No longer covered, Asher's bare skin bore a sheen of sweat, and goosebumps blossomed over his arms and chest.

In the low light, sprawled across the floor, Ren pressed his palms to the deckplate, and the systems of the *Star Stream* buzzed through him. He shivered in the cool air. With a thought, Ren sent warmth into the room.

Ren allowed his head to drop and he blew out a calming breath.

"Ren?"

"I'm here."

Asher released Ren's ankle and lowered his foot gently. The mattress creaked, and the sheets rustled, and then Asher sat cross-legged, wrapped in the comforter, facing Ren. He looked like a toddler at story time with his hair sticking up and ensconced in the folds of his favorite blanket. A line of dried drool crusted the edge of his mouth, and he had a mark on his cheek from the wrinkles in his pillow. His forehead was creased, and his lips turned down at the corners.

"Did you hurt yourself?" Asher nodded at Ren's bandage.

Biting his lip, Ren peeled away the tape. Penelope's regular attention to the wound had seen it heal significantly, and Ren could even see differences since he'd woken a few days ago. A trickle of blood slid down his skin from where a bit of medical glue had torn, but otherwise, it looked as it had.

"I'm fine."

Asher's concern didn't abate. Instead, he leaned forward, elbows on his knees, fingers tented in front of his mouth. "Was that real?"

Ren nodded, sorrow and grief an internal tumult. "Yes."

"That was really your brother?"

"Yes."

Asher tilted his head. "Are you sure? Could it have been a trick?"

Liam's pleas for home and his anguished scream echoed in Ren's head. "No," he said, voice soft. "No."

"I'm sorry."

"He's in Perilous Space." Ren picked a thread in the blanket. "Ollie said he might be there, and it made sense, but I was focused on finding you, on getting to you." Ren swallowed. "I've abandoned him."

"No. No, you haven't."

"I've lost him."

"He hasn't been moved yet."

"They could be moving him right now."

"Ren," Asher gripped Ren's hand.

"The Corps has him. They took him from our home. How could… how could you be a part of that? How could you have willingly joined them?" Ren looked up and met Asher's stricken expression. "I don't understand."

"I told you I didn't know. I didn't know until we returned to Erden."

Ren pulled his knees to his chest, but he didn't disengage from Asher's grasp. "Why did you join? You've never said."

Asher sighed. He ran a hand over his brow. "It's complicated."

"My father was going to turn my mother over to a military organization because her eyes glowed. My stepfather likely killed him. They intended to hide me on a planet I didn't want to be on and kept from me the fact that I'm a mythical being. I can handle complicated."

"Fine." Asher rearranged his blanket. "I was sixteen and stupid and wanted to get back at my mother for basically ignoring me for her political career."

Ren raised an eyebrow. "Seriously?"

"Rowan was already off-drift. She'd saved up credits and bought a ship. Penelope went with her. I was lonely and bored and didn't want to be either. I went to the recruitment office and signed my life away for five years. I went to introduction training at the facility and made some friends. I specialized in tactical operations, and the first few years that meant a lot of travel and the occasional skirmish. And by skirmish, I mean arguments between drifters and the need for protection of a trade route from marauders. It was easy. It was *fun*. I had friends. And then we received an assignment on a planet."

Ren winced. Asher had barely taken a breath. His words were coming fast and clipped, as if pouring it all out as quickly as possible would allow him to outrun the underlying emotions.

"Erden."

"Yes, and we were ambushed. And I was injured but kept alive because of my mother's influence. I was in a cell for a year wasting away."

Ren closed his eyes. "And your friends?"

Asher's trip tightened. "Dead."

"I'm sorry, Ash."

Asher snorted. "Don't apologize. I'm the fool. I should've known the Corps didn't care the minute they let me stay in that cell for as long as they did. Then I trusted VanMeerten about you and I shouldn't have." Asher shuddered. "At first, I thought the Corps was too overwhelmed and bureaucratic to see the consequences of their actions on their soldiers and the civilians they encountered. And that hurt in a way I didn't expect. But now, I know it's indifference. They don't care, as long as they get what they want. They don't care who they hurt or who gets in their way."

Opening his eyes, Ren tipped his face toward Asher. "Ash—"

"It's funny, actually. I didn't understand Vos at all. His motives were foreign to me. Why would a duster baron concern himself with the drifts? But I get it now." Ren made a face. "I'm not saying he's right either. He shouldn't have captured you from your home and raided your village. The way he went about things was wrong. But I get it—that feeling of powerlessness in the face of a military machine."

"We can change things."

"We can try." His voice dipped low. "We'll find your brother. We'll find him. Even if they move him, he'll contact you again. Or we'll find the files from the Corps. We'll do something. For now, though, we have to tell Rowan. We have to let the crew decide what to do, and then you and I…"

Ren turned his hand over and threaded his fingers through Asher's. "You and I?"

"I'm not leaving you again."

The corner of Ren's mouth quirked up. "I don't want you to."

"Then you and I will find a way."

Ren hunched forward. "Perilous Space," he said, squeezing his eyes shut. "The prison on the edge of the cluster near where the technopaths broke the sky. Heavily guarded and impossible to escape from."

"We'll free him. I promise."

Ren believed him. Asher always kept his promises.

⊣⊢

"Ren's brother is in Perilous Space prison. He came to us in a dream, and I met him. The Corps will be moving him soon because of an increase in revolts. Ren and I will be formulating a plan, and you're welcome to join us. If not, you'll need to let us off at the next drift."

Rowan blinked. Her mouth hung open. The food on her spoon slid off and splattered on her plate. Drops of sauce flew over her shirt. "You want to *what* now?"

"So, he is there?" Ollie asked, unfazed. He passed the bread basket to a stunned Darby, who allowed it to drop through her hands.

"Um… can you please repeat that?" Penelope asked. She dabbed her face with her napkin.

"Yeah, same. Because it sounded like you want us to storm an impenetrable prison to rescue someone we've never met who can talk to you through dreams." Lucas took a bite of his food and chewed obnoxiously. "I'm just saying a little more explanation is needed."

Ren hunched down in his seat.

Darby picked the scattered bread from the table and tossed it into the basket. "Is this about freaky science-magic?"

"No." Asher shook his head. "Well, yes, kind of. A little bit."

"My brother," Ren said softly, and all attention turned to him. "My brother can manipulate dreams and gather information. I'm not sure how it works. But the Corps has been using him against Vos. He's tired and frightened." Ren's brow furrowed. "I don't expect you to come with us, especially after everything."

"I said we'd talk about it after finding Ash," Rowan said as she wiped her shirt with a napkin. "But you're right, Ren. I've allowed our lives to be interrupted since you came aboard. We've been stuck on a drift for months, we've been involved in firefights, and we've been on planets where we don't belong. I don't think we can do it anymore."

"I understand. It's fine."

Asher slammed his fist on the table. Everyone jumped, and the plates and cups rattled. "No, it's not fine. Don't you get it? We can't stay out of this. The conflict between Vos and the Corps will only spread. It already has. First it was Erden and then Mykonos and Phoebus and now Bara. This is escalating with or without us, and soon there will be no safe space for anyone."

"You're right. It's going to happen with or without us. I'd prefer without us." Rowan lifted her chin in the face of Asher's betrayed expression.

"Rowan—"

"Do you get what you're asking of us?" Rowan jammed her fork in Asher's direction. "Not only is Perilous Space prison a maximum-security facility run by the Phoenix Corps—the very same organization that we blew up a camp to rescue you from, but also the same one that *killed* Ren. And not only that, but we'd be releasing other star hosts into the cluster who may not be as well-meaning as Ren and who may be even more powerful. We'd be stepping right between VanMeerten and Vos and embroiling ourselves in a situation that you've already said was dangerous beyond what we can imagine."

"We're already a part of it. I don't understand how you can't see that?"

"I know! But I'm not ready to choose a side. I don't know who is right and who is wrong. I only know that both sides have tried to kill us."

"We don't have to be on either side. We can be our own side!"

"We'll lose! We are no match against the Corps or Vos, especially if he has Millicent."

"We have to take the chance."

"We don't! And we're not!"

They shouted at each other over the length of the table. Rowan was almost out of her seat, and Asher bent his fork with his grip.

Ren placed his hand on Asher's trembling fist. "It's okay."

Asher yanked his hand away. "How are you so calm and meek? Why are you not mad? Why are you not threatening to take over the ship and take us there anyway?"

Ren recoiled. "Because I'm not a jerk. The Ren that did those type of things *died*, remember? Yes, I want to rescue my brother. After finding you, it was the top of my list. It still *is*. I'm terrified about what's happening to him. But I'm not forcing your sister and Ollie and Pen and Lucas into anything. They've already done so much for me. *You* have done so much for me."

"Why don't you ask them?" Darby asked, dark eyes darting between Asher and Rowan. "Don't they get a say, or are you going to make their decisions for them?"

"Why don't you stay out of it?" Rowan's voice was sharp. "We'll take you to Echo drift as we promised and drop you off, but you have no say in what happens aboard this ship. Got it?"

"Wait a minute, Darby did risk herself to rescue Asher." Ollie planted his elbows on the table and met Rowan's hard gaze. "You can't discount our opinions on this, Rowan."

"I can. I'm the captain. You've placed your trust in my decisions since you became crew so many years ago. I've bent over backward for the past year to accommodate these two. I've disrupted all of our lives. I'm *done*. There is no discussion."

Darby stood from the table. "Right. Thanks for the food." She shoved a few extra pieces of bread on her plate and picked it up. "I'm going to eat in my quarters. Let me know when we reach Echo drift." She paused at the doorway. "I thought you all were different, but you're just like everyone else. Out for themselves. Good luck with your brother, Ren." And then she left.

Ren sighed. He pushed his fingertips against his closed eyes. The pressure felt good in contrast to the budding headache in his temples.

"We'll be disembarking on Echo too."

Ren dropped his hands and stared at Asher. "What?"

"We don't have time to argue. They're moving Liam, and we have a small window if we want to get to him."

Ren's throat closed. "Okay. We can do that."

"If that's what you want." Rowan's palms were flat on the table top. Her shoulders were tense; her green eyes glittered.

"I'm coming with you." Ollie pushed his plate away. He raised his hand to silence Penelope's inevitable protest. "You're my sister, and, if it were you, I wouldn't hesitate. I'm going to help Ren and Asher and make sure they come back."

Lucas's face was paler than normal. "You should get ready then. We'll be there in a few hours."

Guilt weighed heavy on Ren. He was the catalyst. He was the reason Asher was captured. He was the reason Liam sat in a prison. He caused the crew to fracture.

Ollie nodded and stood. Asher followed, and Ren pushed his chair back from the table. "Thank you, and I'm sorry."

Rowan didn't respond. She pushed her food around her plate. Lucas put his arm around Penelope's shoulders and squeezed.

Ren turned on his heel and followed the others out of the common room.

-||-

They approached Echo drift. A heavy solemn stillness pervaded the ship, and Ren couldn't help but feel responsible. Guilt weighed on his conscience, though he couldn't own Rowan's stubbornness or Asher's passionate assertions. This wasn't the first time the siblings had butted heads and it wouldn't be the last. It might be the most significant, especially if Asher's planned assault on Perilous Space prison ended badly. Ren didn't want to consider that either, and he focused on the ship's approach to the spinning metal microcosm in front of them.

Standing on the bridge, Ren watched through the vid screen as the drift became larger. Next to him stood Asher. In her captain's chair, Rowan sat: back straight, legs crossed, looking like a queen on a throne.

"You can change your mind," Asher said, voice low, head pitched toward Rowan.

"So can you," she replied.

Asher let out a sigh. "I'll contact you when we're done. Until then, lay low. I don't know how long we'll be."

She nodded. Casting her glance to Ren, she forced a smile. "Take care of them. Make sure they all come back."

"I will."

Lucas adjusted the goggles on his head, then pushed a few buttons on his console. "Automated docking engaged."

Asher stepped toward the view screen. "Anything weird?"

"Everything is as normal." Lucas spun in his chair. "Ren?"

Furrowing his brow, Ren reached out through the sensors, vision shifting to blue. The drift's many systems spoke to him, all running at capacity. Most importantly, there was no sickly-sweet churn of his stomach, or cold uneasy prickle over his skin. Ren pulled back to the ship. "It's fine."

"Good."

"It'll be a few minutes," Lucas said. "I'll let you know when the seal is complete."

"Thanks."

"It was good to have you back, Ash," Lucas said in an uncharacteristic moment of seriousness. "We'll see you again soon. I'm sure."

Ren and Asher left the bridge. Asher hesitated at the exit, but when Rowan didn't make a move to stop them, he sighed and followed Ren. They walked in silence down the corridor, their shoulders brushing.

Ren and Asher had packed their bags and stacked them by the aft airlock. Ren shrugged into Asher's drifter jacket and tugged it close around him. He flipped up the collar and rubbed his cheek on the fabric, finding comfort in the sensation and the smell. It grounded him, and he'd need that leaving the *Star Stream*, the ship that had welcomed him and became his home in a way that only a technopath could understand.

Ollie and Darby waited for them in the bay. Darby had had nothing when brought on board, and now only had the few things Penelope had given her. Darby hadn't said much since the confrontation in the common room. Ren didn't know her plans. He doubted she'd go with them.

Penelope was there as well. She handed Ollie a bag. "There is medical glue and tape, antiseptic, and bandages in there just in case." Ollie took it from her hands. She smoothed the collar of Ollie's shirt. "You make sure you pick a reputable ship. Check the registration and last drifts visited."

Ollie raised a dark eyebrow. "No reputable ship is going to take us where we need to go."

She chuckled nervously. "No, I guess not. Well, pick a ship and a crew you can easily overpower if needed."

Darby stroked her chin, her expression contemplative. "Huh. That's not bad advice."

"You could always ask Darby to steal one for you, too." Penelope grinned, but it didn't reach her eyes. Her gaze cut to Darby, who leaned against the airlock. 'I'm sure she'd do it, if not for any allegiance, but for the thrill."

"Aw." Darby placed her hand over her heart. "You know me so well and only after a few days too." She shook her head. "But I don't think I'm sticking with your gang. Assaulting a prison full of career soldiers with magic-wielders as prisoners? No thanks."

Ren was inexplicably sorrowful at Darby's words, but it was expected. She'd been caught up in their lives by accident. He couldn't blame her for going her own way. It seemed to be her nature.

Ollie frowned and turned away from Darby. He focused his attention on Penelope and wrapped his hand around her fingers. "We'll be all right. We'll contact you when we're done. Take care of Rowan."

"I will."

Penelope and Ollie hugged. Then Penelope grabbed Asher and Ren in succession and squeezed. Ren winced from the force of her hug. "I'll see you soon." She wiped the moisture from her eyes and stepped away.

Lucas's voice came over the comm. "Pressurization completed. Have fun, you four."

Darby was the first out of the airlock. Ollie was quick to follow. Asher lingered.

"Are we making the right choice?" Ren shuffled close to Asher's body. "We could wait until Liam is moved. Trust that he contacts us again. It might be an easier location to—"

Asher clasped Ren's hand. "It's taken us this long to know where he is. He's important to you. He's obviously important to the Corps. Retrieving him isn't only serving a purpose for you, but takes away one of the Corps' ways of finding information. And if he's there, think of who else might be."

Ren leaned into Asher's side. "Rescuing my brother is going to start a war."

"The war is already started."

Asher squeezed Ren's hand then departed the ship. Ren followed, fingers curled tight around the handle of his small bag.

The docking bay's large outer doors to the drift were closed. A small doorway off to the side was ajar. Asher walked through, hefting his bag higher on his shoulder.

Ren cast a last glance to the ship that he called home in more ways than one. His heart ached. He'd miss the systems and the circuits, and he hoped he'd traverse them again.

With a slump of his shoulders, he went through the door.

It shut behind him, obscuring the *Star Stream*, and bathing the drift floor in a wash of dim yellow light.

Ren squinted and stopped short.

A group of soldiers in black body armor waited for him. One held a struggling Darby and had guns trained on both Asher and Ollie.

"Welcome to Echo drift," the tallest one said, stepping forward, resting his weapon on his shoulder. He smirked. "There's been a change in management."

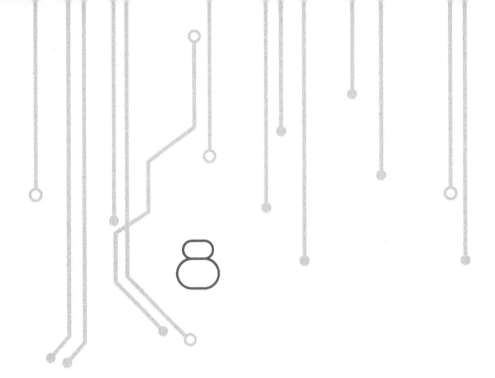

8

"Help! Help! I'm being kidnapped! *Again!*" Darby kicked out with the thick heel of her boot and caught one of the soldiers in his shin. He cried out, dropped his weapon, and grabbed his leg as he hopped up and down. Darby smirked but she wasn't let go. In fact, her wiggling and fighting made another soldier grab her other side.

Asher zeroed in on the pulse gun, which clattered to the ground, but he couldn't move before it was swept up by another guard.

"Quit squirming!"

"I'll stop when you tell me what the stars is going on!"

The four were clad in black with body armor and helmets reminiscent of Vos's citadel soldiers who had taken Ren from his home. But those soldiers wore scavenged armor and shabby equipment. These guards were polished and equipped with tech that pinged in Ren's senses with power and capability. Ren didn't sense any snares or hiccups in their comm system or in the power emanating from their prods and pulse guns. There were no bastardized components or systems holding together by spit and will. Vos had upgraded exponentially.

Standing just on the other side of the large, closed doors that led to the bay of the *Star Stream*, Ren sensed the lowering of the forcefield barrier. His connection with the ship stretched as it left the hangar, and lessened as the distance between them grew. He bit his lip to hide his distress at the loss of his home. He blinked, and the thread which bound them snapped, and tears gathered in the corners of his eyes.

Asher nudged him, and Ren shook the turmoil away, packed it down inside, and focused on the situation in front of him.

The drift was dim, but not shut down like Phoebus. Ren looked up to see blank communication boards; the overhead system remained quiet. But the grav and air recyclers hummed. The essential systems ran on minimal power, but all the superfluous ones were shut down, possibly to conserve energy. Ren wasn't afraid that all the system would fail as he had been on Phoebus. This seemed deliberate. He searched out Millicent's signature, and, though he caught remnants of her and his stomach churned at the sick caress of her power against his, she wasn't there now.

The tension that had twisted his insides slowly eased. He was still standing at pulse-gun point, but soldiers were easy compared to her.

Ren glanced at Asher and found him staring down the small group with his gaze laser-focused on their weapons. Asher narrowed his eyes, assessing, and his hand drifted over to Ren. He placed his palm on Ren's forearm and shook his head slightly. Ren took that as a signal to wait and not reveal himself. He hadn't planned to, not without knowing more information, but Asher's agreement was a reassurance.

"Who is the new management?" Asher asked, voice calm.

Asher's voice startled the soldiers, and their weapons snapped up. "Hands up where we can see them!"

Ren dropped his bag at his feet and reluctantly raised his hands as did Asher and Ollie.

"No problem." Asher pointed to Darby. "Please release our friend."

The leader was taller than the others. His words exuded confidence, but his body language lacked the marks of a career soldier. He didn't hold himself like Asher. He didn't move like Asher. But it didn't mean he wasn't dangerous.

"We're only holding her because she tried to run as soon as she saw us."

Ollie's eyebrows shot up. "Wouldn't you?"

"Everyone has to be processed when they enter the drift. We'll release her if she promises to stay with you."

"She does," Asher said, cutting Darby off. He glared at her, and she snapped her mouth shut. She shook her head so black and purple hair sprayed over her forehead and cheeks.

"Fine!"

They dropped her, and she scuttled across the small gap between the groups. She situated herself slightly behind Ollie and next to Ren's shoulder.

"Now," Asher said, hands still raised, "answer my question. Who is the new management? Who do you represent?"

"We represent the planets under the divine guidance of our leader, Millicent, Mistress of the Stars."

Shock hit Ren full-force. He staggered back. "What the coggin' what? *Millicent*?"

The soldier who previously held Darby lit up at her name. "Do you know her? Isn't she amazing? She took over this whole drift in seconds."

Another spoke up, grin wide under his face shield. "She touched my arm once."

Ren gaped, mouth working uselessly. Not only had Millicent somehow supplanted Vos, but her soldiers were... groupies.

Asher asked. "How long was I gone?"

"I don't know. I've been asleep."

"Hey, stop talking." The leader jabbed his prod under Ren's ribs, dangerously close to his wound.

Ren recoiled, and Darby stepped in front of him. "Hey, don't be a cog. We're not resisting." She sighed, then amended. "Anymore. Not resisting anymore. We're not going to resist. Okay?"

Ren inhaled shakily. The prod brought up memories of his capture, of watching Jakob killed by Vos's trained army. The poke was too close for comfort to his wound. And Millicent's name carried its own weighty connotations of fear and manipulation. Panic hovered close, but Ren steeled himself, gritted his teeth, and took a few deep breaths. He ducked his head into the collar of the jacket he wore, but even with its familiar smell and fabric, he shivered, and his skin went clammy. He had Asher with him and Ollie, and, despite her questionable allegiance, Darby was there too. He'd be okay. He'd be okay. He'd be okay.

The soldier shifted and dropped the tip of the prod. "All new visitors to all of our leader's empire must be processed. Those are the rules."

Asher stiffened. "What do you mean processed? Who are you looking for?"

"Phoenix Corps, mostly, and any known traitors to the cause."

The leader elbowed the speaker. "They don't need to know that. Only the basics to civilians, remember?"

The soldier bowed his head, effectively cowed.

Ren and Asher shared an incredulous glance.

"Is there anyone else on your ship? The registry was blocked when you docked."

"A pilot," Asher confirmed. "But he already left. He shuttled us from Phoebus."

The leader nodded. "Good. Phoebus was the first of the leader's new empire. You will be familiar with the new protocols on Echo as well."

"Right. See, we've already been processed on Phoebus. So, we shouldn't have to do it again." Darby smiled, bright and wide.

"Do you have your badges?"

"Oh, we left them on the ship. I didn't think we'd need them here."

"Too bad. But if you passed last time, then no worries here."

Darby mouthed an expletive.

The comm on the leader's shoulder crackled. "We have another ship docking in bay seven, slip two. No one has disembarked yet, but ship has three registered passengers that will need to be processed."

The leader responded. "Send Bravo Team to the slip. We're bringing four to the processing center right now."

He nonchalantly rested the tip of his prod on Ren's sternum. His finger slipped close to the trigger. Ren's whole body tensed; power automatically surged in his middle. He trembled and resisted the impulse to cut the power or to turn the weapon against the soldier.

The voice came back over the comm. "Acknowledged."

"Come along then," he said to the group. "No more stalling."

The end of the weapon slid down Ren's body, caught on his shirt, then dropped away. Ren let out a stuttered breath.

Millicent's army moved with surprising precision as two took the lead in front of Ren and the other two swooped behind them. With a pulse gun at his back, Ren stumbled forward. Asher caught his arm, steadied him, gripped tight; his mouth was pulled down. Ren shook his head and straightened. His stomach roiled. His heart pounded. His throat tightened. But he held on, took Asher's hand in his and squeezed back, taking comfort in the sensation, grounding himself with physical contact. It helped.

The soldiers marched them through the drift. Asher stayed close to Ren's side. Darby and Ollie closed in around him as they navigated the corridors and passageways.

Clustered together, Ren dipped his head. "Do any of you have a plan?"

"Not yet," Asher said through gritted teeth. His jaw clenched. His gaze darted around the drift, taking everything in. The corridors they walked were empty save for soldiers. The vibrancy usually found on drifts had been either snuffed out or regulated to certain areas.

"We don't have a lot of time," Ren said. "You're a *birdman*. They're going to figure that out."

"Well, I'm pretty sure you're a traitor to their leader's cause. So yeah, we're cogging crunched."

Darby tripped forward and caught her balance on Asher's shoulder. "What are we going to do?" she whispered quickly.

"We?" Ren asked. "I thought you weren't sticking with us?"

"Better with you and freaky science-magic that I trust than freaky science-magic from a person I've not met. Worse yet, a person who you seem scared of. And that scares me."

"She doesn't scare me," Ren muttered. "She *concerns* me."

"She's terrifying," Asher said. "She literally cares about no one other than herself. And I want to know what happened to Vos. He might not be the leader, but he's still around I'm sure."

"Without Abiathar to control her…" Ren trailed off. That was it. Without someone who could control her, she'd broken the hold Vos had over her. She'd gone rogue. She had deposed Vos and taken over his army for herself and turned them into zealots following a higher power. Vos wasn't behind Phoebus or Echo. It was Millicent.

"If she ditched him," Ollie said, "what if he could be persuaded to our side?"

"I wouldn't trust him at all."

"No. I wouldn't either. But he's not evil. He's misguided, yes, and grandiose. But he had a goal and a purpose. Millicent has neither." Asher glanced around. The guards weren't paying them any attention. "If she's building an empire without him, what would be the last thing she'd want?"

Ren perked up. "The prisoners from Perilous Space released. Not only is Abiathar there, and he could regain control over her, but there might be someone else there who could challenge her."

"Also, you," Asher said, gripping Ren's hand. "With you gone, she's pretty much invincible. And if you're processed here, and she finds out…"

"I'm dead. Again."

"Cut the power," Darby said. "Then we can run. Or you take over the drift. You can do that, can't you?"

Ren winced. "I could, but…"

"Millicent makes Ren sick." Ollie coughed into his fist when one of the guards looked back.

"What do you mean sick?"

Ren crinkled his nose. "Her power affects me physically. It's… not good."

"Great."

The group stopped in front of a lift and waited. The conversation was suspended for the time being. They crowded in and went up several floors in tense silence.

The energy and the signatures of the weapons thudded under Ren's skin. He could disable them. Then they could run. To where? Rowan was already gone. All the docks were monitored. And surely Millicent had planted traps in the systems. She could incapacitate him, and then where would they be?

Wrapping his arms around his middle, Ren bent forward at the thought of the way Millicent could pull him in and push him out and how it affected his body.

"Hey." The leader pushed his prod into Ren's shoulder. "Is he okay? He looks sick."

Asher draped his arm over Ren's shoulders. "He's fine."

"He doesn't look it."

"What happened to the Corps on this drift?" Asher changed the subject away from Ren. He tilted his head and eyed their weapons. "I don't expect they gave up the drift willingly."

"Some did," he answered with a shrug. "When they saw what our divine leader could do with a blink of her beautiful, glowing eyes, they laid down their weapons. Those that didn't were vented."

Asher's expression didn't betray him, but he his grip on Ren's shoulders tightened.

They were spared any further conversation when the bell dinged and the doors opened. They shuffled out, and Ren received a push in the back when he didn't move fast enough. He stumbled into Darby and apologized.

They approached the processing center. A large black drape flapped over the Phoenix Corps symbol that blazed from the top of the entrance. The red phoenix rising from ashes with wings spread shone through the thin fabric despite the attempt to hide it, and its imposing figure burned across the whole floor. Orange and red symbolic flames rose and curled on either side of the archway. Ren was reminded of the fire that lit the sky on Bara as they fled the Phoenix Corps encampment.

"I could do it." Ren fluttered his eyes shut. "I could do it. Shut it all down and take over."

"You're not. We'll just have to escape without..." Asher rolled his eyes upward. "...using freaky science-magic."

Ollie snickered.

Darby looked around the area. She spied something and her frown bloomed into a crooked smirk. Her dark eyes lit up. "I got this, fellas. Leave it to me."

"Four for processing," the leader said to a woman at a large reception desk. She wore matching body armor but no helmet. Her dark hair was in a messy knot at the top of her head, and her nails clicked on the equipment as she typed. Dark makeup lined her eyes, and two bright violet circles colored her cheeks. She scanned the leader's data pad with a wand and huffed as she spun in her chair and hovered to a data screen.

The leader pointed his weapon toward a row of seats in a waiting area and addressed the group. "Wait over there."

Asher raised an eyebrow, but they walked over, his arm still draped across Ren's shoulders.

"Got that plan yet?" he asked Darby.

Darby grinned. "Oh, yeah." She lifted her chin at the guard-acting-receptionist. "That one is the mark."

"Why that one?"

"For as dim as the ones who picked us up on the dock are, the ones left behind are always dimmer."

"You'll bet our lives on that?"

Darby winked, dark eyes sparkling. "Who do you think I am, birdman?"

"I honestly don't know."

"Well," she flipped her chin-length hair. "Your loss."

Darby waited until the group who'd arrested them left. She looked around the area until her gaze settled on the guard waiting at the entrance. That one held a pulse gun and leaned against the doorway with his ankles crossed. She pursed her lips and stood.

With a saunter of her hips and an arch of her back, she approached the desk. The receptionist narrowed her eyes. "Hey, don't come any closer."

Darby frowned but stopped. "Seriously?"

"You need to step away and go back over there and wait."

Darby nodded. "I understand, but I have a problem." She ignored the previous order and closed the distance to the desk. She leaned across the surface, propping herself up on her elbows. "It's just… you see the little one over there?" She jerked her head toward Ren.

Ren tried not to take offense, but in comparison to Ollie and Asher, he was indeed the smaller one.

"Yeah? What of him?"

"Well," Darby said, sliding even farther across the desk. She dropped her voice. "I don't want to alarm anyone, but he's a duster."

"So?"

"He's a duster who had to leave his planet due to a sickness."

The receptionist's eyebrows knit together, and her purple lips thinned into a line. "So? I'm a duster. I had to leave my planet because it was crowded, and we all had to stay under the ground because of weeds generations ago who destroyed our environment."

"Ah, you get it then. I picked up that you were smarter than the others. What was your name?"

"Fawn." She tapped her long, red nails against her lips. Her suspicious expression eased into confusion. "I get what?"

Darby raised an eyebrow. "I would think that a duster from an overcrowded planet would understand the implications of a plague, Fawn. Especially in a confined space."

"A confined space?" she asked slowly.

"Like a drift for instance. *This* drift. *You* get it though, right?" Darby shook her head. "I told those cogs that brought us in not to break the ship's quarantine. I mean, it's only been a few days since we left his planet, but they wouldn't listen. They pulled him right out of his little plastic room." Darby sighed. "He watched his sister die, and then we took him on the ship. His fever hadn't even abated yet. I still think he might have one. Doesn't he look pale to you?"

Ren saw the moment Fawn got the implication. Color drained from her face, and her eyes widened. Ren coughed into his fist and curled even smaller, leaning heavily against Asher's side.

"It just takes one highly contagious individual with a disease from planet-side that most drifters wouldn't be immune to. And he would infect the whole drift. Actually," Darby said, looking sorrowfully over to Ren, "you're not from Stahl, are you? You're probably not immune to it either. Few people are."

Fawn leaned away from the desk and scooted her chair away. "His sister died?"

"Oh yeah, he told us all about it. She turned green and she started vomiting this thick, black disgusting stuff. It was as if she was liquefying. She ran a fever so high that it cooked her internal organs. It sounded gruesome."

"What?" her voice was a whisper.

"Can you imagine the population of an entire drift slowly turning to liquid?" Darby waved her hand in Ren's direction. "It happens suddenly too. Like one minute you're sitting there and the next you're doubled over." She shot a significant look at Ren.

Ren took his cue. He clapped a hand over his mouth and bent in half, almost toppling out of the chair. His back bowed and he made a muffled noise—part groan and part gag.

Fawn shot to her feet.

"Get him out of here!"

"Are you sure? We haven't been processed yet…"

"Yes!" She pointed to the door. Her arm flailed wildly; her intricate knot of hair fell to the side. "Go! Get out of here."

Asher pulled Ren to his feet.

"Do we need anything to…"

Fawn threw a handful of green tags at them. They fluttered to the floor, and Darby scrambled to pick them up. She stood and waved as Asher and Ren hustled for the exit.

"Thanks so much, Fawn. You don't know how many lives you saved today. In fact—"

Ollie grabbed Darby by the back of her collar and dragged her toward the door. Darby continued to spout platitudes and grandiose statements about Fawn being a hero and how Darby would tell all her superiors about how smart she was and considerate of her fellow dusters and the arrogant drifters.

"You're a hero, Fawn!" Darby yelled as they stumbled out of the recruitment area and walked quickly to the lift.

"Laying it on too thick is going to get us caught," Ollie said, snatching a green tag from Darby's hand. He snapped it on his pocket.

Ren took one as well and clipped it to the collar of Asher's drifter jacket. It flapped against his chest with every step.

"Let me have a little fun," she said, flipping them a smile. "It was one of my finer performances. But Ren, I have to say, you really sold it. Looking all pathetic and then pretending to spew was genius."

"I try," Ren said dryly.

Darby skipped through the hallways and spun around. A wide smile split her face. "It's been a while since I've had people," she said out of the blue. "I've forgotten how fun it can be. Think of what we could accomplish together. Think of the scams we could run. I want to stick with you. Can I stick with you?"

"That's fine with us," Ollie replied. "But maybe tone it down a little so we don't draw attention. And we'll have to discuss the scamming part."

Darby laughed. "Manipulating attention is what I'm good at."

"Enough," Asher said. He took Ren's hand, and guided the four of them to a corner of the drift, in the shadows. He inspected the ceilings. "This might be a camera blind spot, but I don't know what good that will do. If Millicent is monitoring the feeds here, then we're already crunched."

"She's not." Ren leaned against the wall. "I sensed it when we first got here. This drift is running on its own. She's set it up to conserve power and run efficiently by itself, so she doesn't have to come back."

Darby scrunched her nose. "Why would she do that? Wouldn't she want to check in on her empire?"

"She's only one person. And even as a star host, she's not powerful." Ren flexed his free hand. "The last time we interacted, she still had to be touching an object to control it."

"Which is why she needs zealots like those so-called soldiers. She showed them something amazing, and they followed blindly." Asher blushed and looked to Ren, and Ren heard the similarities and truth in Asher's words. "They believe in her."

"Well, yeah," Darby said. "I have seen some shit since I was kidnapped by you losers and I have to say that if Ren asked me to jump out of an airlock, I might actually do it."

Ren raised an incredulous eyebrow.

"Okay, fine. I wouldn't do it, but I did get us out of jam with my superior acting skills when I could've bolted and left you in the atmosphere."

"We're glad you didn't do that, Darby," Ollie said, resting a hand on her shoulder. "Thank you for rescuing us by nonviolent means."

She beamed.

"Now," Ollie said, rubbing his hands together. "We need a ship and a way out of here."

"One with crew we can overpower if needed." Darby said echoing Penelope.

So much for nonviolence.

"Or one we can steal." Ollie smacked Ren on the back. "Are you up for it?"

"If I need to be."

Asher's smile was rueful. "I think we need you to be."

"Okay, then. I can do it."

With a sinking feeling, Ren led the others toward the lift. They didn't pass anyone, and the lift was empty when they boarded. They went down and exited on the dock level.

"Where is everyone?" Darby's energy had settled and now she squinted as she surveyed the drift. A few citizens milled about, all wearing green badges, but they eyed the group suspiciously and didn't engage them. "This place should be bustling. Especially since drift time would be about the middle of their cycle."

"Hiding."

"From those jerks?"

"They still have prods and pulse guns. And someone untrained is more dangerous than someone who is."

"I don't know, you're pretty scary, Ash," Darby said. "The way you move definitely gives you away. Efficient and precise. Like power barely controlled. To a trained eye, like myself, you'd be the opposite of what we'd look for in a good mark."

"I'm going to take that as a compliment."

"Oh, you should. Only green meat would try to pickpocket or scam you."

Asher led them toward the entrance to the docking bays. Ren held his breath as they passed a group of soldiers with the same black uniforms and body armor. The soldiers looked up and down at Ren, scanning his body, noting the green badge. They continued on their way without incident, and Ren almost collapsed in relief.

Ren wished he could merge with the drift's systems. He wished he could burrow into the vid feeds and scout out the dock. He wished he could search the ship registries and find one that would meet their needs and purpose. He wished he could save this drift, dig in and root out all of Millicent's snares and protocols, and free the people. But he got one inkling of her star signature and nausea rolled over him, and his body went weak in his joints.

"We'll start in the bay where we came in. I thought I saw a good ship we can *borrow*."

Darby grumbled about semantics.

They entered the docking bay, and Ren was flooded with sensation. He stopped short. Asher bumped into his back.

"Ren?"

Ren ran. He sprinted around a corner. Asher was a half-step behind him.

"Ren! What are you—" Asher skidded to a halt beside him. "Rowan?"

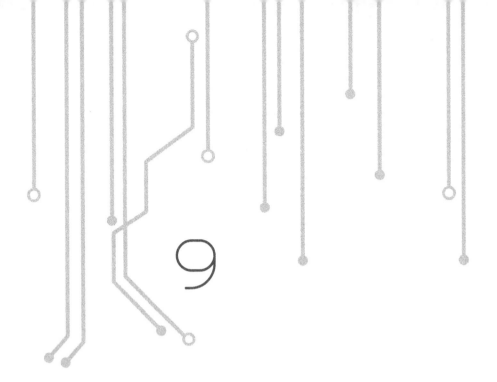

9

Rowan startled at the sound of her name and dropped the prod in her hand. It clattered on the ground. She kicked it away from the prone guard's outstretched fingers, though he was in no condition to reach for it. "Oh, good," she said, with a smug grin. "I don't have to rescue you then."

"What are you doing here?" Asher sputtered.

"We made it to the trade route and turned around." She shrugged and looked away, unwilling to meet Asher's gaze. "Pen's disapproving silence and Lucas's forced humor were enough of a punishment."

"You didn't have to come back." Asher crossed his arms. "We had it under control."

She toed the guard and rolled him to his back as he groaned. "Sure, you did."

Darby and Ollie jogged up to join them, and Darby huffed. "We were about to steal a ship, but I guess that plan is off."

Asher clenched his jaw, and color rose in his cheeks. "Borrow a ship."

Rowan raised a perfect eyebrow. "Completely under control, huh?" Asher didn't respond. Rowan tugged her braid. "Also, what the hell is this about the divine leader *Millicent,* Mistress of the Stars?"

Ren wrinkled his nose. "We'll explain later. Let's get out of here."

"What did you do?" Darby asked, peering down at the guard. She studied him, eyes narrowed, fingertip tapping her chin. Once gauging he was not a threat, Darby went for his pockets and rifled through them. No one stopped her.

"He was talking cogging strangely about a divine leader and how I needed to be *processed.* So, I stole his weapon and sparked him with it."

"Reasonable course of action," Darby said. She pulled out a credit chip and pocketed it. "Oh, ID card! Nice! Might need this later." That also disappeared into the depths of her pockets.

"Look, I'm sorry, okay? I shouldn't have let you..." Rowan addressed Ren, Asher, and Ollie, then nodded her head to Darby. "I shouldn't have let you four leave. It was a bad decision. Though..." She held up a finger. "...I still maintain that this whole scheme of finding Ren's brother is reckless. I may have found a change of heart, but it's entirely dependent on if you can come up with a decent plan." She tossed her braid over her shoulder.

Asher lightly punched Rowan in the arm. "Apology accepted. And yes," Asher glanced at the groaning guard. "We have new problems."

"And a new resolve," Ren added. "But can we leave first?"

Darby straightened. "Yeah. This drift is creepy, and I want off. Besides, I need to hear more about this divine leader that you all seem to know."

Rowan nodded sharply. "Right. Let's go. And put the prod down, Darby. That thing is not coming on my ship. Honestly, I don't understand the appeal. A pulse gun does the job just as well and from a distance. It's elegant."

Darby frowned, but dropped the prod. "Did you just call a weapon elegant? Rowan, I feel we may have missed out on some bonding. We need to remedy this."

"Later. Follow me."

They crept down the row of bays. The *Star Stream* called to Ren as he approached. It welcomed him as it always did, and Ren's power engaged. His vision went blue, and he opened himself to the systems and circuits.

"You're glowing," Asher said in a low voice. He knocked his shoulder into Ren's arm.

"I'm home."

Asher's grin widened into a full-blown smile. "Good to know."

Aboard the ship, the tension Ren carried in his spine and shoulders eased. Penelope and Lucas waited on the other side of the airlock.

"Good to see you," Lucas said, with his goggles on his head and his brown hair sticking up. "Long time no see."

"Shut up," Rowan said, stepping into the ship, heading for the stairs.

Lucas's grin only widened. He pounced on Ollie when he walked in, and Penelope followed suit. Someone snagged Ren's arm as he tried to maneuver around them, and he was swallowed in a bone-crushing hug. Asher rolled his eyes and grudgingly joined in.

"You cogs are weird." Darby followed Rowan up the stairs and dodged Penelope's attempt at scooping her into the group hug.

"Lucas, get us off this hunk." Rowan rested her crossed arms on the railing above them. "The rest of you, common room. Now!"

Gathered in the common area, Ren sat on the couch with his legs draped over Asher's lap. Asher absently rubbed Ren's leg over the fabric of his trousers; the heat of his palm bled through the cloth to Ren's skin. Even as light and nonchalant as it was, his touch helped soothe the tremble of fatigue in Ren's muscles. The casual intimacy of their position was not lost on Ren, and his body warmed, and his pulse quickened. Their relationship wasn't a secret, but they'd not been this openly tactile. If anyone noticed, they didn't comment, but Ren kept his head ducked to spare himself from knowing looks. He tucked his bare toes under the arm of the couch and waited for Rowan to ask questions.

Lucas and Penelope sprawled in the dining chairs. Ollie sat on the deck plate with his back to the front of the couch, and Darby perched, cross-legged, on the table.

Rowan stood, arms crossed, posture straight.

"Feet off the table," she said, giving Darby a stern look.

Darby rolled her eyes but kicked out her legs, so her boots hung off the end. "Yes, Captain."

"Captain?" Asher sputtered. "Just call her Rowan, or she'll get a bigger head than she already has."

"I thought it was appropriate. She did come back for us in kind of true, badass lady fashion. I mean, she did take away the opportunity of Ren and I stealing—" Ren coughed. Darby blew out a breath. "Really? Fine, *borrowing* a ship, but, you know, can't win them all."

"We would've returned the ship. If we could've."

Darby scoffed. "You stopped me from stealing this ship and you stopped me from stealing another ship. You are a killjoy, Ren. I don't say that lightly."

Ren rolled his eyes. "You're a menace."

"Whatever, blue eyes. Maybe turn that down a little bit, okay?"

Ren hadn't realized he was using his star, but at her words, he did find himself unconsciously running through a systems diagnostic. Everything was in working order, which was to be expected as he had only left a few hours ago. There was not much Lucas could do to break the ship in that time, and Penelope could've fixed anything minor.

Asher put his arm around Ren's shoulders and lightly tousled the longer strands of Ren's hair.

"I was checking the systems."

Rowan shifted her weight and cocked her hip. "Anyway, now that we've left the empire of the divine leader Millicent, does anyone want to fill me in on how the hell that happened?"

"We don't have much more information than you do unfortunately." Ollie stretched his back, then dropped his hands. "Those soldiers on Echo are zealots under the thrall of Millicent."

"That's unsettling," Lucas said. Penelope elbowed him. "What? *She* was unsettling. I don't think anyone is arguing that point. And it's not like she's here to hear me say that I found her creepy behavior unsettling. She was the definition of *unsettling*."

"Okay, so like, how do you people know this lady?" Darby spread out her hands. "Is she a friend or something?"

"No."

"Ex-friend."

"Kind of."

Darby looked at Asher, Ren, and Penelope, and made a face. "Which is it?"

"I met her when I was trapped on Ren's planet under the reign of an autocrat named Vos. She left before Ren arrived. We ran into her again on Mykonos, and she was under the control of Abiathar, a star host who can control other stars with his voice. We released her, and she agreed to become part of the crew, until she betrayed us on Crei and was instrumental in my capture by the Phoenix Corps and Ren's mortal injury."

Darby's mouth dropped open. "Wow. Okay. So, she's the one who," she waved her hand.

"No, Corporal Zag shot me."

"And he's?"

"Phoenix Corps," Asher said. "Like me."

"Oh. That's... complicated. I'm sorry I asked."

"Millicent is obviously no longer under Vos's control," Rowan said. "She's taken over Phoebus and Echo. Who knows what other drifts she hopes to target. And for what purpose?"

"Power," Asher said.

"No." Ren shook his head. He shared a look with Ollie. "Millicent left Crei because of the opportunity to escape her situation. Power isn't what drives her."

"What is it then? It's not for anyone's benefit but her own. That much is obvious."

"You're right on that front," Ren said as Asher drummed his fingers on Ren's shin. "She's not in it to make friends."

Ollie frowned. "She wants freedom."

"She doesn't want to be confined to a single drift. She was confined on Crei, in more ways than one. She wants to move freely and by taking over several drifts she's able to maneuver." Ren laid his hand over Asher's, stilling the movement. "She's building a base."

Asher squeezed Ren's hand.

"What does this mean for us?" Rowan paced, her boot heels clicking.

Asher sighed. "It means we can't run and hide."

Ren threaded his fingers with Asher's. "The best way for a star host to be able to have freedom from the Corps and from Vos is to destroy both the Corps and Vos."

"We have to stop her," Ollie said.

"I agree." Darby propped her head on her crossed knees and put her boots back on the table. "I don't want to live through another Phoebus and, as much fun as Echo was, I don't think the hilarity would hold when she decides to vent everyone because being a ruler doesn't suit her anymore."

"What can we do to thwart someone who can control tech and makes our own technopath ill when they interact?" Rowan asked more to herself than the group.

Ren rubbed his eyes. "Free Abiathar."

Rowan stopped pacing. "What? Free that cog? So he can turn you against us? I don't think so."

"He's in Perilous Space with Liam. It's worth a try."

"Or we could get an ancient gun like Zag did and shoot her. It worked on Ren." Ren narrowed his eyes at Lucas, and Lucas raised his hands. "What? It's a valid option. *Unsettling!*"

Penelope raised her hand. "Maybe we should figure out a way for Ren to be able to… override Millicent? Do you think that might be possible?"

Asher resumed his rubbing of Ren's legs with more focus and with more pressure. Ren bit off a gasp when Asher's fingers dug into a tender spot on his calf.

Ren cleared his throat. "I could try?"

"Sorry, Ren," Asher said with a frown, "but that's not a good enough plan. That's not a plan at all. We don't even know what we're going to do when we get to the prison."

"We're puttering in that direction, right now," Lucas said. "In case anyone cares."

Rowan scrubbed her hands over her face, then dropped them, fists clenched.

"We need to talk to Mother," Rowan said.

Asher recoiled into the cushions. "Do we have to?"

"I'm missing something," Darby said. "Who is your mother?"

Rowan and Asher shared a glance, and Rowan tugged on her braid. "Our mother is the esteemed Councilor Morgan of the Drift Alliance."

"Your mother is a politician?"

"Yes."

"Huh. I guess that makes sense."

Rowan rolled her eyes. "Unfortunately. She has to know what is happening to the drifts. And if what those cogs said was true, if Millicent vented those Corps soldiers, Mother needs to know that as well. She can pass the information on to VanMeerten."

Asher laughed without humor. "Do you think she'll tell the general anything? They hate each other."

Rowan shrugged. "It's worth a try. Especially if Mother can send help. Maybe she can convince the Corps to release the prisoners in Perilous Space without us having to get involved."

Ren raised an eyebrow. "Does she even know what they're using Perilous Space for? And last time we talked to your mother, before she met me, she didn't even believe people like me existed. Now, we're going to tell her Millicent is killing people and taking over drifts? And that's somehow going to convince her to allow the star hosts in Perilous Space to be released?"

"You have to admit that you *are* farfetched," Darby chimed.

Ren glared.

"What?"

Lucas stood. "I'll get the comm set up."

"I'll get ready." Asher gently pushed Ren's legs from his lap. He shot him an apologetic smile, then kissed Ren's cheek.

Ren's heart raced, and his blush deepened.

Darby whistled and grinned ear to ear. She raised both eyebrows in quick succession and laughed at Ren's mortified expression. Asher made an impolite gesture with his fingers when he left the room.

"Rude!" she called after him.

Ren buried his face in his hands.

⊣⊢

Ren stood at Asher's shoulder while he and Rowan prepared to face their mother. Rowan brushed imaginary lint from Asher's shirt. Throat bobbing and jaw working, Asher swept the ends of his blond hair from his forehead.

Ren tentatively placed his hand on Asher's shoulder and squeezed.

"You should be out of sight," Asher said and immediately pinched the bridge of his nose. "Sorry, that came out badly. But you shouldn't be where they can see you."

Ren admitted it stung, but he understood. By all accounts, he was dead, and they needed to keep it that way. "I'll be right over there."

"Okay you two, show time. Best smiles," Lucas said, pressing buttons and flipping switches.

Ren left the bridge but hid behind the doorway. He tucked himself into the small space at the top of the stairs between the sliding door and the entrance. He brought his knees to his chest and wrapped his arms around his shins. His stomach flip-flopped when he reached into the systems.

He boosted the signal as Lucas put in a message request with the councilor. Through the comm system and the vid feeds, the screen was a blanket of interference and snow until the ship connected and a clear picture slowly sharpened.

Councilor Morgan looked remarkably like her children. She had the same light-blonde hair and the same vibrant green eyes. She had their strong jaws and straight noses and light brows. Wrinkles spread out from the corners of her eyes, and she had frown lines around her mouth. She was beautiful and strong and terrifying when she forced a smile at her children.

"Good morning, my loves," Councilor Morgan said as she smoothed her hair from her eyes. "I haven't heard from you in months. Asher, I thought you were back with the Corps."

"I left," he said flatly.

Her smile didn't move, but her eyes gave her away. "Is that wise? They'll court-martial you."

"I'm fine."

Her smiled wavered. "I'm sorry about what happened to your little friend. I know he was dear to you."

Asher didn't move; his expression seemed frozen. "He was. I loved him."

Ren's breath caught. Warmth was like a live wire in his middle, and he shivered and pressed a smile into his knees. The fabric of his trousers felt coarse against his mouth.

Councilor Morgan's expression remained placid. She changed the subject. "And Rowan? Still drifting from place to place with those friends of yours?"

Rowan's smile was frightening. "Yes, Mother. Actually, I wanted to talk with you about that. We've recently been to Echo drift and—"

"Oh? You're far out in the cluster, my dear. I've not been to Echo in years. It's almost as quaint as the planets Asher is fond of."

"Have you heard anything about Echo? Or about Phoebus? Or any others?"

Their mother shook her head. "No, dears. You understand there are so many drifts these days that it's difficult to keep up with them all. Echo and Phoebus are so small and far out from Mykonos. Why? Are they having trouble?" Her eyes flitted to stare at something off screen.

Rowan and Asher shared an uneasy glance.

"Yes," Asher said.

Councilor Morgan's gaze slid off screen again, and Rowan stepped forward.

"Who's there with you, Mother?"

"What?" Her manicured fingers rested against her throat. "No one is here with me."

"Don't lie to us. Is it Corps? Vos? That girl Millicent?"

She sighed and put her hands on her hips, all pretentions vanishing. "You're too perceptive for your own good." She addressed the individual off screen. "Well, Grace, might as well come out from hiding."

Grace?

A shadow moved across the screen, and Ren clapped a hand over his mouth to stifle a gasp.

She looked different with her iron-gray hair falling around her shoulders rather than pulled back in a severe bun. Her scar was unmistakable, stretching from her ear, down the line of her jaw, then stopping at her chin. She wasn't wearing her uniform, and the shapeless dress she wore made her appear softer than normal, though her gaze was as sharp as ever.

Asher jolted back. Ren jerked, and moved to run to Asher's side, but stopped himself. Asher made a movement with his hand, and Ren recognized it as a signal to stay put. He crouched behind the door.

"Private Morgan," VanMeerten said, peering down her nose. Her eyes seemed hard and glinting with disapproval. She swished a glass of wine; the red liquid swirled like blood. "There you are. The last I had heard, you were lost in a commotion on Bara that was blamed on the residents of the nearby city. Now I must conclude that it was your sister who destroyed the generators and aided in your desertion. I'll be issuing a warrant for both of your arrests."

"You will do no such thing, Grace." Councilor Morgan slammed her hand on the table. Her tone dripped with venom as she continued. "You leave my children alone. Whatever truce is between us extends to them."

VanMeerten eyed Asher and Rowan. "You're lucky your mother has the means and power to stay my hand for the time being, but, as far as I'm concerned, you're a deserter and a traitor, Asher, and you, Rowan, are a pirate."

Rowan lifted her chin. "And you're a bitch, but name-calling isn't going to bring us any closer to figuring out how to stop the attacks on the drifts. We've encountered two drifts that have been sieged by zealots."

VanMeerten set her glass of wine on the councilor's desk. "No need to worry. We have the situation well in hand."

"Right," Asher said. "And how do you plan to stop her? Are you going to use the prisoners in Perilous Space to do so? I know you have someone there that can manipulate others with his voice. His name is Abiathar, if you've forgotten. We captured him on Mykonos."

"Why would we need to utilize that ancient cog?"

"Oh, do you have another trick up your sleeve? Is Zag going to hide around a corner and shoot her with an ancient projectile, like you did Ren? Kill her from a distance? Like a coward?"

VanMeerten's eyes flashed. "I don't have to justify Corps decisions to you."

"No, you don't." Asher strode forward, hands clenched. "That's the problem. You have no accountability to anyone and indiscriminately make decisions that affect others with no regard to the consequences on dusters and drifters alike!" His chest heaved. His voice rose, banged through the silence, echoed around the small area of the bridge. "You're the real villain."

"How dare you lecture me! That star host was *dangerous*. He was bringing that tunnel down around you all, and you would have let him."

"He was afraid."

"He was wild and out of control. He was possessed!"

"He was a teenager!" Asher pointed a shaking finger. "He was doing the best he knew how to do. He was frightened and unsure and only wanted to go home, but he couldn't, because the Corps had taken that home away. And you've done the same to others, and now they're rebelling and trying to make a safe haven for themselves. You're not the only one to blame, but you've as much of the burden to shoulder as anyone else."

"We already have the suspect in custody." She placed her hands on the table and loomed over them. "I won't deny that you're passionate, but its best to know the facts before you jump onto a soap box."

Asher bristled and shrugged off Rowan's placating touch to his shoulder.

Councilor Morgan spread her hands; her mouth twisted into a frown. "Asher and Rowan, please, leave this business to the general and myself. We are aware of the situation in the outlier drifts. We have no plans to allow it to escalate further. You two should find a place to relax for a few weeks while we rid the drifts of these ridiculous dusters and their dreams of grandeur."

Asher didn't move, but Rowan knuckled her eyes in exasperation.

"Mother, we're dealing with something you don't seem to understand."

"Who do you have in custody?" Asher asked.

"Don't answer," VanMeerten snapped. "That's need-to-know, and a deserter doesn't need to know."

Rowan threw up her hands. "Mother—"

"Rowan, please, don't do anything rash." Councilor Morgan picked up her own wine glass. "I know it's been a tough few weeks for the both of you. Please find a nice spot to rest. I'll send you the credits to cover the cost, of the whole crew even, for you to have a nice relaxing vacation."

"A vacation? Are you cogging—"

"Cut it off," Asher said, waving his hand to Lucas. "Cut it off."

The screen went dark. Ren pulled out of the systems and hurried through the entranceway to Asher's side.

"Well," Lucas said with false cheer, "at least they don't hate each other anymore. That's something, right?"

Rowan looked to the ceiling. Asher shook his head and sighed.

"Don't do anything rash," Rowan muttered, echoing their mother's words. "A vacation. A vacation! And offering to pay for it! Who does that woman think I am? I've been on my own since I was seventeen! I don't need her credits!" She wagged her finger in Ren's face. "We're going to Perilous Space. We're going to find your brother. And we're going to stop Millicent. I swear to the stars, a *vacation!*" Rowan stalked off, yelling over her shoulder. "I'll tell the others!"

Lucas shot to his feet and followed, loudly talking about coordinates and space routes and the estimated time to arrival.

Asher leaned hard against Ren's side. "I feel a headache coming."

"Come along, then." Ren threaded their fingers and gently tugged Asher off the bridge and down the hallway.

+⊦

Asher closed the door behind them and leaned against it, allowing his head to fall back against the metal. "Finally, we're alone."

Ren smiled. "Too much?"

"My mother is always headache-inducing, not to mention the general. Also, Darby talks more than Pen and Lucas combined. Once you get her going she won't stop."

"Darby is something."

"She is. You didn't tell me she tried to steal the *Star Stream* out from under you."

"I was kind of passed out on the deck and pretended to be a ship. Not my most brilliant moment and not something I'd want to share with the cute guy who likes me."

Asher ducked his head and laughed. "You forget that I met you in a cell. I've seen it all, and you're not going to scare me off."

Ren sobered. "Thank you." He shucked off his shirt and tossed it to the floor. "Thank you for what you said to your mother. I needed to hear that."

"You're not going to scare me away, Ren. I'm with you." Asher crossed the room and placed his large hands on the jut of Ren's hips. He rested his forehead against Ren's, and his green eyes fluttered closed. "It's going to take much more than a little freaky science-magic and glow-action to scare me away."

Ren looped his arms over Asher's shoulders. "And I'm with you. Always. I messed up before, but not again. You're all I have."

Asher huffed. "That's not true. I think Rowan likes you more than she likes me. Ollie certainly does. And Darby is in awe of you."

"Rowan would fight the universe with her bare fists for you; don't start."

Chuckling, Asher nuzzled his nose along the line of Ren's jaw up to his ear. "She might." He kissed the line of Ren's cheekbone.

Ren let out a stuttered breath. "She would."

"You too are scarily alike. Maybe that's why I fell for you." Asher's grip on Ren's waist tightened. "Do you miss your family? Do you miss Erden?"

"No," Ren lied. He missed his brother, but that was no secret. Sometimes, in the night, when memories filled the spaces in his head, Ren missed the simplicity of the village: the sense of knowing where he belonged; the structure and familiarity of the homes and the lake and the work; the seemingly petty village politics. He missed his mother—the person he had thought she was, not the one he knew now. He missed the secret visions of his father, the man he'd never met. He missed the small moments when his stepfather treated him like a son. He missed Jakob, the brash naïve boy who carried himself like royalty, and he missed the man he'd become, the protective and supportive friend. He missed Sorcha, the beautiful girl with the spine of steel, the fiery leader he'd left behind to rule. "No, I always wanted to be in space and here I am. I may miss a few things, like the smell of the earth after the rain and the sunrise over the lake. But I'm happy the *Star Stream* is my home now. I don't want to be anywhere else."

"You're my home."

The sound of that was small and vulnerable, and Ren's heart ached. He tucked Asher closer in his arms, and slid one hand into the thick strands of Asher's blond hair. "I'm tired. Let's sleep."

Asher nodded. "Good plan."

"Come on."

They dressed for bed and climbed into the small bunk together. Asher curled on his side and Ren spooned around him. His arm wrapped around Asher's body; his palm pressed against Asher's chest so the steady beat of his heart was beneath Ren's hand.

Ren kissed Asher's nape as Asher pulled the blanket over them. Asher fell asleep quickly. Ren stayed awake, measuring the passage of time by Asher's heart beats and the small snoring sounds he made when he turned his face into the pillow. Ren never wanted to move. He never wanted to be anywhere else ever again except in this bunk on this ship with his past firmly behind him and his future ahead, uncertain and frightening, but thick with potential in the promises of Asher's kisses and the faith of the crew. Even without that, Ren was content to lie there, in the questionable softness of the bunk, with his back pressed against the metal wall and his feet sticking out the other end of the blanket and his arm trapped beneath Asher's body so fingers were slowly becoming numb. Ren could become used to this and he would revel in the magnificent predictability of an unextraordinary life.

This is what Ren wanted: a soft place to land at the end of the day, Asher right beside him, and all the domesticity and routine and happiness of a life filled with love and certainty.

He squeezed his eyes shut and hoped and hoped and hoped it was possible.

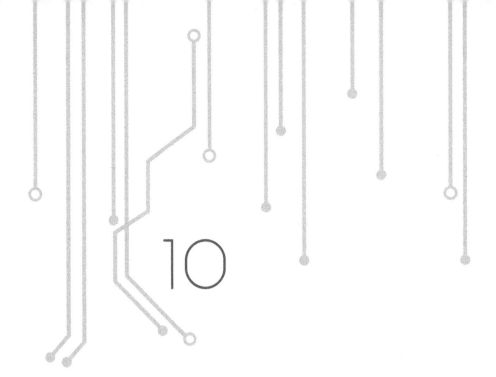

10

"We'll be close to Perilous Space soon," Lucas said, plopping into a chair at breakfast. "There is a debris field a few hours out, and the prison is beyond that."

After three days of uneventful travel, knowing their destination was so close spiked Ren's anxiety. He sipped his coffee, and Asher rubbed his back. Asher sopped up egg with his toast as his palm swept up and down Ren's spine. Ren took comfort in the familiar touch and consciously eased the tension from his shoulders.

They had a semblance of a plan. The specifics were hazy at best, but they'd get close enough for Ren to create a blueprint of the prison and go from there. Asher and Rowan had scoured the archives they could access, and Ollie and Darby had made plans which involved weapons and bombs that Ren hoped they didn't have to use. Penelope ordered Ren to have daily check-ins regarding his wound and his fatigue. With regular use, Ren's muscles had stopped seizing and constantly feeling weak, but he was far from one hundred percent. Exhaustion was a constant threat, and Ren spent most of his time either working out or sleeping.

He didn't mind that much, since Asher joined him when he was able.

Penelope dropped a plate of food in front of him. "Eat," she ordered. "You need the protein and the energy."

Ren rolled his eyes fondly, but took the fork from Penelope's outstretched fingers. Digging in, Ren chewed as the others filtered in. Darby shuffled by, barely lifting her feet, with her hair standing on end, and wearing pajama pants with little dogs on them, obviously Penelope's. Lucas stifled a laugh, and Darby mustered a glare that was tempered by the picture of a tiny barking dog on her shirt.

Asher pulled his hand away, laced his fingers over his empty plate, and put his elbows on the table. Ren missed the warmth of his touch, but he couldn't be greedy. He'd spent the last three days in Asher's bunk, napping and exploring all the ways they fit. It was the most corporeal he'd felt in weeks. His consciousness was firmly within his body, and the ship was merely an occasional echo in his head. It was wonderful.

Smiling dreamily, Ren shivered as someone passed behind him; their touch whispered over the base of his skull. He snapped his head around to find... no one.

"You okay?" Asher asked.

Ren squinted, confused. "Yeah. I'm fine, I just thought..." he trailed off. He shook off the phantom touch. "Nothing."

Asher raised an eyebrow, but went back to sniping with Lucas and Ollie.

Ren snatched Asher's toast crust and popped it in his mouth. As nervous as he was about approaching Perilous Space, he was excited as well. Soon he'd find Liam, and then they could focus on their future— the crew's, his with Asher's, Liam's as well.

A thought caressed the back of his mind, a fleeting murmur that was not his own. He jerked in his seat. "What did you say?"

The room was quiet. "Ren?" Asher asked.

A new ship is approaching. Older model. It doesn't look like one of the Corps.

Ren's ran a hand over his head. "Did you say something to me?"

"No, Ren, we haven't said anything."

"Is there another ship out there, Lucas? I swear I thought I heard something."

Lucas shook his head slowly. "Not that I saw before I came down here. I would've seen it. Are you picking it up on the sensors?"

Ren bit his lip. "I'm not in the ship."

"Are you sure?"

Ren gave Lucas a pointed look.

"Well! You tend to do weird things. I don't know."

A wrinkle appeared between Asher's eyebrows. Ren absently smoothed it away with the pad of his finger, then dropped his hand to his lap.

"I'm fine. I just…"

I wonder what they're doing all the way out here. They don't belong. Don't worry. I doubt it's anything exciting.

Ren stood abruptly. "Did you hear that? Tell me you heard that!"

The wrinkle deepened. Darby's wide eyes and Penelope's open mouth told Ren otherwise. They didn't hear it. What was happening? There had to be a ship. Ren jumped into the sensors and raced through the wires. He pinged outward, but there were no ships and no communications in the area, only the beginnings of the rings of debris. Ren raced to find Rowan in her quarters, but she wasn't on the comm system, or on a data pad.

Asher took Ren's hand. "Ren?"

"I'm in the sensors on purpose. And Lucas is right, there are no ships." Ren slotted back into his body. Confusion and fear formed a knot in his stomach. "I'm… I'm going back to bed."

He scrambled out of the common area, leaving his dirty dish on the table, and stumbled toward Asher's bunk. He was hearing things. He was stressed. He was tired. He hadn't eaten well. He wasn't slipping. He couldn't be slipping again. Millicent wasn't there. She was off courting disaster on drifts, and he'd been securely in his body for the last several days. He stretched his fingers and curled them toward his palm. He sat heavily on the bunk and counted his heart beats, inhaling and exhaling, feeling his lungs fill and expand, then empty. Running his nails over his scalp, Ren dropped his head in his hands.

"Please don't be slipping. Not now." He was on the verge of panicking. He could feel it, crawling into his throat, tightening around his neck. Sweat formed at his temples and nape. His heart raced.

The door opened, and Ren startled.

Asher held out his palms. "Hey," he said, shutting the door behind him, then sitting next to Ren on the bed. "What's going on?"

Do you sense that? There's one of us nearby.

Ren clapped his hands over his ears. He didn't want to worry Asher, but he'd learned that keeping things bottled up was worse for him than telling Asher the truth.

"I'm hearing things," he whispered. "And it's not another ship or any of the crew sending messages."

Asher made a low noise. "Are you stressed?"

Ren's shoulders hunched near his ears, and the food he ate a few minutes ago swirled in his stomach. "Yes, of course."

"Are you panicked?"

"No. I mean, yes, but it's coming from the voices." Ren dropped his hands and ran his palm up and down his thighs; the rough fabric of his trousers chafed against his skin, grounding him. "The voices aren't a symptom of my panic attacks. But apparently they're a trigger." His breath hitched.

"It could be a new symptom, Ren. Despite the rest we've had the past few days, you've been running nonstop since you woke up. You were inside the ship for weeks. You're fatigued. You might be feeling a few strange aftereffects."

"Maybe," Ren said, unease an unpleasant thrum beneath his skin. "You're not wrong."

Asher sighed. "Let's take a nap."

"We just woke up," Ren said, lips tipping up into a half-smile.

Asher shrugged. "We didn't sleep much the night before."

"I'm not going to argue with a nap."

"Good. Shove over."

Asher manhandled Ren into where he wanted him, with Asher on his back and Ren tucked along his side. Ren's arm was slung over Asher's waist; his head rested on Asher's shoulder.

"When this is over," Asher said, tugging up the blanket, "we're buying a better blanket and a new pillow."

Ren snorted. "I don't disagree. Your pillow is horrendously lumpy."

Asher dug his fingers into Ren's rib and made him squirm closer. Ren let out a breathless laugh, and the curl of Asher's lips into a smile did more to abate the clench of his heart than anything else.

"It is. We'll have to buy at least three pillows for our bed. And a bigger blanket, since you steal."

Ren made a half-hearted protest, but closed his eyes and reveled in the warmth and comfort of Asher's body. "It'll be the first thing we do. After we storm a prison, save my brother, and stop a powerful technopath."

"Go to sleep, Ren."

Ren snuggled in and, between one breath and the next, he fell asleep.

⊣⊢

The hollow thud of metal debris hitting the hull echoed through the *Star Stream*, but that was not what woke Ren from his dead sleep. It was the sound hidden within, the *voice* of the debris' occupant. The bed was empty except for Ren and a tangle of sheets. He swung his legs over the side and didn't bother taming his hair or putting on shoes before he was out into the hallway. Vision blue, Ren ran to the bridge.

Do you think they know we're here?

Sprinting through the hallway of the crew quarters, Ren passed the open arch to the common area. He didn't stop when Asher and Darby called his name. He jumped up the steps to the bridge, ducking at the last minute.

He was already connected to the ship; his star bled out of the soles of his feet into the sensors and outward. With every step he took, they became louder, and his connection with reality stretched and dimmed. Voices. So many whispers in his ears. Talking. To each other. Not to him. Do they know he was here? Do they know he can hear them? Was he eavesdropping? Was he picking up something on the sensors?

No, this was different. This was... surreal.

Lucas swiveled in his chair. "Ren?"

"What is that?" Ren asked, pointing to the debris that surrounded them.

"The debris field around Perilous Space. Where the last of the technopaths were destroyed in the war between them and the organization that became the Corps."

Asher and Darby walked onto the bridge, and Asher clapped his hand on Ren's shoulder. "What's wrong?"

"The voices." Ren closed his eyes and opened himself. It was like a zipper being pulled, a revelation of power and energy, and, with that one action, the universe opened.

"Do you hear them?" Ren asked.

Ren turned his head to find Asher staring at him with wide eyes and a concerned frown.

"Ren? Are you okay? What's going on?"

Ren squinted. Asher was beautiful bathed in blue.

"Can you hear that?"

Asher's lips turned down farther. "Hear what, Ren?"

"The voices. They're talking."

Lucas opened the shipwide comm. "We're approaching Perilous Space. All crew to the bridge. We may be having a situation."

Asher crowded close to Ren's side and placed his hands on Ren's shoulders; the action was slow and deliberate. "Ren, tell me what's going on."

"It's… voices. I hear voices."

Biting his lip, Asher asked. "Is this panic? What do you need?"

"No, this isn't an attack. This is…" How could he explain it? Murmurs and absent thoughts whispered in his head. The hairs on his arm stood up, and he trembled. Power shivered down his spine. He moved to the vid screen and studied the shapes and scraps of metal and circuits and wires which floated around them. They were ships. Dozens of ships, their components singed and tortured, twisted hunks of metal that gently bumped the *Star Stream*'s hull. They spoke to him. It was them. It had to be. "I'm hearing someone else's thoughts." No. That wasn't right. Not someone's. Several different… beings.

Ren allowed Asher to guide him to Rowan's chair while they waited for Rowan and the rest of the crew. He blinked sluggishly and walked with delicate steps, conscious of not much other than the heat of Asher's grip on his body and the voices swelling in his head. Asher ran his fingers through Ren's hair and gripped his hand as if he might float away.

"Look at all this debris," Lucas said, sweeping his hand toward the view screen. "It surrounds the prison on three sides. No wonder it's impenetrable."

"We can get through," Rowan said, stepping onto the bridge followed by Ollie and Penelope. She raised an eyebrow at Ren in her chair, but then stopped short, mouth dropping open. "Ren? What's going on?"

Tongue thick in his mouth, Ren closed his eyes. "Do you hear them?"

"Uh oh," Pen said softly.

"Is he going glowy?" Darby asked, inching away. "Is that what's happening?"

"Ash?"

"He looks like a ghost."

"He's not a ghost."

Ren tilted his head. The voices were clearer now. They spoke to each other and they weren't talking to him. Did they know he was there? Could they feel him? Could they recognize him for what he was?

Ren surged out into the debris field.

They saw him then.

Hello, there.

"Hello. Are you real?"

Of course. As real as you are.

"Are you like me?"

We are you.

"What is going on?" Asher shook him, and Ren's body swayed. "Ren?"

With squinted blue glowing eyes, Ren turned to the group on the *Star Stream.* They watched him warily, and Darby appeared ready to bolt with her body angled toward the exit.

"They're out there. Technopaths. Like me. In the debris. I can feel them."

Asher's eyebrows shot up on his forehead. "Are you serious?"

Why are you here?

"To rescue my brother."

Asher kneeled in front of the chair and filled up Ren's vision. "Don't talk to them. We don't know what they want."

"My boyfriend says I shouldn't talk to you."

Why? Is he afraid of us? Many people are. But in this incarnation, we are hardly worthy of fear. We were vanquished and forced to live scattered in this debris.

"Wait. I don't understand." Ren slumped in the captain's chair. "You've been here all this time?"

The rest of the crew exchanged glances. Rowan joined Asher. "Ren, we can't hear them. Can you feed them through our comm system?"

Dipping farther into his star, Ren split his concentration between the voices emanating from the debris field and the systems of the *Star*

Stream. He fed the sound through the sensors and into the comm system. It crackled to life, and the bridge filled with the sounds of noncorporeal beings. Their voices flooded the small metal space.

They talked over each other and they talked in unison. It was a cacophony of tones, low and high, slow and fast, bleeding into one synchronous and resonant voice echoing with the power of dozens.

"Holy stars," Darby whispered. She moved closer to Ollie, Penelope, and Lucas. They all stared at the ceiling of the bridge. They should have looked out at the remnants of the ships and drifts which spread like asteroids and dust across the wide expanse of the cluster.

If Ren concentrated, he could pinpoint the faint glow of the ones that housed the voices which spoke to him. They pinged in his chest, reverberated through his flesh and bone, echoed the stuttered heartbeat in his chest. They were pure power, stardust incarnate, basic elements of life made sentient. They were his kin, more like him than any human.

Asher grasped one of Ren's arms with both hands. Rowan took the other and held on. Ren saw their fingers wrapped around the sleeves of his shirt, saw their pale skin contrasting with the dark cloth, saw their nails dimpling the fabric. Were they scared? Were they afraid Ren would float away with the voices? That he'd become as incorporeal as they were? He'd done it once. He could do it again.

He didn't want to do it again.

He didn't want to leave Asher.

Ren placed his hand over Asher's and eased his fingers over the straining tendons of Asher's fingers. His skin was dry and cool against Asher's clammy sweat.

"It's okay."

"Where did you go, little technopath? Are you still there?"

The crew jumped at the voice directed at Ren.

"I'm here. My friends can hear you now. I'm funneling you through our systems."

"Very clever. Are they afraid?"

Darby nodded vigorously. Asher's grip tightened, and his brow furrowed. Ren smoothed his fingers over the wrinkle between his eyebrows.

"They are worried for me."

"Ah, they should not be. We are no danger to you. We can sense you are powerful. Not many can feel us in the expanse of space. Others have recently passed by and did not sense our presence."

Ren's blood ran cold. Did they mean Millicent?

"Who are you?" Asher's voice ran out strong and clear.

"We are the losers. We are the victorious. We are the immortal. We are the perilous."

Rowan slowly released Ren. Her fingers left creases in the fabric of his shirt. She tossed her braid over her shoulder, and Ren saw the second her fear subsided and turned into annoyance. "That's not who you are. That's a bunch of ominous titles which mean dust. We don't deal with frauds and tricksters."

The laugh that boomed over the comms was in a lower register than the other voices. The equipment popped and sizzled under the strain, and Ren ran to repair the imminent overload.

"We're the remnants of the army that lost to the Phoenix Corps."

"How is that possible? You were destroyed."

"Obviously not. We have been here, existing in the debris. Your friend understands."

Ren did. He'd lived in the systems and circuits for weeks. He'd lived as star and electricity and constituent elements and atoms, haunting the relays from the cargo bay to the bridge, watching as his body slowly healed. He had lived as energy and sparks and power. When he'd entered his body again, bound by muscle and skin and bone, he'd found it clumsy and inelegant. Is that how they saw him?

"I do. I understand."

Asher leaned as close as possible to Ren. "You've been orbiting the prison for years. Can you help us?"

"We stay out of the affairs of humans."

"It's my affair," Ren said quickly. "My brother—he can walk in dreams—is trapped in there. There are others too. A man who can compel and a woman who has visions of the future."

The voices scoffed. "They are no friends of ours. They abandoned us when it came to fight. They left us alone to fend off the humans who would see us destroyed."

"They left you?"

"When the war brewed, our kind was targeted as the threat due to our power. To control technology and energy is to control information and systems. The fledgling drifts were terrified of falling under our control. At first, they tried to cast us out. Then they tried to shut us away in their walls. And when we fled, they followed. We had no choice but to fight. The others hid."

"But you were dangerous," Asher said. "You lost your humanity. Is that true? That you lost your balance between power and blood?"

Another huff. "History is written by the winners. But it is not wrong. We gave in to our power and forgot ourselves. Our physical forms became worthless to us."

Ren shuddered, remembering the times when he'd walked a dangerous line in his own balance. Millicent had almost forced him away from his own humanity. And sometimes he'd given in gladly: on Erden when Zag had threatened his friends, and on the ship at the siege on Mykonos. Ren was lucky he had Asher to ground him or he would've given in and become like the remnants floating in space around them. Ren clenched his fists. "And you were destroyed?"

"The Corps could not destroy us. They were nothing but flesh caged in ships when we were energy caged in flesh."

"Then what happened?"

A shrill laugh broke over the comm system. Darby clapped her hands over her ears. Penelope flinched, and Lucas stood abruptly and stepped away from his console.

"We self-destructed. Our vessels were worthless, and they'd never let us be."

"That makes no sense," Asher said, expression livid, cheeks red. "You died, and for what? To live as memorials to a rebellion? You accomplished nothing!"

The comm crackled. The vid screen lit up with static. The hull shook and clanged. Objects thumped against the airlocks. Warning claxons blared, and the red emergency lights flashed.

Ren flooded the systems and pushed them back. Blue tendrils gathered in the corners of the ship. A swell of power and electricity rushed through the wires and systems as he chased out the would-be intruders. He flung them away, his rage at their invasion and their presumption was a palpable thing.

"Stay out of my ship!" His voice thundered outward. It shuddered through the comm system and into the cluster of debris, shook through their circuits, and bounced from one metal hunk to the next.

After a long silence, Darby cleared her throat. "Are they gone?"

Ren restored the systems on the ship to normal, but he hadn't chased the others away. They hovered nearby. "No," he said, eyes blazing. "They're regrouping." He settled his gaze on Asher. "You insulted them."

"They deserve to be insulted."

"That's the Corps talking. Not you. I don't blame them for their actions. If what they say is true, then they were as stuck as we are. Not able to rest. Not able to hide. Not able to just be. They chose their way out."

"Is that what you'll choose, then? If there is no rest for us after this?"

Ren was split between his body and his star. He felt the energy racing through the circuits and felt his blood race through his veins as his pulse quickened. He took Asher's hand.

"No. I've chosen you."

The voices edged back into the comm system, and Ren allowed it.

"You are too powerful, little technopath."

"My name is Ren."

"We will not help you, Ren. We owe nothing to you or to those in the prison. And you side with the wrong individuals."

"And you'll leave them to their fate? You'll do the same to them as they did to you? You were forced to abandon your humanity. That must have been a terrible decision to make. But I won't do that." It wasn't wise for Ren to challenge them, as it wasn't wise for Ren to allow them into the *Star Stream*. But the crew had come so far, he wouldn't allow these beings to stand in their way.

"We do not meddle. The Corps meddles. We are not the same."

"Then get out of our way." Ren burst outward, cleared a path through the field, and tossed the debris to the farthest bounds of the orbit.

"Feisty," the deepest voice said. "You are determined. We have not met one like us in so long. It's only been us and we've forgotten our flesh and the bonds of our mortal coils."

Asher's throat bobbed. "You'll help us?"

After a long silence several voices spoke in a merged statement. "We'll assist you with moving close to the prison. We'll act as your camouflage, but we will not assist you with the prison itself."

"That's better than nothing," Rowan muttered.

"That's a generous offer," Ren said. "We accept your assistance."

"The dock for the prison is along the back as you approach, with the deepest piece of the debris field surrounding it. We can guide you through and hide you from their sensors."

"We'll go slow," Lucas offered, sitting back in his chair and punching in the coordinates. "Thank you."

"Good luck, Ren and humans."

Ren nodded. "Thank you."

There was a flicker of static in the comm, then they were gone.

⊣⊢

With large pieces of debris hovering near the hull, the *Star Stream* crawled toward the prison. It would take hours.

Ren wandered to the cargo bay. He folded down next to the aft airlock and pressed his fingers along the seal. There were many systems in place to keep the seal from breaking and causing a loss of pressurization. Opening the ship to the vacuum of space would be disastrous for the structural integrity and for the crew. But would it be for Ren? Would he be like those that surrounded him? Could he die? Or would his body turn to dust and his energy remain, trapped in wires? Was his star his soul? Or was it separate?

When Millicent was on board, she'd tried to teach him to meditate, and he echoed her pose now. He breathed in past the knot of panic in his middle, and breathed out against the tension in his muscles. He sank into his body and released a stream of star. It rushed outward, finding the path of least resistance, and with that, Ren was out in the debris.

I'd like to talk, he said, hoping they heard him. *I want to know more about what we are. How to control what I am. What else I can do.*

They echoed. *We don't have much time to teach you.*

Please. Anything.

A whispered conversation happened between several of the glowing pieces.

What do you need to know to help you in your foolish quest?

Ren swallowed. Gathering his memories of Millicent and the way she manipulated him, hurt him, he sent those thoughts and feelings into the ether, converted them into electrical impulses, willed them to feel how he felt. *How do I stop her?*

You wish to harm one of our kind?

I wish to stop her from hurting anyone else.

Another rapid conversation and then a new voice, old and scratchy, like the sound of his stepfather's music player scratching over the antique vinyls he coveted.

She is a technopath, but she has secondary powers, just as you do. She can push and pull like the moon on a tide, or like the fluctuating gravity on an orbit. You haven't discovered your secondary power, though you've used it without knowing.

Ren steeled himself. *What is mine?*

Can't you feel it? She may be able to influence you, but you can **overwhelm**.

That's a function of my power?

Yes. Wield it. Think of how you pushed us out. How you swarmed into us and blackened our coils and wires. You are powerful, and you burned us.

I didn't mean to hurt you. I only wanted you out.

Focus on what you want, on what you've lost. Focus on your grief and your anger and your turmoil. Focus on your love and your happiness and your ambition. Those are your strongest emotions; use them to scorch.

I don't want to hurt anyone.

You are a supernova. You will collapse.

Ren froze. A supernova. He read about when massive stars died, how they would collapse into their cores, then explode outward. Their blasts were so powerful they would send their elements into space, seeding the universe for a new generation of stars. That was the myth of the star hosts, how they gained their power from the stardust that drifted until finding its way into the bodies of their hosts and imbuing them with power.

If I can overwhelm her, if I can burn her out, will I die?

There was no answer. Ren didn't expect one.

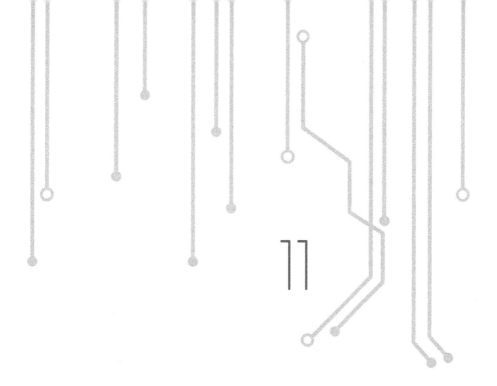

11

Perilous Space prison didn't look like a drift. It wasn't a stack of levels that spun gracefully in the vacuum of space creating its own gravity. Absent were the large viewing windows or the different-colored lights along the floors. No cheery welcoming message repeated from the communications tower with docking instructions and mentions of drift-specific sites to see or stores to visit. Instead, it sat as a square block, stark and intimidating, which didn't look as though it belonged floating in space at all. Ren pegged the architecture as something he would've found on a planet, squat and cube-shaped and ugly, positioned in the middle of a field encompassed by a high fence. The only light came from a beacon on top of a spindle at the very center. It sat perfectly still in the middle of a large sea of broken parts, and broken ships, and broken dreams.

"That is the weirdest thing floating I've ever seen." Darby leaned close to the view screen and squinted. "Is it real?"

"Yeah, it's real." Asher sidled close to Ren's side. "Ren?"

The room Liam had shown them fit right into the overall look. It was a prison after all. Ren hoped his brother was still there and this wasn't a snipe hunt. He needed it to be real. This was his only shot.

He couldn't ask Rowan to continue to put everyone at risk, especially with the stakes as high as they were.

Reluctant to reach out, Ren scrunched his features and closed his eyes. The low hum of despair vibrated in the depths of Ren's veins along with the bare minimum of systems needed to keep the occupants alive—air and gravity. A large weapons system singed the outside of Ren's consciousness, and he recoiled from the power it drew from the generators, draining and straining the grid even at rest. He'd hate to feel the weapons when they were engaged, and the thought made him shudder. It would destroy the ship with one shot, and Ren wasn't certain he could stop it.

"See if you can check the validity of the information from the voices. Scan for the docking bay."

Ren surged outward using the *Star Stream's* sensors. He felt the brush of the other beings as they hovered close and cloaked the ship in debris. No external communications pinged his senses. The docking bay was tiny and hidden around the back of the structure, where it faced the ring of junk, which floated on three sides, caught in the small gravitational pull.

"Found it."

You're doing well. Keep going. You're on the right trajectory.

Ren nodded. "They say we're on track."

"Good," Rowan said from her captain's chair. "Thank them for us."

Thank you.

The ship moved through the debris, and the group of technopaths moved the large pieces out of their way and otherwise kept close to the hull, acting as a shield. The *Star Stream* moved achingly slow to avoid attention.

It wasn't fast enough for Ren, and his anxiety welled within him and made his skin crawl. Even Asher's hands on him, grounding him to the present, didn't keep his stomach from twisting and his body breaking out in acrid sweat. He clenched his eyes shut and focused on his job.

Lucas piloted. Asher and Ollie scanned the sensors and comms. Darby and Penelope readied for the physical assault and liberation of the prison. Ren scanned for blueprints.

"I have a map," he said.

"Can you cast it on the screen."

Ren nodded, and, with a flick of his wrist, the layout of the block appeared. It was straightforward, with few twists and turns. Each floor had the same basic layout of hallways, except the lowest, which was the docking platform, and the top, which appeared to have larger rooms—maybe offices? Or labs for the experiments Liam had talked about? The four layers in between just small rooms next to each other with single exits into a large hallway.

Liam was in one of those rooms.

Ren was sure of it.

"This looks straightforward enough," Asher said, flipping through the pages. "I only wish we knew what room Liam was in exactly. We'll have to open the doors to them all and hope we find him."

"Or he finds us," Darby said. She moved from her spot by the outer vid screen to Asher's console. She leaned over it and dragged her finger over the map. "If we could separate the guards from the prisoners, then we could have the prisoners all come down to the docking bay. Maybe trap the brass on the top floor?"

"That's not a bad idea," Asher said. "We lure the officers to the top and have Ren shut them in. Then we open all the prison doors."

"Two problems," Rowan said. "One—we don't know where the star host prisoners are versus the actual bad guys that are housed there for things other than a little pickpocketing. And two—Abiathar. He'll have Ren or one of the others turn on us as soon as he can speak."

"I'll be fine as long as Ash is with me," Ren ground out.

We'll be with you as well. We'll not allow a coercer to harm you.

"So we'll go door-to-door. We'll lock most of the guards on the top floor, enter through the dock, and then work our way through. Maybe Ren will be able to access records and get us the right door."

"I don't like the idea of you all being on there for a long time," Penelope said. "The longer you stay, the higher the chances of being crunched."

"And I don't like the idea of docking there long either. Don't forget we have disembodied voices that are helping us. Who knows where their allegiances lie and what they'll do when they get a chance." Lucas kept a tight grip on the piloting controls and his gaze on the screen, but he grimaced as he said the words. "Did they hear that?"

"No," Ren said. "They're locked out of systems right now. I put up a barrier."

"Smart thinking."

Rowan stood and came over. "That's our plan, then? Ash, is there a Phoenix Corps code or signal that would get everyone to congregate in one place?"

"Yes."

"Really?"

Asher nodded, face grim. "Yeah. There's a few."

"Great. We're doing this."

"We're doing this," Ash agreed.

"I can't believe we're doing this," Darby said, rubbing her hands together. Her dark eyes glittered. "This is the big one. The one all thieves and cons talk about and laugh that no one would be stupid enough to do."

"That's... not reassuring."

She shrugged. "It wasn't really meant to be."

"Ren?" Asher asked. "Are you ready?"

Heart lodged in his throat and his body trembling from excitement and panic, Ren nodded. "Yeah, I'm ready."

"We're with you, Ren."

We're with you.

⊣⊢

They left the bridge when there were only a few meters left of the approach. The debris had peeled from the ship and spread out toward the docking bay to cover their route.

We'll stay as long as you need us.

Thank you.

Dressed in black, hood pulled up over his head and a pulse gun strapped to his side, Ren fidgeted as the others prepared. Darby took the offered pulse gun with a reverence Ren hadn't seen her display for anything else. She slid it in an arm holster Rowan had tightened across her back. She also had over her shoulder a bag of tricks and gadgets that she and Ollie had developed. Ren hadn't asked, but he would wager that included explosives. Darby did have an enthusiasm for blowing things up.

"Don't use the pulse gun unless you absolutely have to." Rowan patted Darby's shoulder in a sisterly fashion. "Let Ren disable them first if he can. He's good at it. Follow Asher's and Ollie's leads when it comes to shooting."

"Yes, Captain."

Ollie clipped his own guns at his hip and shoulder. "Don't shoot if you can run."

"We'll be fine," Asher said, tone flat, not at all reassuring. "If this goes right, we won't run into anyone other than who we're looking for. Search and rescue. Do not engage."

Lucas's voice came over the comm. "We're five minutes out at this pace. Be safe out there. Come back to the ship as soon as you can, and we'll blast out of here."

Ren rolled his shoulders. "The star hosts in the debris are going to hover nearby until we're ready to depart. And they'll continue to cover us."

"Okay, Ren, send the announcement."

Ren took a deep breath and squeezed his eyes shut. He focused past the hull of the *Star Stream*, and reached out until he met the circuits of the prison. He trickled in and stopped abruptly. A large barrier loomed in front of him. It was a wall of static and code, built upon more static and lines and bricks of programming. He poked it tentatively, and electricity bloomed out in a webbed pattern encompassing the whole of the system. Unperturbed, Ren pushed slightly harder. It resisted, and the code thickened and spread farther and wider so that it was difficult for Ren to find a way around. It was a deterrent, a way to keep the technopaths housed at the prison from taking over.

Face scrunched, Ren pushed against the wall, and it repelled him, sent him scurrying back into his body. He gasped and took a step back and fell into Asher.

"It's blocked."

"What do you mean?" Asher asked, gripping Ren by the biceps. "Are you okay?"

"I'm fine but… it's going to take me a minute. There's a…. wall."

Rowan arched an eyebrow. "A wall? Of what?"

"Code and… I'm sure there are going to be traps and snares once I get through that. I… should've known. It's meant to hold star hosts and that means technopaths too."

Rowan and Asher exchanged a glance. "We should pull back," Asher said. "It's too dangerous."

"No! I've got it." *I need help.*

What's wrong, little one?

There's a wall and traps. I might not be able to get through.

Burn, Ren. Burn as we showed you. Focus on your strongest emotions and overwhelm.

"Ren?" Asher's hand wrapped around the back of his neck. His thumb ran over the straining tendon. "What's the plan?"

"One more try. That's all I need."

"Hurry. We don't have much time to sit out here."

Ren dove back into Perilous Space. He encountered the wall and stopped. Gathering his power in his chest, he concentrated on his fear, and his hope, and his desire for peace. His power welled within him, and he *burned.*

He'd always associated his power with blue. His vision would go blue. His eyes, he was told, would glow blue. The sparks and webs of electricity would tangle in blue lines and drip like water from his body in blue drops. The hottest stars radiated blue, but he already bathed in blue. As he drew power to him, coaxed energy from the generators and from his core, he burned *darkly.*

Blue deepened to violet, then black consumed him and wrapped around his virtual self. His back arched, and his fists clenched. Ren pushed through the barrier, and it burst in a shower of sparkles of red and orange and purple like fireworks booming against the darkness of the sky. Ren broke through the barrier; code scattered like leaves on the wind. He raced into the wires, scorched out of snares and traps, and left a trail of shadow behind him.

He sorted through the active systems. Information pounded at him from all sides, and tricks and catches awaited him. There were codes and blocks to sweep aside and break through. He slid into the communication system and found the mechanisms he needed. Using the prison's normal computer alarm system, Ren sent claxons blaring and bathed the prison is flashing red lights.

"Forcefield failure. Imminent pressure loss. All personnel seek emergency shelter on level five."

Pleased, Ren set the message on repeat, then returned, retreating in waves. He checked the vid feeds. Corps guards and officers headed to the top floor scrambling for the lifts and stairs.

Secure in his body, he grinned at the others. His vision was shadowed. "Message delivered. Everyone is fleeing from the imminent forcefield failure."

"You are entirely too pleased with yourself," Darby said. She knocked his shoulder. "I like it."

"Did you hear that, Lucas? The dock should be deserted. Take us in."

"I hear you, and we are almost there. Okay, Ren, can you get that forcefield down?"

Ren checked the security cameras and confirmed that the dock was deserted. He sensed the field at the forefront of his star sense. He powered it down, and Lucas slid the ship into the empty slip with precision. As soon as they passed the threshold, Ren flipped the field back on.

"Pressurization achieved. Good luck."

Asher nodded to the group. "Let's go. Darby, stay behind Rowan and Ollie. Ren, you're with me. Liam is priority. Anyone else is a bonus. Understood?"

They nodded. "Good. Anything weird, head back to the ship."

Asher yanked the door open. They slid out, one by one. Asher, Ollie, and Rowan had their weapons drawn and ready. "This way." Asher gestured, following the blueprint Ren had downloaded.

Ren's message bleated overhead. He resisted the urge to silence it because that would be suspicious. He tugged his hood closer, though the fabric did nothing to block the noise.

"How's it looking?"

Ren checked the feeds. Everyone had evacuated to the top floor. There were several people in a single, large room. "They're all on the top floor. All of them."

"Are they locked in?"

Ren cocked his head. "No. There is something going on. Other than us. They… they have someone up there. They have… someone important."

"Millicent?"

Ren shook his head. "No." Peering through the security channels, Ren saw the familiar form of the man who left him to bleed on Crei. He saw the man who had taunted him in a hologram in the citadel. He saw the man responsible for setting all the wheels in motion. "They have Vos."

"Vos? That's why VanMeerten was so smug. She thought she had the leader."

Ollie shouldered close. "What's the plan now?"

"The same. Find Liam. We can leave Vos to rot. Ren."

Ren snapped his head toward Asher, his vision no longer blue but a mixture of shadow and light. "Yes?"

"Lock them in."

Ren flashed like a crack of lightning from the sky and sizzled through the circuits. Finding the locks, he took satisfaction in engaging them all. The doors that were open swung closed, and the bolts slid home. He singed the relays and the protectors. No one would be able to undo what he'd done, unless they were a technopath.

"Done," Ren said, his voice monotone.

"Ren? What's a man who knows everything but admits he knows nothing?"

"A paradox," Ren answered. "Don't worry, Ash. I'm here."

"Your eyes are black. But you're right. I'll be worried later. Where's Liam?"

Ren was searching through the information, sorting through files, looking for his brother's name or his power. He flipped through code and tossed lines aside, until only notes on Liam and his missions remained. While looking for his location, Ren sent the pertinent information to the *Star Stream* through the tenuous connection the ship shared with the prison.

"We need to go up. Second floor, third door on the left. Nadie is next to him. Abiathar is down the hall. There are others as well. Several others. I can't open the doors. They're not on the system. They're not electronic locks."

Asher placed his hand on Ren's arm. "It's okay. We'll figure it out. But we need to hurry." Asher ushered them to the stairs. "Do you have the comms?"

Ren nodded. He held out his palm, and energy dripped from the whirlpool of power in his hand. "Right here."

Asher inched closer; his breath seared the skin of Ren's fingers. "You're hot and scary at the same time. We'll talk more about this later."

Ren blushed and shrugged. Taking control of the communications, he fed everything to the physical comms they all carried. They'd all be able to hear what was said through the prison's communication system. Right now, the channel was silent.

Asher pushed open the door to the stairwell and, with pulse gun raised, he peeked around the frame. He waved them all in, and the door closed behind them, leaving them in relative darkness. Ren switched on the lights with a blink, keeping them dim. Crouching, Asher lead the group up the stairs. They didn't meet another soul, and, on the first-floor landing, Asher paused.

"Ren, can you lock this door?"

Pushing past the webs of code that wanted to ensnare him, Ren engaged the automatic lock.

"Done."

"Good." Asher relaxed. "Darby and Rowan will stay here and guard our exit. With no one at the dock and with this door locked, the only attack will come from above. Stay on the comms, and let us know if you hear anything."

Rowan swept her braid from her shoulder. "I'm not staying behind."

"You're not," Asher agreed. "You're protecting our exit. And you have Darby with you in case we need any kind of fancy explosion to aid in our escape."

Darby rubbed her knuckles on her shirt. "You know me so well."

"And if we get pinched, you can come save us," Ollie said, with a sly smile.

"Fine," Rowan said. "But I'm not happy about it."

"You never are," Asher muttered. He looked at Ollie and Ren. "Ready?"

The three of them crept up the second set of stairs. Ren kept one part of himself in the prison systems and the other alert in his body. Spread thin, he had less control over his anxiety, and his blood pounded. Panic crawled in his veins but did not take root, not yet. He remembered he needed to breathe, evenly and deeply, to keep everything under control, but his exhalations were staccato, as his concentration focused on not hitting a trap in the system.

"Second floor," Asher whispered. "There will be a long hallway and then a cross corridor. Ollie, you'll hide around that corner and protect our flank and our way back out."

"Got it, Ash."

"Ren, you'll get Liam."

Ren closed his eyes. Something was going on. Something… a warning pinged in his chest. The locks! Ren raced to the top floor but the locks he'd previously engaged were now encased in code. They were open.

"Ren?" Asher said forcefully. "Everything okay?"

Ren bit his tongue. "Yeah, but we need to hurry. Something is weird upstairs."

Asher read the lie in Ren's face, but didn't call him out. He shook his head and frowning. Instead of pushing the door open slightly, Asher kicked it open with force. The door swung outward so hard it hit the inner wall.

Asher and Ollie jumped out, back-to-back, weapons raised. But there was no one. No exchange of fire. They moved silently, and Ren followed Asher down the corridor. Ollie broke off as Asher had instructed.

After a few feet, Ren counted one door. Then two. Then three—

"This one," Ren said. "This one. This is it." He peered through the small window blocked by a shaky forcefield but couldn't see through the static with his human eyes. He pressed his palm flat next to the door and concentrated. He looked, but there was no electronic mechanism on the door, and, parsing through the circuits and systems, he could find no power source. He powered down the forcefield, but he couldn't open the door. No, no, no! They were so close. His brother should be in there. Liam was in there.

He snapped back into his body. "Ash," he said, his voice desperate, twisting Asher's name into a plea. Excitement and panic made him tremble, and he touched the door. He tugged on the handle; his palm was slick with sweat, and his fingers trembled. "I can't open it. I can't."

Asher waved to Ollie and kept his pulse gun raised as Ollie crossed from the last intersection to where they stood. Asher covered his movement.

"Ren, calm down. Ollie, it looks like the lock is manual."

Ren had missed the obvious—a large metal bar sheathed in a metal container crossed the face of the door. Ollie studied it before grabbing a knob. He pulled, his muscles strained beneath his dark skin, and the bar screeched until it crossed the crease of the wall. Ren grabbed the handle, and they pulled the door open. It scraped across the floor, and Ren winced at the sound.

It slowly swung open, and, when the space was big enough, Ren slipped into the room.

A figure lay on the bed, unmoving, and Ren raced to the bunk. His shin smacked into the bed frame, and he shook the body's shoulder. Oh, please. Oh, please. Oh, *please*.

Liam rolled to his back and blinked up, confused, his eyes blurry, and his forehead crinkled. "Ren?" he croaked. "Is this a dream?"

Ren smiled so wide his cheeks hurt. His heart pounded, and joy flashed through him; his eyes stung with tears. "Get up. This isn't a dream."

Liam shot up, and Ren jumped backward to keep from knocking their heads together. Liam swung his legs around. The white of the medical scrubs he wore washed out his complexion, and his eyes were shadowed with lack of sleep and worry, but he grinned when he staggered to his feet.

"Ren?" Ren caught him in a hug and held on. Liam sagged into his arms. "What are you doing here? What have you done?"

"No time to talk. We need to go."

Ren swung Liam's arm over his shoulder and grabbed his waist. They hobbled to the door, and Ren peeked around the frame.

Ollie and Asher waited, scanning the hallway, weapons up and ready.

"Got him?" Asher asked, casting a glance over his shoulder.

Ren beamed. "Yes. Yes, I have him."

"Good. Let's go."

"Wait," Liam rasped. "Wait, there are others. There are others here, and they're going to move us or kill us. I'm not sure which but, please."

"Sorry, kid, but we don't have time." Asher raised the comm to his mouth. "We've got Liam. How are you doing?"

Darby's voice came back. "We're clear, but we heard chatter on the comms that Vos is loose in the facility. He got away in the commotion."

"Stars," Asher cursed. "Is that what you hid in the stairwell?" he said, gaze cutting to Ren.

Ren shrugged. "I didn't know he was loose. I did feel the doors open on the top floor."

Asher clutched his gun and dipped his chin toward his comm. "Eyes open. We don't want to run into him or anyone who is hunting him."

"Gotcha, boss," Darby said.

"Ren? What's going on?" Liam rasped. He was heavy on Ren's shoulder, and his weight threatened to pull Ren to the floor. But he wouldn't let Ollie take Liam. They needed Ollie for protection, and Ren wasn't going to give up. Not now. He hauled Liam closer.

"We've got to get out of here before we're crunched by one of the Corps."

"Like me?" The figure that stepped out from the cross section wore the Corps uniform and a smug smile. He stopped in the middle of the hallway to block their path to the docking bay.

"You," Asher said, voice hard.

Corporeal Zag smirked. "Me."

"How'd you get free?"

"Manual override," Zag said, with a shrug. "This base is not technopath-friendly. And you may be navigating now, but I guarantee you'll make a mistake. It's a matter of time."

Ren scoffed. "Stars. Figured we'd run into an utter cog," Ren said. Liam hung on his arm like a limpet and squinted at Ren. Ren thrust his chin at Zag. "He killed me."

Zag pressed a hand to his chest. "I didn't kill you." He reached for his hip, and Asher raised his weapon and trained it on Zag.

"Don't."

Zag stopped, smirk still firmly in place, and raised his hands. "The gun in my holster killed you." His hand fluttered, and Asher moved forward, stepping between Ren and Zag. "You're interrupting the reunion, Morgan. I'd love for another bullet to find its way to your friend. Maybe this time, he'll stay dead."

"Out of the way," Asher said, gesturing with the tip of his gun. "Back the way you came and maybe focus on the real threat."

Zag smiled. "You mean Vos, that duster playing leader? He may have escaped, but we'll catch him again. Just as I've caught you."

"You haven't caught us yet. And I promise you," Asher said, body trembling with rage, "you don't want to catch me."

Ren reached out but there were no weapons on Zag he could use. And the hallway was only equipped with cameras—no weapons for technopaths to turn on their captors.

"Is that a threat, Morgan?" He tapped his chin. "What are you doing here anyway? I thought you were doing grunt work on Bara? We're taking that planet over, you know. The Corps is done with you foolish dusters coming up here to space and mucking up the drifts. It's not just techies and star hosts we're imprisoning now."

"A police state. Nice. Except you won't be able to police anything once you're all vented."

Zag laughed. He dipped his head and met Ren's gaze. "You going to vent me?" He swaggered closer. "What will your little brother think about you killing soldiers on Erden? Or the ones on Bara? That was you, wasn't it?"

Ren narrowed his eyes. The longer they stood there, the longer Zag stalled, the greater the threat of capture or worse. Liam was already weakening, his pressure on Ren's body was becoming a dead weight that he wouldn't be able to support.

"It's not Ren you have to worry about."

"Vos? That cog? He's a duster cog. He's not a threat to me." Zag cocked his head and peered over Asher's shoulder. "And neither are you, Ren. Is that your name? Take away the access to tech, and you're a scared, little, village boy."

Liam rolled his eyes. "This guy is a dick," he said out loud. "Why are we listening to this? I don't know you and I don't like you." Liam turned to Asher. "Shoot him."

Asher didn't hesitate. The first shot glanced off Zag's knee, and he fell to a kneeling position. The second hit him in the shoulder and sent him sprawling on his back. Asher strode forward, bent down, and slipped the gun from the holster on Zag's hip. He pocketed it and kicked Zag's injured leg. He hissed, eyelids fluttering, hanging onto consciousness by a thread.

Asher leaned close to Zag's face. "Don't interfere again. Next time, I won't miss." Asher stepped on the burn and the smoking fabric on Zag's knee. "Understand?"

Zag grunted and squirmed on the floor. "I get it," he gritted out.

"Good." He grabbed Zag's hair and slammed his head onto the hard floor. Zag's body went limp.

"Your boyfriend is awesome," Liam said, with a wide grin. "I like him."

"You're entirely too snarky for someone who has spent the past year locked in a maximum-security facility," Ren said. "Let's go before anything else happens."

"My brother can do anything," Liam said with a smile. "And so can his boyfriend. And you." He looked at Ollie. "You look awesome and intimidating. I bet you can do anything you want as well." Liam listed to the side, and Ren staggered. "I'm happy!"

"I think you're loopy," Ren grunted. "Are you... are you drugged?"

Asher grabbed Liam's other side. "Let's get out of here."

"The others!" Liam insisted. "We can't leave them."

Asher furrowed his brow.

"Ren! We can't leave them. They drugged us all."

"To make you easier to move," Asher said. "Okay, we'll figure something out. Ren? Any ideas?"

They staggered toward the stairwell door. "One." On the other side with the door closed behind them, Ren pushed Liam over to Ollie. "I have one idea," Ren said then dove into the circuits and found Vos on the vid feeds.

Vos hurried down a hallway, looking harried and pale, not the man Ren had known.

"You. Vos," Ren's voice echoed over the comm in the hall, "go to the docks and wait for me there."

Vos looked at the ceiling, eyes wide. "*You*," he said. "You're dead."

"No, just a ghost. Hurry. You don't have much time."

Vos frowned, but nodded.

Ren retreated to his body and found Ollie, Asher, and Liam staring at him.

Asher leaned close. "What did you do?"

"Found us an ally."

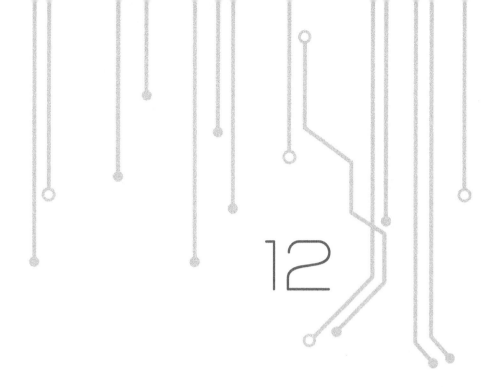

12

"WHAT'S GOING ON DOWN HERE?" Asher sailed down the stairs. Ollie, Ren, and Liam followed like ducklings.

Rowan and Darby offered twin forced smiles. Darby held a smoke bomb. She and Rowan had their backs to the door, holding it closed as soldiers beat against the other side.

"Oh, you know," Darby said, with gritted teeth, "holding the fort like you said. But they are right here, if you couldn't tell. I thought you said the only attack would be from above."

"I was obviously wrong," Asher replied.

"That's awesome, Ash. Really awesome." As she spoke, the door heaved inward, and, in an acrobatic move, Darby jumped and spun and threw the bomb through the crack. Ollie, Rowan, and Asher threw their weight against the door. Smoke billowed in around the edges, but the pounding was replaced by the sounds of coughing and gagging.

Palm flat on the wall, Ren reached in and engaged the lock but, despite tying off the ends of the circuits and burning out the mechanisms, he couldn't keep it held for long.

"There's a manual override on the other side of the door."

"Great." Rowan pushed a stray hair away from her face with the back of her wrist. "Let's go then."

Darby eyed Liam with a squint. "Is this him? He doesn't look like you. Maybe around the nose, but… no, not really. You look nothing alike."

"Half-brothers," Liam said with a goofy smile on his face. "I'm Liam."

"I'm Darby."

"And I'm out of here," Rowan said. "There's a regiment on the other side of this door and probably one down at the docks too. We have to go."

"Vos is going to meet us there."

Rowan stutter-stepped. "What?"

The door creaked and shuddered.

"No time. Let's go," Asher grabbed Ren's bicep, and Ollie had Liam tucked close to his side. Stealth no longer an option, they thundered down the stairs and burst onto the docking bay. It was deserted, except for a lone figure waiting in a swath of light next to the aft airlock of the *Star Stream*.

"Vos," Ren said.

He turned on his heel and gave Ren a wan smile. "You."

"Me," Ren agreed.

"Rumor was that you died."

"I did, but I got better."

Rowan and Asher had their weapons trained on him, but Ren could tell he was unarmed. His complexion was sallow, and his cheeks were sunken. His eyes were circled by dark rings, and his hair and beard were uncharacteristically unkempt.

"Space is treating you well."

"Better than you did," Ren said. "But enough, we don't have time to reminisce."

"No, we don't."

"Third floor," Ren said. "I can't open the doors. They're manual. But on the third floor you'll find your general, a seer, and a few others."

Vos's eyebrows ticked up. "And how am I going to get there?"

"With me."

Asher protested, but Ren shook his head. "We have Liam. Get him on the ship with the others. You too, Ash." Ren glowed, eyes darkening to black, his power flowing out of him in waves as he entered the prison and flooded the systems. "Vos and I will rescue them."

"No," Asher's fingers around Ren's wrist were iron. "This is a dumb idea. They are not worth your capture. And we cannot trust him."

Vos spread open his hands. "I can't do anything to your friend. His power eclipses any I've seen. I have no weapons. I have no idea how to navigate this place."

"Ash—"

"Not without me." Ash leveled Ren with a glare. "If you feel like we must rescue them, then fine. But we promised each other to stay together. We're staying together."

Ren softened. They had promised, and Ren wouldn't break it, not after Crei, not after Bara. "Fine, but we have to hurry," Ren said, surging through the systems, and camera feeds. "There are guards swarming down from the top level and coming around to flank us."

"Get on the ship," Asher told the others. "If you need to leave, then go. We'll follow."

"And where will you run?" Vos asked, walking forward. "Where will you and your crew go? Now that you have his brother? There's nowhere safe for you, except with me."

"This guy sounds like the other guy," Liam said, holding onto Ollie. "Shoot him, too."

Asher raised his gun, but Ren stayed his hand. "What we do after this is of no concern to you. But for right now, we have similar goals."

Vos smiled, and it was more like an animal's show of teeth than a gesture meant to endear him to them.

"Stars, you're disgusting," Rowan said, making a face. "Come on," she said to Ollie and Darby, then she wagged her finger at Asher as she pulled Darby along. "Don't do anything stupid. Be back here as quick as you can."

Asher allowed a small smile. "Have Pen look at Liam!"

Darby mock-saluted and the four of them raced to the ship. Ren was surprised at their quick acquiescence of him and Asher staying behind with Vos of all people, but they understood what Ren needed to do. They understood that, in good conscience, Ren couldn't leave other prisoners behind.

"We'll use a lift," Asher said. "It's a quick way up, and Ren can control it. Right?"

"Yes." With his concentration split, Ren rerouted his power to the lifts and found the nearest. Except, in his rush, he missed the trap laid for him in the code. It snared him, like a rabbit rope around his foot, and he stuck fast amid a tangle of circuits and a rush of encryption. His physical body stiffened, and he fell to his knees, palms on the deck. He tried to pull out, but the virus leeched into him, began to smother him with code, locked him behind rapidly building virtual bars.

"Ren?" Asher was by his side, his hand on Ren's shoulder, but it was far away, secondary to the trap squeezing tighter and tighter around him. "What's wrong?"

"Stuck," he forced out. "Trap."

"What do you need?"

Ren shuddered. The more he fought, the tighter the snare wrapped around him, squeezing his electric self. He couldn't hold awareness in both domains, and there was no way for him to pull out of the prison and back into his body. With gritted teeth and fingers curled against the deck, Ren let go, and trusted Asher to protect him. He left his body behind and focused entirely on his technopathic self.

From the video feeds, he saw his body on the deck squirming and thrashing and Asher hovering over him, holding him, but he couldn't stay long. He had to free himself, had to untangle from the snare wrapping tighter around him, trying to snuff him out.

He fought, but with every piece of code he unfurled or peeled away, two more took its place. He was trapped, as Zag had warned. Trapped in more ways than one in the prison built to hold people like him. They'd have to leave him behind. Asher could drag his physical body to the ship, but his other self would be stuck.

Help!

Ren thrust the plea out into the universe.

Help! Help! Please!

He had seconds left. The cell walls stacked higher and thicker, and Ren was almost completely covered. He had nowhere to run. He lost access to all the systems including the cameras. The chains and strings of code wrapped tighter and tighter around him, crushing him. And Asher ran out of time as well. Those guards would be descending on the dock in minutes. Asher was left alone with Ren incapacitated and Vos right there. He had to get out. He had to get out. He couldn't get out.

Panicking, Ren struggled to do what the others had told him. He was a supernova. He could explode. He could overwhelm. He had to. He had to. He had to. Focus. Focus! Hold on to the anger. Hold on to the hope. Hold on to the love. He thought about Liam and the joy he felt seeing his brother again. He thought about Asher and his faith and determination. He thought about the crew and how they'd folded him into their family and accepted Darby the way she was. He thought about Jakob and Sorcha and their resilience and how he ached to see them again. He tapped it into it all, the power of his star, the power of his humanity. He gathered it in, collapsed inward, and he expanded and pushed and struggled against the wires holding him captive.

It *hurt*.

It hurt so much.

He couldn't do it. He *couldn't*.

We're here!

Ren felt them in the system. He had no idea how they'd gotten in, no clue how they had left their debris, unless they had butted against the prison itself. But they were there. The other star hosts. Four of them, pinging against his senses.

Help!

They swarmed him, broke down the trap, ripped away the barriers, and Ren could metaphorically breathe again. When the last piece snapped away, Ren ran; the others followed.

Thank you. Thank you. Thank you.

You're welcome. Get out of here.

The weapons system. The guards have escaped. They can access it. They'll blast us out of the sky.

We have it. We'll disable it. Go quickly!

What about you?

We're fine. The guards are almost there. You must go, Ren. Run!

Body arching on the deck, Ren gasped and slotted into his body. He grabbed Asher's wrist; Asher's hands clenched in the fabric of his shirt. Eyes open, legs twitching, he gulped in a lungful of air.

"Run. Out of time."

Asher's gaze flicked away, and Ren followed it to see Vos standing there, face pale. Asher unholstered his pulse gun and slid it across the floor to a far corner of the deck.

"You're on your own. Good luck."

With a strength that surprised him, Asher hauled Ren to his feet and threw him over his shoulder. Vos ran for the gun, and Asher, yelling into his comm as he went, ran for the ship. The aft airlock swung open. Ollie waited on the other side. Asher's strides ate up the expansive distance. Ren's body jostled with each step.

With a few meters left, the door to the docking bay flew inward with the force of an explosion, sparks and metal skittered across the deck surface, and Ren's senses pinged with a barrage of weapons. Ren raised his hand, and, despite the weakness he felt in his own power, he locked on to the weapon signatures. He twisted and yanked and cut the power supplies to all the tech.

And then Ren was tossed into the *Star Stream*.

"Go! Go!" Darby yelled into the comm to Lucas. "We got them!"

Ollie closed the airlock and ensured the seal, just as ship left the ground.

"Ren! Can you get that forcefield?" Lucas called over the comm, his panic evident in the crackle and the static.

We have it. Go!

"The others have it," Ren rasped, from his prone position on the deck.

Ren felt the tingle in his body when the field powered down. The ship rocketed out of the docking bay, leaving the prison behind. Ren pushed to his feet and ignored the calls of Asher, Ollie, and Darby. Stumbling along the way, he pulled himself to the bridge with Asher on his heels. He lurched onto the bridge, knocked his head since he forgot to duck at the top of the stairs, and hurried to the vid screen.

"We're not being followed," Rowan said, from her captain's chair. "Other than by a few pieces of debris."

Ren flicked his wrist, and the sensors showed four large pieces of debris right next to the hull. He reached out and found the weapons system dark.

Are you okay?

We're fine. Are you?

Ren smiled ruefully. *Maybe.*

Did you save him?

Now that they were back in the belt of wreckage, Ren allowed his body to relax. He breathed and rolled his shoulders. Liam was in the common room with Penelope looking him over. Lucas piloted them away.

We did.

Congratulations.

What will you do now? Ren asked.

We'll protect you until you move on.

What about beyond that? Will you always be here?

We will exist, until we dissipate and float away in the blackness of space with hopes to reform into a new star or planet or new being.

Thank you. Thank you. We wouldn't have been able to free him without you.

You're welcome, little one. And what will you do, Ren? You've found your brother. You have escaped.

Ren sucked in a breath. *I'm going to stop her.*

We do not wish harm on another of us, but we understand your conviction. Be careful, Ren. You are stardust. You are part of the universe, and the universe exists within you. And while your constituent atoms are immortal, you are not.

I wish you well.

"Are they talking to you?"

"Yes," Ren said. "They saved me."

"What happened?" Asher tentatively lay a hand on Ren's shoulder. "Was it a trap?"

Ren patted Asher's hand. "Yes. I tripped something, and I couldn't... couldn't leave the prison systems. It was like... it was like a chain wrapped around me and squeezed while a cell was built to close me in."

Asher moved closer to Ren's back and dipped his head; his breath was hot on Ren's neck. "Are you all right?"

"I think so. I feel... shaky."

"Well, I don't think we need you right now," Lucas said, navigating the debris. "We're going to hide in here and, with your friends around, we should be okay until you're ready to transport us where we are going next."

"Once we figure that out," Rowan said, ruefully. "Vos was not wrong. With Millicent knocking off drifts one by one and the planets crawling with Corps, we don't have many options."

"We'll think of something," Asher said. "Keep an eye out for anything coming out of that prison. Vos didn't have great odds but he's slippery."

"Lucas and I have it. Go say hi to your brother, Ren." Rowan smiled. "You have him back. Enjoy it."

The truth of that slammed into Ren, and he smiled in return; his eyes crinkled. "I do."

Asher's hand tightened on Ren's shoulder, and Ren couldn't help but kiss Asher's echoed grin.

⊣⊢

Ren walked into the common area and found Liam sitting on the couch with Penelope looking him over. She took his temperature while he drank a glass of water.

Liam.

Liam was here.

Ren's throat closed up. The last time he'd seen his brother had been at the lake, after a stupid playfight where they had rolled around on the sand, and Ren had talked about leaving their home for a place among the stars. They were there now, but at what cost? What had Ren lost to achieve his dream? And what kind of dream was it? It certainly wasn't the one he'd hoped for all those years living in the dirt and wishing for stardust.

Liam didn't look well, but he'd been imprisoned for almost a year. Was it a year? Over a year? Ren had lost track of time. Between planets, and drifts, and space, and death, Ren didn't even know what season it was on Erden now. Had he had a birthday? Had Liam? Ren rubbed a hand over his face.

Liam wore medical scrubs, and the dark circles beneath his eyes stood stark in his pale face. His red hair had turned more blond, and his skin, which used to be covered in dark freckles from the sun, had evened out to a waxy complexion. But he was there. In the flesh. Not in a dream. And Ren's mission was complete. He had Asher. He had Liam. He had Penelope and Ollie and Lucas and Rowan and now Darby as well. But there was one last missing piece—a safe place to land. Vos was right—where could they go?

Liam caught him staring, and a smile broke out over his wan features. "Hey there, big brother? Are you going to keep staring or come over here and save me from beautiful women poking me with instruments?"

Penelope laughed and swatted Liam's arm. "Asher's orders to make sure you're okay. Other than a little malnutrition and sleep deprivation, you appear to be in good health. The drug should be working its way out of your system, but you might feel a little… off for a few hours." Penelope smirked at Ren. "Sound familiar?"

Liam's eyebrows raised.

Ren shoved his hands in his pockets. "I went through a few months where I kind of… well… I wasn't well. I didn't sleep much and kind of… lost myself in my power." Ren shrugged. "I'm better now."

"Really? You didn't just have a seizure on the deck of a prison drift?"

"That was an anomaly. A trap. I'm okay."

"Liar," Liam said, smiling easily. "But keep your secrets. I'm just glad to be out of there."

"Me too. I'm glad you're safe."

Penelope packed up her equipment and touched Liam's shoulder. "I'll make you a sandwich or soup, if you want to eat?"

"Yes, thank you."

Penelope smiled gently and excused herself to the kitchen area.

Liam crossed the small space between them, staggering every few steps, then threw his arms around Ren's shoulders. Ren grabbed him tight and held on. Liam had had a growth spurt since the last time he'd seen him, and he was the same height as Ren, maybe a tiny bit taller, not that Ren would ever admit it.

"I can't believe you've become such a badass," Liam said, laughing. "And you have scary-competent friends. And your boyfriend shot a guy for taunting you."

Ren laughed. "The company I keep, right?"

Liam pulled away, and his green eyes twinkled. "You got what you wanted. You found your place in space. You're stardust. It's everything you used to talk about. How are you not bouncing around like a bunny?"

Ren's smiled faded. "It's not that simple, Liam. There's so much going on, and so much has happened and…" he trailed off. "But that doesn't matter. You're free. We're together. That's what I've been striving for since that day at the lake when we were separated."

Liam took a deep breath. "I know we can't go home right away, but I really want to be back on solid ground."

Ren rubbed the back of his head. His hair stuck up. "We can't go right now. Maybe when it's all said and done."

"I look forward to it. Until then, can I eat and maybe meet the rest of the people on this ship? I feel like they're all standing right on the other side of that door."

There was a cough, and Darby stumbled in. Asher was right behind her.

Seeing their caught-out expressions, Ren laughed. He wrapped his arms around his middle and threw his head back and laughed.

Asher chuckled. "We've met," he said.

Liam waved him off. "I know you. You make my brother happy."

"I try."

Asher crossed the room and caught Ren in a hug. He spun him around, and they landed on the couch. Ren's laughter echoed in the common room. He didn't know if it was relief from escaping the prison or finally finding his brother, but Ren was giddy. He cupped Asher's face and kissed him, hard, lips smacking. Asher tightened his arms around Ren's waist.

"Get a room," Darby called. Ren felt a cushion hit his back.

He broke away and made a face.

"We have a room," Ren said. Asher tipped him to the side, and he fell from where he had perched precariously on Asher's lap. Asher caught him before he slipped all the way to the floor and hauled him back to the cushions.

Settling on the couch, Ren sat close to Asher's side and tangled their legs together. His head rested comfortably on Asher's shoulder.

"I'm Darby," she said to Liam, shaking his hand. "I tried to steal the ship from your brother, but he did his…" She wiggled her fingers. "…thing on me and I ran away. Scared the stardust right out of me."

A knife in her hand, Pen waved from her place by the counter. "I'm Penelope. Some call me Pen, but it sounds like Ren, and that can get confusing. I'll answer to either. And that big man is my brother, Ollie."

"Nice to meet you, Liam. We've heard a lot about you."

Liam raised an eyebrow. "Well, that is unfair. I guess that means I get to tell stories about Ren while I'm here."

"No!"

"Yes!"

Liam rubbed his hands together gleefully. Ren buried his face in Asher's chest.

"Well, there was this one girl named Ezzy who *adored* Ren and followed him around…"

Ren groaned. "Please, stop."

"He was so oblivious! He had no idea." Liam grinned.

Liam gratefully accepted the bowl of vegetable soup and a plate of meat-spread sandwiches and plopped down at the table. He shoved one in his mouth, and Ren was happy for the quiet.

"We met her," Asher said. "She fawned over Ren with big, moon eyes."

"Not you too," Ren said, hiding his face in his hands. "She did not."

"Oh, come on," Darby said, settling next to Liam and elbowing him in the side. She stole a half a sandwich. "You have to have better stories than that. Granted the only planet I've been on was Bara, and that teemed with weird animals the likes of which I've only seen in exhibits. But I guess that your home planet was about the same. Right?"

Liam snorted. "Hardly. There were fish in the lake. Some of them were weird, like the eels. And there was a bear that liked to sleep on our back porch in the spring."

"Boring," Darby said, drawing out the vowels. "Tell us something else."

The conversation droned on, each of them sharing stories, and Ren smiled, content to listen and to rest on Asher's chest. The rhythm of his heartbeat was a comfort in Ren's ear.

"You okay?"

"Yes," Ren said. He touched his forehead, where he had a small purpling bruise from hitting his head on the way to the bridge. "Except this."

Asher chuckled low, the sound of it tingling in Ren's ear. "How long have you been on this ship? You know you have to duck."

"Not long enough apparently," Ren grinned lazily.

Asher's arm tightened around Ren's waist and pulled him closer.

The sound of the crew's voices ebbed and flowed as Ren reveled in the warmth of Asher's embrace. He melted into it and didn't care when Ollie teased them or when Liam cast him knowing glances. And for the hour that they gathered with Ren's brother and his boyfriend and the rest of his family, he didn't have a care. He was happy and he was grateful the universe allowed him to have that moment of peace.

‑‖‑

Trouble.

Ren stirred from his relaxed posture on Asher's chest. "What?"

"What?" Asher echoed.

They're coming. You need to run.

Who's coming?

Phoenix Corps. Leaving the prison.

"Hey, guys! A few ships just rocketed out of the prison dock. And they're heading right into the debris field," Lucas's voice crackled over the comm.

Ren shot up and abandoned his place at Asher's side. He ran from the common room, leaving a stunned group behind, and strode quickly to the bridge. He remembered to duck at the top of the stairs.

A small ship barreled into the debris field with abandon. And, even though the *Star Stream* was well hidden with the other hosts gathered around them, it would only take one misplaced weapon's blast to reveal them or obliterate them. Three ships followed the fugitive ship, only seconds behind it. All the ships bore Phoenix Corps insignias, but clearly the three were after the one. It had to be Vos.

"I hope you had time to figure out where we're going next," Lucas said, "Because we need to flee."

Rowan tugged her braid. "Any ideas?"

"Yeah," Ren said. "I have an idea." He placed his hand on the navigational system. He didn't need Lucas to program coordinates. He didn't need any guidance to get where he was thinking. He just had to think of a lake surrounded by a small wood.

He sent his goodbyes out into space.

Goodbye, Ren.

Ren gathered his power, and it came to him more easily than it ever had. Light and sound trembled around him, and, between one blink and the next, they were gone, and then they were in orbit around a broken moon.

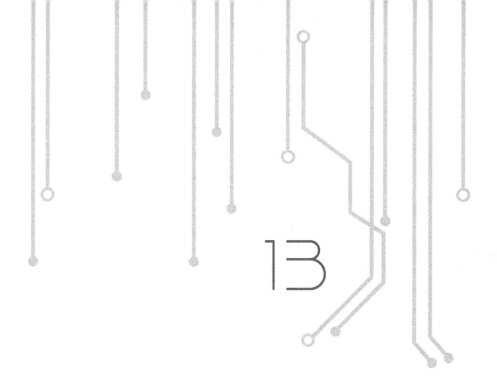

13

BLINKING AWAY THE STREAKS OF blue in his vision, Ren stared at the moon of Erden. A jagged slice through the rock separated the two largest pieces, and debris floated around it in a loose array. The moon was small compared to the planet and the larger drifts Ren had seen, and thus the gravity was less heavy. Ren had stared at this very rock for many of his formative years, wondering what the view would be from another angle. He had it now, and, for all the mysticism that surrounded it on Erden, seeing it this way, a hunk of rock spinning slowly amid a backdrop of stars, much of that mystery was lost. Yet, it was no less beautiful—a reminder of the home Ren once had.

"Erden," Liam said, from behind Ren.

Ren startled and turned his focus away from the moon. In the corner of the vid screen, Erden was a blue and green sphere. It was stunning, but the memories of the last time Ren had been there bombarded him and made his gut sink to his knees.

"Ren, what did you do? How did we get here? Was that you?"

Darby, for all her glitches, was probably the most socially aware, and pulled Liam away and off the bridge. "Let me tell you all about your brother's freaky science-magic."

"You okay?" Asher asked.

"Yeah," Ren answered. "It was the farthest place I could think of, and there aren't any drifts nearby for Millicent to attack."

"We can hide in the fissure," Lucas said, arms straining as he piloted the ship closer to the moon. "Good call, Ren."

"Thanks."

"Now what?" Rowan asked, lounging in her chair. "We can't keep running. The Corps will eventually find us, and, after that stunt, we're wanted fugitives."

"Asher and I were already wanted."

"We were all wanted once the Corps figured out it was us on Bara," Lucas added. He piloted the ship into a cove between the two parts of the moon. The rough rock cast the ship in shadow, but Ren could still see Erden on the view screen.

"True," Rowan tapped her foot. "We need a plan."

Ren was at a loss. He had pledged to help everyone he could, but he had his brother back now. He had Asher and the crew. He didn't want to risk them, and any action that put them at risk was that much harder.

"Um…" Lucas said, tapping on his console. "We're getting a message."

"From whom?" Rowan tapped her mouth.

Lucas spun around in his chair. "Your mother."

"Oh." Rowan and Asher shared a glance. "That can't be good."

Asher wiped his hair from his forehead, then caught Ren's hand in his own. He laced their fingers, and Ren held on.

Rowan crossed her legs and straightened her posture. She cleared her throat and gestured toward Lucas. "On screen."

Ren held his breath. The screen blinked on, wavered, and then focused on Councilor Morgan and General VanMeerten. Dressed in her uniform, her gray hair pulled back in a severe bun, VanMeerten loomed. The harshness of her scar was matched by the cruelty of her frown.

"What have you *done*?" she shouted.

Rowan tented her fingers. "I have no idea what you're talking about."

"Don't play coy with me, Rowan. I will have you thrown into prison. You and your brother and your crew and—" she sucked in a breath, "*you*." She eyed Ren as if he was a bug under a magnifying glass. "You were dead. I saw the footage of your bloody and lifeless body. How are you alive?"

"Don't answer that," Rowan snapped. She stood and crossed her arms. "Do you need something, General, or are you here just to yell at me and threaten my crew?"

Her face went nearly purple with rage. "Perilous Space housed dangerous criminals and star hosts and you have set them loose on the Corps and the drifts to fall into league with *that girl*."

"That girl is your problem. Not the people you had falsely imprisoned. And we didn't do anything criminal unless correcting an injustice is considered wrong. We freed a young man whom the Corps had taken from his home village planet-side. Last time I read the law, not only was kidnapping a crime, but planetary affairs were out of Corps' jurisdiction. You didn't belong on Erden, you didn't belong on Crei, and you didn't belong on Bara." Rowan tapped her foot. "Now, if you are only here to scream, I'll end this call now."

Councilor Morgan reached out. "No, don't. There's more." She looked worse for wear. Though she was dressed in her usual finery, the lines around her mouth and eyes had deepened in the days since they'd last talked. She wore her makeup caked thick to hide the stress evident under her eyes. She swirled a wine glass and took a gulp. "There's more," she said, quietly.

"Get on with it then. I have a business to run."

VanMeerten narrowed her eyes. "Since your little stunt, the star host named Millicent has attacked yet another drift. She continues to vent Corps soldiers and then uses her power to take over the electrical and mechanical systems on the drift. She scares the residents into complying and has an army of zealots behind her. Our efforts have been ineffective."

"What?" Ren asked. "Zag hasn't been able to shoot her? How surprising."

"It worked on you," VanMeerten said, the lines around her mouth deepening with her frown. "Except it seems death didn't stick."

Asher's hand flexed around Ren's own. "You mean when you betrayed me and instead of going after Vos and Millicent, the very girl who is exacting her revenge on you right now, you decided to attempt murder on the person who was not the threat."

"Not a threat?" VanMeerten scoffed. "As I understand it, he's more dangerous than the others combined."

"You betrayed us." Asher said, not yielding. "You betrayed *me*."

"You were working both sides from the beginning, Morgan." She slammed her fist on the desk. "Don't think I didn't know that your allegiance was always with him and never with the Corps."

"That wasn't always true, General. But when you left me in a cell for a year on a planet, injured and afraid, a hostage to a man who wanted to build an army and wage war, then yes, my allegiance changed to the person who actually cared enough to free me." Asher's eyes flickered to his mother, who had grown even paler. "But instead of rehashing everything the Corps has done wrong since the beginning, let's talk now. What do you want?"

"She's powerful," Councilor Morgan said. She finished her glass of wine and poured another one. "And you're right, the Corps efforts have been unsuccessful. We need help. You can help."

"We decline," Rowan said. She smiled sweetly. "Sorry."

Councilor Morgan squinted at the screen. "You'd allow one of your kind to wreak destruction on innocent people."

Ren bristled. "That's implying that Corps soldiers are innocents. She's otherwise left the residents alone. And why would I want to interfere with a duster doing good?"

Ren lied. He lied and kept a smile plastered to his face, but his stomach churned. He hated the idea of Millicent killing anyone. He hated the idea that she was using her power for her own gain and scaring people and giving people reason to fear technopaths. He planned to stop her, but it would be on his own terms, on his own time.

"I think you have your answer, Mother, and General," Asher said, clutching Ren's hand tighter. "Unless, well, we may be persuaded."

Rowan tapped her chin, sharing a glance with Asher. "You know, you might be right. We *could* be persuaded. But so far all I've heard is a bunch of yelling and no offer."

VanMeerten sputtered. "Pirates! You are nothing but filthy pirates!"

Rowan cocked her head to the side. "So you've said. But I also know that I've lost a lot of potential jobs because of your incompetence. And I wouldn't mind a little compensation."

"If you don't assist, then there will not be any drifts left for you to run trade between. Your living will become obsolete."

"There are planets and, so far, I have a fairly good reputation with all the dusters I know." Rowan shrugged. "There may be a little longer transit time, but, hey, when I have a technopath on board, I don't foresee that as being much of a problem." She winked, and her lips pulled into a smug smile.

General VanMeerten put her hands on her hips and huffed. Councilor Morgan hid a grin behind her glass.

"What do you know about her?" Councilor Morgan took another long drink of the dark liquid, then set the glass on her desk. She brushed her blond hair from her shoulder. "What is her weakness?" She zeroed in on Ren. "What can we do to defeat her? Or persuade her from continuing her rampage?"

"Don't answer that," Rowan said. "I haven't heard a number yet."

"Rowan!" her mother snapped. "This isn't a game."

"No, it's not. We offered information last time, and you dismissed us. We tried to warn you a year ago, and again, you dismissed us. If you want our help, then we want a deal."

"Fine!" VanMeerten glared. "What do you want?"

Ren swallowed. "I want my brother and myself to be left alone. I want a place on a drift, and your promise that the Corps will stop trying to imprison myself and other peaceful star hosts. I want the planets to be left alone and allowed to govern themselves without interference from the Corps unless that's requested. I want you to apologize to me and the others."

"I want credits," Rowan said. "Lots of credits."

"I want an honorable discharge." Asher's shoulders tightened. "And an apology wouldn't go amiss either."

VanMeerten pressed her lips together in a tight, white line. "I can arrange a discharge. I can arrange credits. I cannot speak to the other requests."

Ren inwardly wilted, and his face drained of color. He should've known. Even if he bargained, he'd never be free.

"You can't apologize?" Rowan asked. "I find that hard to believe."

VanMeerten clenched her jaw, and a tremble appeared in the hinges. "I can't speak to Corps policies. I cannot grant blanket amnesty to dangerous individuals and I cannot withdraw all the troops on planets as I am not the only individual who makes those decisions."

"Ren is not dangerous," Asher said. "Neither is his brother. And neither are the ones who had lived quietly in hiding until the Corps began to drag them out. Vos took advantage of a situation the Corps created. Surely, you see that."

"I can give amnesty to Ren and his brother. No one else. And I will remove troops from Erden."

Ren shook his head. "I won't advocate just on my behalf. It has to be all or none."

"Can you even stop her? You can't expect us to bargain so much away when we don't even know the extent of your power. And will you stop her? We can't trust you. You all lied, and you attacked an encampment."

"Ren," Rowan said, lifting her chin, "show them."

Ren swallowed. He disentangled from Asher's hand, not wanting to hurt Asher's mechanical shoulder accidentally. He took a deep breath and called upon the anger that welled within him due to this conversation, the frustration, and the fear and he concentrated on shaking apart, vibrating into pieces, as he collapsed inward. It came to him more easily, and his vision went blue, then violet, darker by degrees as he crumpled, and then his star exploded outward. A rainbow of sparks dripped from his fingers, and his vision swam in technicolor.

The comms crackled with energy and power, and he reverberated across the cluster, stretched along the communication feeds, and into the councilor's office. It was the farthest he'd ever gone, and he was weak scattered out along the lines, but he flickered in their lights.

"What are you?" VanMeerten asked, voice breathless with horror.

"I am a star."

"Ren," Asher took his hand. "Come back."

Ren retracted into his body in seconds and let the power go. He heaved in a breath and locked his knees to keep from staggering. The action left him weak, but he refused to show it, not in front of VanMeerten.

"Impressive," Councilor Morgan said. "But can you stop her?"

"I don't know," Ren admitted. "She has abilities that I don't. But I've learned more since I last faced her."

"Then what good are you?" VanMeerten sneered. "Why should we waste our efforts on you?"

Rowan raised a finger. "Because everything else you've tried has led to people being killed. You've been utter dirt at protecting the drifts. We've seen it. And you need help."

"We have another ally," Asher said, shouldering forward. "And he won't work with you without us. Without Ren. Between the three of us, we can work something out."

VanMeerten sniffed, but the apprehension in her features softened. "And what? You'll arrange a meeting?"

"Yes," Ren said. He caught the look Asher and Rowan shared, but ignored them for the time being. "Yes, if you promise. Promise me you'll back off and let us live."

"A moment." Councilor Morgan placed her palm over the camera and Ren heard a hurried whispered conversation. Rolling his eyes, Ren boosted the sound, and the conversation came loud and clear over the *Star Stream's* comm.

"Handy," Rowan said with tight smile.

With a huff, Councilor Morgan pulled her hand away. "Speak, Grace."

The general straightened the jacket of her uniform. The medals on her chest gleamed; the braided ropes over her shoulders pulled taut.

"An honorable discharge for Asher. Credits for Rowan." Her left eye ticked. "And a pardon for the technopath and his brother. Warrants and files deleted. That's all I will promise. If you succeed, we'll negotiate for the other pieces." She cleared her throat. "Does that sound fair?"

"You forgot the apology," Rowan said sweetly. "I think we all deserve one, but especially Asher and Ren."

VanMeerten grumbled but the councilor knocked her arm into the general's back. "Fine. On behalf of the Corps, I apologize for the treatment you've both received."

"Work on the apology," Asher said. "For when we arrange the meeting. I'd like it to be more specific and sincere."

"Otherwise? Do we have a deal?"

Asher wrapped his arm around Ren's shoulder. "What do you say?"

It wasn't enough. It wouldn't ever be enough. But his family would be taken care of. Maybe… maybe she would bend when Millicent and Vos were finally dealt with.

"Fine. With further negotiation understood once the threat has been neutralized."

"Yes," VanMeerten agreed. "And how will you arrange this meeting? It needs to happen fast and—"

"We'll take care of it," Ren interrupted. "We'll contact you when we're ready."

She nodded. "Fine. Don't dawdle."

Rowan cut he feed. "Don't be such a cog," Rowan muttered once the screen winked out. "Who does she think she is?"

"I think she is the head of a military organization," Lucas said from his seat. "That was intense."

Ren had forgotten he was there, but was glad he was another witness to their deal.

"Did you record that?" Asher asked.

"Sure thing. I hit that button as soon as she popped up on the screen. Damn, she's scary."

"She's not scary when you know what scares her." Ren leaned into Asher's side. "She's afraid of me."

"So," Rowan sat heavily in her chair and slumped, "how are we going to arrange a meeting with an escaped convict and us and a general who would as soon see us all thrown into jail as smile at us. We can't go to them. I don't trust VanMeerten."

"I don't trust Vos. He'll turn on us as soon as he gets a chance. And if he managed to free Abiathar, he could turn Ren against us, or any other star host he may have freed."

Ren bit his lip. "We'll use a dream."

"What?" Rowan stood. "We'll do what?"

"My brother can enter dreams. My powers don't work there. I'm certain he could find Vos. He might not remember, but he's done it before in the prison. And we know where VanMeerten is hanging out."

"That was Mother's office."

"Can he get all of us there? Would it be safe?"

Ren shrugged. "It would be safer than a physical meeting."

"We'll ask him."

"Not now," Ren said. "He needs to rest. He's been through a lot."

"Soon though. VanMeerten is right. We can't dawdle. Millicent has three drifts under her control that we know of. And with each passing moment, Vos is either getting farther into hiding or starting to rebuild his own forces."

"I'll talk to him tonight."

⊣⊢

The rest of the day passed uneventfully. Restless, Ren stayed in the cargo bay, rifled through the crate Ollie had bought him before the incident, and fixed the spare parts he could and trashed the ones he couldn't. Asher left him to his thoughts. Liam rested, and Ren checked in on him often, traveling through the circuits to watch the slow rise and fall of his chest. He slept like the dead, sprawled out, unmoving, leaden in the sheets—the sleep of the truly exhausted. Ren intimately knew the feeling.

Ren dreaded asking Liam to use his power to help them. He'd been manipulated by the Corps, tortured if he didn't comply, and resisted in his own small ways. And now he was rescued, only to be asked to do the same thing. Lost in thought and work, Ren didn't notice the passing of time until Asher touched his arm.

"Ren?"

Ren blinked, and Asher frowned. "I'm going to bed. Are you okay?"

"Yeah, I just… lost track of time."

"Not like before?"

"Huh?" Ren set a piece of tech aside. "No, not like before. Thinking about Liam."

"Ah," Asher sat next to him. "Do you want talk about it?"

Ren scrubbed a hand over the back of his head. "Not really. I need to talk to him."

"You do."

"I don't have much time."

"You don't."

Those were the facts and Ren appreciated Asher for confirming them and not trying to pry anything else out of him or try to offer unwanted platitudes.

"Talk to him, Ren. If he doesn't want to help us, that's fine. It means we have to figure out another way. We can do that."

Sighing, Ren stood. He checked the feeds and was surprised to find Liam was gone from the room he'd been assigned and was on the bridge. Lucas was there as well, tapping away at his console, but otherwise, they were silent.

"Okay. I'll see you in a few minutes."

Asher's mouth tipped up in a grin. "I'll wait for you."

Ren padded up the metal steps from the bay into the heart of the ship. He passed the common area, where Penelope and Darby played a card game, laughing at each other, then walked down the hall past the crew quarters. He jumped up the small set of steps and ducked onto the bridge.

Lucas looked up from his calculations and stood. He didn't say a word, only acknowledged Ren with a tip of his chin and a small pat to the shoulder as he walked past.

Liam stood at the viewing screen, dressed in clothes that didn't belong to him, barefoot, and swaying like an apparition.

Ren waited a few moments before addressing him.

"Hey, how are you doing?"

Liam didn't turn around.

"I'm fine."

"That's good." Ren knotted his hands behind his back. "I need to talk—"

"It's right there." Liam pressed his hand to the viewing screen. "I want to go home."

Ren wandered toward the screen. "I know."

"When you were there last, did you see anyone other than our parents? People from the village?"

Ren crossed his arms. "A few. Our home isn't there anymore, Liam. The village is gone. Our house… well, it was standing, barely, but I doubt it is any longer."

"We'll rebuild it. Dad and I can. I know you two didn't always get along, but between the three of us, we could fix it."

"Liam—"

"You could convince Sorcha and Jakob to move the village back to the lake. They'd listen to you."

"I don't think—"

"Mom told me she was sorry for everything that happened in the laurels." Liam cast a look over his shoulder to Ren. "She wanted me to tell you. I talked to her through my dreams, when I could. She was harder to contact than you were, and I think it had something to do with her power. I've been too exhausted to try for the past few weeks. She'll be worried."

"I'm sorry."

"I want to go home. Please?" He turned wide, wounded eyes to Ren. "We could run down there, and you can drop me off. Or you could transport us. I know you can. I saw that you can."

Ren ducked his head. "We're not going to Erden. We don't know what's happening down there or where our friends are."

"Ren—"

"I said no," Ren snapped. "We're not going. We have other things to deal with. We have other things to do than worry about anyone planet-side."

Liam's features screwed up in anger. His cheeks went red, and his lips trembled. "Just because you don't want it to be your home anymore doesn't mean you can keep me from going. I want to go to the lake. I want to see Mom and Dad. I want to be back on the soil."

"Liam, that's not why."

"Yes, it is! Just because you hate it doesn't mean I do!"

Ren sighed. He scrubbed a hand over his face. "Liam, I don't want to fight with you. I'll get you home. I promise. But later. Too much is at stake right now."

Liam crossed the room and pushed Ren hard in the shoulder. Ren staggered back.

"You just want to use me like they did, don't you? I heard you talking to that general. She needs you, and you need me."

Stricken, tears sprang to Ren's eyes. "That's not true." His voice shook.

"Liar!" Liam pushed again. "Liar! Come on!" He pushed until Ren's back hit the bulkhead. "Fight back! I know you can! You never did at home, but I've seen you now. I know what you can do!"

Pushing his forearm across Ren's chest, Liam pinned him against the metal. Ren's heart slammed against his ribs.

"Liam, stop."

"Why? Why should I? That's how it works up here, right? You got what you wanted by fighting; maybe that's what I have to do."

Ren pushed against Liam's shoulders. "Will you cut it out? You're right. I don't want to go back to Erden. I don't want to take you there. Happy?"

"No! I want to go home! Why won't you let me?"

"Because I just got you back!" Ren shouted. Tears threatened to spill down his cheeks. "You may have spent a year in that prison, but I've been in chains and chased across a countryside. I've been possessed by a ship. I was betrayed, and I was *murdered*, and the whole time I looked for you. I wouldn't stop looking for you."

Liam shoved Ren one last time. His elbow caught Ren in his wound; then he released him and stalked across the deck. The pain stole Ren's air, and he gasped, knees weak.

"What? Is that supposed to make me feel guilty?"

"No," Ren said. "It's supposed to make you feel loved."

Liam bowed his head and covered his eyes with one hand. His shoulders shook. Tentatively, Ren came up behind Liam and touched his back.

"You're my brother. You're my family. You're the only family I have."

"That's not true," Liam said, voice thick.

"Our mother and your father aren't… they're not… I don't think…"

"Not them," Liam said, saving Ren from having to find the thoughts and feelings associated with his mother and stepfather. "The crew. This crew are your family. Asher is your family. I… don't have that."

"You could have that. They've spent almost as much time looking for you as I have. They welcome everyone who wants to be a part of the crew."

Liam shook his head. "I don't want them to be my family. I have one." He pointed to Erden. "There."

Ren closed his eyes and blew out a breath. "You're right. It's not just that we don't have time. I need you. I need your power. I can't let you leave, yet."

"I know." Liam shrugged. "You want me to arrange a meeting between those people."

"I do."

"So you can kill her."

"I don't want to. I don't want to kill her. And maybe we can disarm her and keep her from hurting anyone else."

"And if you're not able to."

"That's why we need to have a meeting. To go over our options."

"I thought you hated the Corps and Baron Vos."

Ren smiled ruefully. "The enemy of my enemy is my friend. And VanMeerten promised she'd let us go if I do this. If I help them, they will let you go home and they'll give Asher a discharge, and Rowan will be able to do business again."

"And you?"

"I'll get to be free."

Liam's brow furrowed. "What are you planning?"

"I'm not planning anything."

Liam's defensive posture dropped. "You're a bad liar." He waved his hand. "Don't. I just... you need to consider Asher before you make any big sweeping decisions. He loves you."

"I am considering him."

"Okay. I just think he'd be happier with you than without you."

Ren didn't have any intention of leaving, of dying again. But he wasn't naïve. He was a supernova, destined to explode. "I'm sorry for not telling you everything," Ren said. "You're not a child anymore."

"Neither are you." Liam smiled sadly. "Sorry for pinning you against the wall and thanks for not frying me or something."

"It doesn't work like that."

"Sure, it doesn't. You could've totally toasted me, and I would've deserved it."

Ren ruffled Liam's hair, and Liam ducked, laughing, and batted Ren away. "Go to bed," Ren said. "You've had a trying day."

"Yeah, in a bit. I want to stay and look a little longer."

Ren knocked his shoulder in Liam's. "Okay. Night."

"Night, big brother."

Ren left the bridge and headed to the crew quarters. In the crew hallway, Asher waited, feet twitching on the deck plate, arms crossed over his bare chest, hair sticking up.

"I heard shouting."

Ren looped his hand through the crook of Asher's elbow. "Everything is fine." He tugged Asher back toward their room.

"Are you lying to me?"

Ren stopped short.

"We made a promise we would be upfront and wouldn't hide things anymore. You lied to me at the prison."

"Come on," Ren said. "I want another night of sleeping with you before things get out of control again."

Asher followed, frowning. Once inside their room, Ren guided him to the bed.

"I'm not lying," Ren said. "I didn't tell you about feeling the trouble on the top floor because I was scared you'd have us abandon Liam when we were so close. I was afraid. I'm sorry."

Asher sat heavily on the edge of the bed. "I wouldn't have done that."

"I know."

"And now?"

Ren lowered next to him, their bodies flush from hip to knee. "The others in the debris told me that I am a supernova."

"What does that mean?"

"It's what I did on the bridge. If I allow myself, I will collapse and explode outward. It's why everything is burning darkly now. It makes me more powerful, and it's how I can defeat Millicent. I can overwhelm her, maybe."

"But?"

Ren winced. "Supernovas explode."

"You'll… explode."

"Not literally," Ren said. "I don't think. My power might become too much and I'll…" Ren mimed a blast with his hands.

"Huh," Asher said. "So, you're at risk of losing your humanity if you become too entrenched in the ship, which I've seen and is frankly terrifying, or you might tear your star to pieces trying to defeat Millicent." Asher laughed. "Nothing is easy with you."

"You're not mad?"

"I'm confused and frightened, to be blunt." He shrugged. "But what can I do? Other than protect you and be at your side." He twined their fingers. "I'll be your anchor when you need one. And I'll piece you back together like a puzzle if I have to."

Ren blinked. "Are you serious?"

"Absolutely."

Ren smiled, the relief of Asher's words a balm to his worry and anxiety. "I can't believe you."

"I told you, Ren. You're it for me. And I'll want to be with you in all your weirdness, whatever form that takes—star host or supernova. Get it through your thick skull, you idiot duster."

Laughing, Ren tackled Asher to the bed. "I love you, you arrogant drifter."

"You better," Asher said, rolling Ren off of him.

Propped up on his elbow, Ren faced Asher. "I can't wait to have a life with you. When this is all over, I want you and me, on a drift, living together and being us."

"Sounds perfect." Asher pulled their clasped hands and hugged them to his chest. "But until then, get some rest."

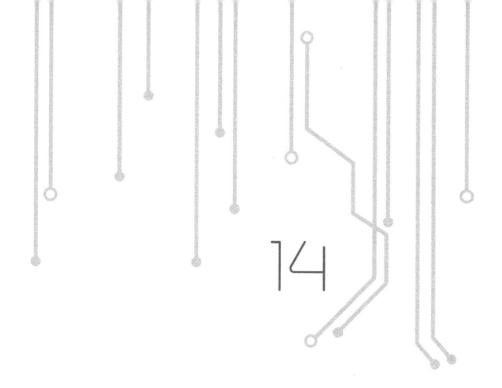

14

"Do you know what you're doing?" Rowan asked, eyebrow raised, as Liam plumped a pillow and dropped it on the floor.

"Yes. I've been doing this for a while."

"And you're going to be able to find Vos and VanMeerten and pull them into your dream?"

Liam nodded. "I can make it a nightmare if you prefer."

Rowan smiled and patted his shoulder. "My kind of kid. We'll talk later about that option."

Smirking, Liam lay down, limp red hair splayed across the crisp white pillowcase. "My kind of captain."

Rowan laughed. Asher rolled his eyes as he shouldered past her into the room.

The entire crew stood around the bare floor in the common room watching as the three of them prepared to meet their enemies. The room was tense with questions and disbelief and nervous banter, but Ren trusted Liam, trusted that his brother could pull this off. He'd spent the last year manipulating dreams. He had the experience.

Ren rubbed his brow, as Lucas cracked a joke about damp dreams, then crouched to the floor, squeezing into the space between Liam and the couch. Asher flopped onto the cushions; his arm fell off the edge to grab Ren's hand in his own.

"This looks like a bizarre sleepover game." Darby bent at her waist and squinted. "Like that game where you pretend to levitate someone with your fingers but turn off the grav instead and freak everyone out."

Rowan pressed a hand to her chest and appeared vaguely scandalized. "What kind of party game is that?"

"The fun kind."

Ren rolled his eyes. He squirmed trying to find a comfortable position. The deck plating was cold, hard, and flat, and reminded him of the medical cot where he'd spent weeks asleep. His hands went clammy where his palm pressed Asher's and where he gripped Liam's wrist.

"Hey," Liam said, head turned, voice low. "I'm sorry, by the way."

Ren furrowed his brow. "For what?"

"For losing it on the bridge last night." He scratched his ear where it was tinted red in a blush. "I… uh… have things to deal with. And I shouldn't have taken it out on you."

"It's okay," Ren said, squeezing gently. "I've been there. I still am there, dealing with things. Don't forget that I'm here if you need me."

"Yeah," Liam said, rolling his head back to look at the ceiling. "I'll remember that for next time."

"Please do."

"So what now?" Darby asked. "You fall asleep?"

"Yes and no. I have learned how to enter dreams on command by accessing my power. I'm going to pull them in with me." Liam jerked his chin toward Asher and Ren. "Hopefully. We'll see. It might work."

"You don't sound very confident," Darby said.

"It'll work," Rowan interrupted. "We know VanMeerten is on the same drift as our mother and it's the middle of their sleep cycle right now. She should be asleep and be easy for Liam to find."

"And Vos?" Lucas asked. "The dude we really need to be there."

Liam shrugged. "If what you've all told me is true, then I've met him before. I already have a connection with him through my star. I should be able to grab him and suck him in."

"Even if he's not asleep?"

Liam nodded. "Yeah. It's something I learned since the last time we talked," he said, casting a glance at Ren. "It's easier when someone is asleep or relaxed or if I'm touching them, but I've been successful with nabbing someone who was wide awake. I did it once at the prison."

"That's terrifying," Darby said, eyes wide. "Utterly terrifying."

"More terrifying than freaky science-magic?" Ren asked, craning his neck.

"Yes!" she said with a sharp nod. "Can you imagine going about your day and suddenly you are pulled into an alternate reality created and controlled by someone else?"

Liam cocked his head to the side and scrunched his brow. "I never thought about it that way."

"That's because you're the one doing it!" She flung her arms to the side. "Honestly, what would you all do without me to be your moral star chart in these situations?"

"I think we'd make do," Rowan said, drily.

Darby huffed. "I think you've been living in star host reality for too long and forgotten what it's like for us normal people."

"Normal?" Penelope waltzed in, blankets in her arms. "Who's normal? No one on this ship surely." She passed the blanket pile to a confused Lucas, then pulled the top one off and shook it out. Stepping through the small crowd, she draped it over Liam, then tucked him in tightly. "In case you get cold. I know how Ren can sometimes play with the environmental controls when he's stressed, and we'd hate for a chill to disrupt negotiations." She took the next one and did the same with Ren, laying it over him and jamming her fingers around Ren's body, tucking the thick fabric close while Liam looked on in confusion and vague horror. The last one she tossed in Asher's face. He sputtered, and she grinned.

"Thank you, Pen," Ren said.

She waved away his thanks and turned to the group. "Okay, let them get to it. The rest of you have things to do. Right?"

"No," Darby said, jumping up on the table and kicking out her legs. "I'm watching this."

"Out," Asher barked, pointing his finger to the door. "Liam needs to concentrate."

Darby groused but hopped off the table and followed Ollie and Lucas out the door. Rowan crossed her arms. "Do you need someone to stay behind and wake you up?"

"No," Liam shook his head from his blanket cocoon. "We'll be fine."

"Fine then. Come find us when you're done." She said it as if she wouldn't be hovering as soon as they were asleep. Ren knew otherwise.

Penelope was the last to leave. "I'll check in periodically." She smiled warmly. "Good luck."

With Penelope's departure, the common area went quiet. Their breaths and the creaks of the ship were the only sounds in the room.

"Are you nervous?" Ren asked Asher.

"No." It was a lie. "You?"

"No," Ren lied back.

Liam rolled his shoulders and closed his eyes. "Relax," he said.

Ren followed suit, snuggling into the blanket, and closing his eyes. He made sure he had a tight grip on Asher's hand on one side and Liam's wrist on the other and took a deep breath. He tightened his muscles and relaxed them, starting with his toes, then his calves, then his thighs, moving up his body as he slid deeper toward sleep.

One moment he was in the common room drifting on the edge and the next—

They were at the lake. The soft sounds of the waves ebbing and flowing on the shore were as familiar to Ren as the feeling of Asher's hand in his. The coarse sand pricked the bottom of his feet, and the sun shone on him, bright and hot.

"Really?" Ren asked, turning to find Liam.

Liam sat on a large rock at the line where the beach met the forest. Long grass tickled his ankles and wisped in the breeze. He shrugged. "I figured it was neutral ground, and this is where I want to be."

Asher's body slowly came into focus as he stood by Ren's side. "I hope this works."

Ren dug his toes in the sand. "Me too."

"Liam?"

"I'm good. I can hold it for a while." Liam scrunched his face. "I've got VanMeerten."

As he said it, VanMeerten coalesced a few feet down the beach. She wore her uniform and shielded her eyes from the harsh planet light. She scowled as she approached. "Is this your idea of contacting me for a meeting?"

"It worked, didn't it?" Ren said.

VanMeerten narrowed her eyes, but otherwise appeared unruffled at being pulled into a dream. "Where are we?"

"Erden," Ren said. "Where we grew up."

"Charming," she said with a frown. "Where's Vos?"

"He's slippery," Liam said with a grunt. Sweat appeared at his temples. His brow furrowed; his teeth dug into his lip. He gripped his knees. "Got him."

Ren looked down the beach and watched as Vos appeared. He wore all black and he frantically spun around, kicking up sand, before his gaze lit on Ren and VanMeerten.

"What is this?" he said, walking forward, his black boots sinking into the beach. "Your little dreamwalker here to steal my thoughts again?"

VanMeerten sniffed. "I don't know what you're talking about."

"Sure, you don't, you old hag." He pointed at Liam. "That little weed slid into my dreams and stole my secrets. He trapped me in nightmares and tortured me for nights on end."

Liam waved. "I don't remember doing it. If that helps."

"No, it doesn't. And you," Vos said, turning his attention to Asher and Ren, "left me at Perilous Space."

"You escaped," Asher said, voice flat.

"With no help from you."

Asher shrugged, unconcerned. "I left a weapon."

"With barely any charge!"

Asher smirked.

"Anyway," Ren said, "I gathered you here for a reason. The two of you have a common enemy."

"You?" Vos offered.

A harsh smile tickled the side of VanMeerten's mouth.

"Hardly. I didn't steal your army," Ren said, addressing Vos. "And I'm not venting yours. Though I could." VanMeerten's smug smile flattened.

Vos crossed his arms. "So, you want me to corral Millicent. Is that it?"

"You were the idiot that released her into the drifts," VanMeerten snarled. "You should've known as a star host she was dangerous."

Vos laughed. He pointed at Ren. "This one is more dangerous than five Millicents. And just as you can't control him, you can't control her."

"Neither can you." VanMeerten clenched her fists. "After she blows through the Corps, the planets will be next. You will be next."

Vos huffed and crossed his arms. "She doesn't concern me."

"So, you freed him?" Ren asked. "Abiathar? You were able to get him out?"

Vos smiled. "I did. Is that what you want? Abiathar to stop her? Then what? You throw my friend back into prison where you muzzle him until he's needed again?"

"You created this mess," VanMeerten shoved her finger into Vos's chest. "You need to own this."

Vos knocked her hand away. "Me? Your military regime came to my planet and interfered. I didn't have designs on the drifts until I found a Corps regiment snooping and caught the son of a high-powered drift official with them." Vos nodded to Asher. "How's the shoulder by the way?"

"You're lucky," Asher said, "that I promised Ren I wouldn't kill you here."

"A soldier to the core. Even when branded a traitor."

Ren pinched the bridge of his nose. "This isn't getting us anywhere. I understand that there will be no trust between us. We've all betrayed each other. But we must stop Millicent. If you don't want more Corps dead and if you want freedom for our planet, you'll both shut up and listen to each other."

Vos raised a black eyebrow and stroked his hand over his goatee. "Fine. I'm willing to bargain."

"Not you, too," VanMeerten said with a roll of her eyes to the heavens. "What do you want? A pardon?"

"Hardly," Vos said, strolling around them in a circle like a shark circling its prey. "I want Erden. I want to rule."

"No!" Liam stood. The dream wavered; reality shimmered. Holes opened in the sky and in the ground, revealing stark darkness just beyond the image he created. "You were a horrible baron. You kidnapped my brother and my friends. You stole our food and our livelihoods."

Vos held up his hands, head tilted. "I can't argue."

"We're not sacrificing the planets to save the drifts," Ren said.

"Well, then," Vos said, backing away from the group. "No deal."

"We don't need him, anyway," Asher said. He shrugged. "His army defected to Millicent, so he wouldn't be helpful. And I doubt he knows where she's going to strike next."

Vos stopped his retreat. He looked at Asher and let a slow smile bloom over his face. "You're trying to appeal to my vanity. You think I'd care about what you think of me, a Corps traitor and a little boy who stayed in my prison for a year? I don't."

"But you're not walking away."

Vos clasped his hands together in front of him. "No, I'm not."

"It burns you that your faithful so easily abandoned you for another. Granted, her power is spectacular, but it pales in comparison to Ren's."

Vos tapped his lips with a finger. "I admit it stings. What would my part be in all this? You already have an army," he said, gesturing to VanMeerten. "And you have a star host that can presumably stop her. What do you need from me?"

"We don't need you," VanMeerten said with a frown. "And I am having a hard time understanding why you're here."

"We need a backup plan," Ren said. "I don't know if I can defeat her. She has manipulated me in the past. Vos is a duster. He cultivated the devotion and respect of the people who follow her now. He may be able to turn them back to his side. He also has Abiathar, who can help me. Abiathar can stop both of us if it gets out of control."

"And he probably knows where she is going next."

Vos didn't refute Asher's statement. "And again, we're down to compensation," Vos said. He spread his hands. "I gave you my terms."

"You can have Erden," VanMeerten said, with a wave of her hand.

Ren stiffened. "No."

She spun on her heel, sand flying. "You want the planets to be able to govern themselves. Correct? Well, if they don't want him in leadership then they can revolt. That is their choice of action. Not mine. Not the Corps. We won't interfere if that happens, but if he's so important to this mission, as you seem to believe, then I will not have you and your brother stand in the way of stopping this madwoman."

Ren took a step back. "You'll install him as a puppet?"

"No," VanMeerten said. "We'll give him a ship and his army and will not interfere when he comes back to this," she swept her hand to encompass their environment, "dirt hole."

Liam shot to his feet. "No!" The dream wavered again, the sky turned purple, and the waves slapped against the shore as reality shuddered.

Ren held out a steadying hand to Liam. "It's okay," he said to his brother, then turned back to the group. He bristled. "Fine." He glanced at Vos's arrogant and pleased expression and his stomach churned. "I'll have people waiting for you. Don't think it will be easy."

"Oh, I welcome a challenge."

"Enough." Asher pulled Ren to his side from where he had drifted toward both VanMeerten and Vos. "Tell us where she's going next."

"In my plan, my next two targets would be Nike or Ephesus."

Asher crossed his arms. "Both small and far away from the major routes. Why?"

"Liam," Ren said, keeping his gaze glued to Vos. "Can you bring up a map?"

A large map of the cluster sprouted from the ground between them, then bloomed outward. Planets and drifts spun lazily.

"Highlight Phoebus and Echo. What was the other drift she's taken?"

"Viktory drift."

The three drifts flashed gold on the map. They were all outer drifts, near planets or moons, and scattered near the edges. "And Nike and Ephesus." They also burned gold, and Ren saw the pattern instantly.

"Your plan was to make a barrier. You were going to circle the major drifts and slowly move inward."

"Tightening a noose," Vos said, pleased with himself. He poked at the map and set Mykonos drift spinning. "Until I could get there."

"Last time you tried that, you were stopped," VanMeerten shrugged. "What makes you think you could take it this time?"

"Last time, I was stopped by him," Vos pointed to Ren. "But by all accounts, he was dead. Also, I had devised a much better plan now that I knew the limitations of your regime."

"Great plan," Asher said, sarcasm thick.

Ren ignored them all. "She's following your pattern." Ren squinted. "Evacuate the Corps from Nike and Ephesus."

"That's impossible," VanMeerten sneered. "It will arouse suspicion. It will cause panic."

"Do you want more soldiers to die?"

"No. I do not. If I evacuate those drifts, then what? She will waltz in unopposed."

Ren nodded sharply. "Yes. That's what we want."

Vos's eyebrows shot up. "What are you planning?"

"You and Abiathar will be waiting on one drift, and I will be waiting on the other. Wherever she lands, we'll be prepared, and the others will then converge to support."

"And what will you be waiting with?"

"Traps," Ren said. "I was ensnared in Perilous Space and I can create the same obstructions in the drift systems. Maybe I can capture her."

"And if she goes to his drift?"

Vos tilted his head and smiled, self-confident. "You forget. I have a star host who controls others with his voice. He can stop her. I can stop her zealots."

"And I am supposed to trust you both? Trust that you won't take the drifts for yourselves?"

"Yes," Asher said. "You have to."

"I don't want a drift. I only want this to all be settled," Ren said. He tapped his bare foot and crossed his arms.

Vos shrugged. "As long as you keep your end of the bargain, I don't see why I would want a little outlier drift."

VanMeerten pointed a finger at Vos and then swung around at Ren. "I'll be watching the both of you and will have regiments ready by both drifts. And if you cross me, I'll throw you so deep in Perilous Space neither of you dusters will ever see another planet sunrise. Am I clear?"

Vos smirked. "We've both escaped there once."

"Why you—"

"Yes. Fine." Asher interrupted and waved his hand before another verbal sparring match could break out. "We'll be on Ephesus." Asher gestured to Liam. "We're done here."

Liam nodded, and the dream winked out.

"How did it go?" Rowan asked as soon as Ren woke. Asher stirred next to him and sat up, rubbing a hand over his head.

"We have a plan," Ren said.

"And?"

"And it's the best we can do." Asher mumbled.

Liam jerked up. He glared at Ren as he stood, stomping out of the common room, presumably to his bunk.

"Is he okay?" Rowan asked.

Ren sighed. "We had to make a trade. He didn't like it."

"I don't think I want to know." She sat on the couch next to Asher. "Are you sure about this?"

"No." Asher rested his hand on Ren's shoulder. "I'm afraid any plans we make are going to be thrown out the airlock as soon as we encounter her."

Ren leaned into the touch. "It was worth a try."

"Yeah," Asher agreed.

"So, what now?" Rowan nudged Ren with the toe of her boot. "What's the plan?"

Ren and Asher exchanged a look. "We're going to Ephesus drift."

⊣⊢

Liam stood on the bridge, looking out at Erden through the rocky debris of the broken moon. Ren tentatively approached from behind, as Lucas typed the coordinates to Ephesus drift in the nav console.

"Sorcha and Jakob will stop Vos," Ren said, standing next to Liam's side. "We'll alert them, and they'll be waiting for him."

"He'll have an army," Liam said, voice low, fingertips splayed on the viewing screen. "He'll roll over them."

"He won't. Sorcha has an army too. You should see the person she's become. Jakob too. You'd be amazed."

"And the person you've become?" Liam asked, gaze breaking from the sight of their home planet to rest heavily on Ren.

"Will do whatever it takes to make sure everyone I care about is safe. Including you. Including them. Including this crew."

Liam turned away. "I never thought of you as someone other people would be scared of, but that general, and even Baron Vos, both of them were afraid. Should I be too?"

Ren pressed his lips together and remained quiet. The answer was too complicated for the moment, but Liam took it for an answer anyway.

"Do you think I'll see it again? Erden?"

"Of course." Ren knocked his shoulder into Liam's. "Once it's all said and done, I'll bring you right back. Maybe even you can be part of Vos's welcoming party."

Liam huffed, and the corner of his mouth lifted into a smile. "I'd like that."

"Ren?" Lucas asked. "Everything's ready. We just need a little freaky science-magic."

Ren gave Lucas a small smile. "You too, huh?"

"It's catchy."

Ren grumbled good naturedly and crossed the bridge to the nav console. He nodded to Lucas.

"Hey all," Lucas said into the comm, "we're about to move quickly through time and space via technopathic abilities. Hold on to something."

Several voices came over the comm at once affirming the crew was ready.

Ren glanced to Liam, who sat on the floor with his back against the bulk head and watched Ren with a wary gaze.

Closing his eyes, Ren blew out a breath. He gathered his power and entered the ship, bled into the systems, flooded the circuits with his presence and his will. Electricity crackled over his body and throbbed under his skin, matching the beat of his pulse. Static and power crested higher and higher, built upon itself until both Ren and the ship reached their limit. The power exploded outward, kinetic and powerful, a wave of light and sound. Space folded and time stretched and snapped.

The *Star Stream* burst into existence on the outskirts of Ephesus drift.

"I think I am getting used to that," Lucas said, stretching his arms behind his head. "It beats puttering down a trade route."

Face pale, Liam staggered away from the view screen. "I don't think I'm used to it yet," he muttered.

Lucas laughed while he hit buttons and received information from the docking staff. "Stick with us, and the extraordinary becomes ordinary. Like a year ago, I thought people like you were duster myths, and now, well, I know better." He flashed a wide smile before flipping open the shipwide comm. "Hey all, we're here and in the docking queue. Drift time is the middle of the night, perfect for sketchy activities." Ren frowned. "And reconnaissance. Sketchy activities and reconnaissance."

Ren shook his head. "Darby is a bad influence on you," he said over his shoulder as he left the bridge.

⊣⊢

They docked without a problem. The *Star Stream* eased into the bay and settled on the drift's deck plate. During the entire process, Ren fidgeted, tugging at the collar of the jacket he'd taken from Asher's room. After a few minutes to allow pressurization, Ren opened the back doors of the ship wide, as if they were taking on cargo. His power crackled in the mechanism. He followed Ollie and Rowan down the ramp with Asher at his side and Liam trailing with an open mouth and wide eyes. Darby elbowed Liam in the side.

"Close your mouth, dust bunny, or do you want to be pegged a mark."

Liam snapped his mouth shut. Darby looped her arm through his and tugged him through the doorway from the *Star Stream*'s slip into the dock itself. "Stick with me. You'll be all right."

"I'm not so sure about that," Liam said in return.

Ren bit back a chuckle.

"Remember, we're doing reconnaissance," Asher said, casting a glance at the duo. "Not picking marks or other…" He sighed. "…sketchy activities."

Darby shrugged. "I can't do both?"

Rowan spoke into her comm. "Hey, Pen and Lucas, we're on drift. We'll check in on the hour."

"Okay, Rowan," Penelope's voice was cheery. "We'll be here and will keep an eye out on the docking traffic."

"Alert us when the Corps regiment VanMeerten promised gets here," Asher said.

"Will do. You be careful."

"We'll try," Rowan said with a wry smile.

The group left the dock through a small door and spilled into the drift proper. A few shops and restaurants were open on the dock level. Signs flashed, and drones flew overhead, carrying objects back and forth. The usual announcements were quieter than during the bustle of the drift's day, and only a handful of individuals milled about. Lucas had said it was the middle of the sleep cycle for the drift residents, which left docking parties like their own and a few opportunistic merchants awake.

They stopped at a large observation window, and Ren smiled when Liam looked out as the backdrop of stars rotated around them.

"Holy dust," he whispered.

"Bunny," Darby said, cheeks dimpling. "This is nothing."

Asher nudged Ren's arm. "Reminds me of you."

Ren blushed. "Shut up."

"Anyway," Rowan said, tapping her lips, "there is a reason we are here. We'll split up to cover more ground."

Ollie draped his large arm across Darby's shoulders and tugged both her and Liam to his side. "I'll take these two."

"Good." Rowan adjusted the weapon at her hip. "I'll head up. You three head down. Ren, can you give us a quick layout?"

"Sure thing." Ren swept into the drift's systems, vision washing blue, to pull up schematics and abruptly stopped. The sickly-sweet embrace of Millicent's power rolled over him as soon as he slid into the systems. He stumbled, hand against his chest, a cold sweat breaking out along the back of his neck. He leaned heavily against the drift's bulkhead.

"Ren? What's wrong?" Asher was beside him in an instant and wrapped his hand around Ren's arm to steady him.

He swallowed the lump in his throat. "She's already here."

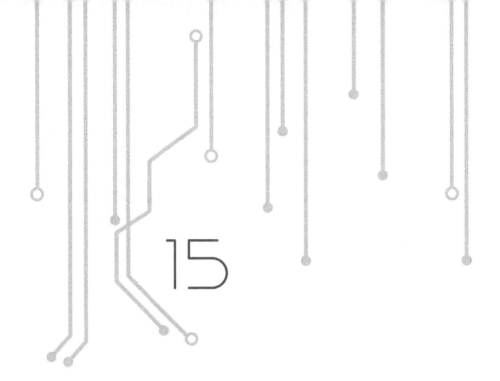

15

"WHAT DO YOU MEAN SHE's already here?" Asher grabbed Ren's arm. His fingers bruised Ren's elbow.

Ren grimaced. Millicent's power pulsed in the systems of the drift. She was there, and her signature crawled in Ren's veins; it ebbed and flowed over him like the tides compelled by Erden's broken moon, and his stomach lurched. This wasn't a series of remnants like he'd felt on Echo. It wasn't a caress of his skin or a touch against his own star. This was an infestation, a sickening surge of her presence everywhere around him. Ren recoiled, and she followed, poking at his star with her own. Wrapping his arm around his middle, Ren closed his eyes and would have doubled over if not for Asher's grip.

"She's here." He gulped down the acid in his throat. "And she knows I'm here too."

"She beat us," Asher said. He turned to the group. "Rowan, get everyone back to the ship! We need to get out of here."

"Too late." Ren trembled.

The sound of boots striking the deck in unison echoed down the drift corridor. Whipping his head, Ren spied a cadre of troops in helmets and body armor, weapons raised, marching toward them from one way. In the other direction, a lift dinged, and the sliding doors revealed a second troop. As the first few filed out, Rowan and Asher exchanged a glance.

Ren's gut twisted as Rowan's hand dropped to the weapon at her hip, and Asher pulled his from his shoulder holster. They nodded to each other.

"Scatter," Rowan said voice low. "Make for the ship if you can or hide and wait. Understood?"

"Yes, captain," Ollie said.

She nodded, body tense like a spring. "Okay, now. Go now!"

Ren engaged his power; his star burst out of him in streaks of blue. He entered the systems despite Millicent's presence. Pain lanced through the base of his skull, and bile crawled up his throat. He cut the lights on their floor. Amid shouts from the soldiers and the crackle of electricity of their weapons, the group dispersed, running in opposite directions. Rowan fired shots into the dark, aiming high to distract and frighten, not injure. Sparks rained as pulses struck the drift walls.

Ren reached out; signatures from the different weapons pinged his senses. He shorted them out as best he could to give the others time. Asher grabbed Ren's hand and yanked him away, pulling him toward the interior.

"Liam," Ren said, craning his neck to check as they ran.

"He's with Ollie and Darby. He'll be fine. We have to hide."

"No, we have to find her."

Chest heaving, Asher tugged open a door to a stairwell and thrust Ren inside. He closed it behind him, and Ren engaged the electric lock, gagging as he did so.

"She's hurting you already. Just from taking out the lights and locking a door. Ren… we have to wait for the Corps."

Ren bent at the waist and sucked in air. "So she can vent them?"

"Better them than us."

Ren raised an eyebrow. "She knows I'm here. She'll flush us out before VanMeerten's regiment gets here. And the Corps stationed here are probably already dead or captured."

As he said it, a loud bang sounded on the other side, and Ren jumped away as more followed.

"They're ramming the door." Asher spread his palms against it.

Ren clapped a hand over his mouth as Millicent jumped into the lock and slid into the mechanism. She slammed into Ren, and his throat went tight. He fell to his knees. The lock slid.

The door banged open, and Asher threw his body against it to slam it shut again. He wedged his gun into the door jamb.

"Up!" He tugged Ren to his feet. "Up the stairs."

They ran. Ren tripped up the steps to the next floor as the door flew open below them. Asher caught Ren's hand, his grip bruising, and pulled Ren along. Up and up they sprinted. The soldiers followed, only a landing below them.

"I have an idea," Ren gasped. He furrowed his brow. It would hurt. It would make him sick. But it was better than continuing to run. He flickered into each door they passed and swung it open, hoping to throw the troops off their trail. But each encounter with Millicent's signature sent a wave of weakness over him.

Panting, Ren stumbled and landed hard on the stairs.

"No stopping," Asher grunted, hauling Ren up. "Come on. Next one. Next one."

Chest heaving, legs trembling, Ren scrambled up another set of steps. Asher's fingers wrapped tight around his upper arm. With a heave, Asher opened the next door, hurled Ren through, and slammed the door behind him.

The floor was empty.

Ren doubled over. "No," Asher said, striding across the floor. "Cameras," he said, pointing to the corners. "She knows where we are. Keep moving."

Ren straightened, features twisted in pain and exhaustion. He'd forgotten how bad Millicent could make him feel, or she'd become stronger—both were possible. "Ash, we can't run forever."

"We're not. We're buying time."

"For what?"

"The longer those troops follow us, the better chance Rowan and the others have of escaping." Asher continued to inspect their location. "And we need to give the Corps a chance to respond."

Ren screwed up his features. "The Corps? You know we can't trust them or VanMeerten. Do you honestly think they are going to keep their promise?"

Asher scowled. "No, I don't. They've left me twice, and betrayed us, but I'd rather have them here to take the pressure off of you." He crossed his arms over his head and took a deep breath. "We need to find a blind spot."

"There's not one!" Ren swept his arms out. "She can see us right now. She knows where we are. I can feel her in my head and in my body." Ren rubbed a spot on his chest. "We're not going to be able to hide."

Asher scrubbed a hand over his head. "Why are you so dirt-bent on facing her alone?" His voice came out anguished and sharp. "Don't you remember the last time?"

"I can't forget the last time," Ren said, pointing two fingers at the wound in his side. "I'm the one who died, remember?"

"Yeah, I do!"

Ren frowned. "You agreed to this plan. You were aware of the risks. What? You don't think I can do it? You don't think I have it in me?"

"I don't want to lose you!" Asher crossed the small distance between them and grabbed Ren by the front of his jacket. "I don't want to lose you." He ducked his head. "I can't lose you."

"You won't." Ren rested his forehead against Asher's. "You won't."

"How sweet," Millicent's voice boomed from the overhead system. Ren startled as she cackled and flooded the drift floor with light, pinning them under the heat and glare. Ren closed his eyes, blocked her out, held on to his last sweet moment with Asher. It didn't last long as she flickered the lights and laughed over the comm. Asher pulled away first.

"I thought you were dead. You should've stayed dead." Millicent sounded accusatory.

"That's not how technopaths work, apparently," Ren said with a wry smile.

"Ren," she taunted, drawing out the vowel, her voice breathy and eerie, like a ghost or a dream. It sent a shiver down Ren's spine. "Ren, I have your friends."

Snapping his head up, Ren looked to the cameras. "What do you want?"

"I can't have you stopping me, Ren. I have a plan and an army and a purpose."

"And what is that?"

"You'll have to come talk to me to find out. Your friends are on level two, waiting for you. I'll vent them if you don't hurry." She laughed. "You know I will."

Ren nodded. "I know."

"Here, this will be quicker than the stairwell." A lift dinged nearby, and the door opened. "You look peaked. Come along, you two. Don't want to keep me waiting."

Ren steeled himself and stepped into the lift. Despite his fears, Millicent didn't drop the elevator out from under them. It descended at a slow pace, but Ren allowed his vision to wash blue, just in case.

Asher's fingers clasped tight around his. Ren wanted to reassure him, but he didn't know what to say. He wasn't certain he could stop Millicent. He wasn't certain he could do what the technopaths in the debris said he could. He only knew that he'd do anything to protect Asher and to save his brother and the others. Rowan had saved him when she didn't know him, and Ollie had welcomed him when he didn't have to. Darby stayed in spite of the danger. Penelope healed him. Lucas made him laugh.

Asher loved him.

Ren's breath caught. He didn't want to lose them. He couldn't lose them.

He wouldn't lose them.

Panic lanced through him as the lift ground to a halt. Ren stalled the doors from opening for a moment and turned to Asher. He gave him a watery smile and kissed his stubbled cheek.

"That better not be a goodbye," Asher said, softly.

"No, it's a promise."

Ren stepped back and let go of Asher's hand, then he allowed the doors to open.

Guards swarmed the area, all dressed in black with body armor and helmets. They had a group of individuals surrounded off to the side, and Ren immediately recognized Liam among them and Ollie as well. His heart sank.

While the guards on Echo drift were inexperienced and comical, these moved in unison and with a coordination that marked them as well-trained. They encircled Ren and Asher as soon as they stepped from the lift. Hands raised, Ren felt the echoes of their weapons in his body and tamped down the urge to turn them against their owners. He wanted to burn out the power sources and send the guards to their knees in agony through the crackling of electricity. He withheld his power. They weren't his real enemy.

"I'm here, Millicent. Don't hurt them."

She didn't respond, but she must have sent a communication to the guards. They parted so Ren could see the group they had cornered, though they kept their weapons trained on them. Ollie, Lucas, Pen, and Liam had their hands raised. Rowan wasn't there. Neither was Darby. Ren's throat tightened. Had they avoided capture? Were they dead?

Millicent's voice crackled over the communication system and echoed in the wide space she'd chosen for their confrontation.

"I have your brother," she sing-songed. "The one you were looking for. I found him for you."

The soldiers pushed Liam forward, and he tripped his way to Ren and grabbed Ren's arm. His lip was bloody, and he had a bruise forming around one eye and a singe in his shirt at the upper arm. Ren caught Liam and pulled him close to his side.

"Okay?"

"Not really."

"We'll be fine."

Liam raised an eyebrow, then was knocked to the side when the guards went for Asher.

"No! What?"

"Our divine leader's orders," the leader grunted. They grabbed Asher by the arms, dragged him away, and shoved him into the small group. Ollie caught Asher in a tight hold and glared at the soldiers.

"Let them go, Millicent." Ren narrowed his eyes.

There was no answer, but the lift on the opposite side of the wide space dinged.

Millicent emerged in a swirl of light. She stepped lightly, her bare feet making no sound on the deck plating, her limbs moving like a puppet with no strings. Her white, formless dress swished about her knees. Her eyes glowed a brilliant blue, and her dark hair fell in tangles down her back to her waist. She lifted her hand, and tendrils of blue snapped from her fingers.

"You can't stop me," she said.

Ren gritted his teeth. "I can try."

She laughed, high and loud, bordering on hysterical. "Why? They took you from your home. They imprisoned you. They tortured you. They killed you. Why stop me from avenging you?"

Straightening his shoulders, Ren dug his fingers into his palms. Sweat beaded along the back of his neck. Anxiety and fear pounded through his body. His breath hitched. "You're not avenging me. You're taking revenge."

"They deserve it for what they've done."

Ren frowned. "You tortured me. You're the one who turned my dreams into weapons and turned me into a ghost. Should I take my revenge against you?"

She laughed again; her open mouth was a red slash in her pale face and her eyes were wild. "You were weak. Easy." She waved her hand, and the life support systems flickered in Ren's middle. "You can try to stop me, but I am a star. You are a human. You made that choice."

His star was a deep well of power in his chest. He gathered it to him, allowed it to flood through his veins and arteries and mix with his blood. His power was a separate heartbeat, a rhythmic pulse of crackling energy. He channeled his anger and his grief and his happiness and his love until he was consumed. He drew on his panic and his desperation and funneled it into his will.

"No," Ren said. His voice was static and power. "I'm a supernova."

Ren released his tight hold, and his star poured outward, the world around him awash in a spectrum of color: reds and blues and purples and darkness as black as the space between the stars in the night sky. Fire and light exploded from his fingertips; electricity arced between his hands, around his torso, and down his legs to the soles of his feet. He tapped into the power of his humanity and into the power of stardust. He dove into the drift's systems.

Millicent blasted into the circuits to repel him and met Ren with her own surge of power. They clashed within the drift. A wall of blue smacked against Ren's own nebula of color. Millicent pushed and pushed; her power strained against the torrent of Ren's own. His stomach roiled, and his head pounded with pain and exertion, but it was secondary to the feeling of being overtaken by the explosion of potential. He overwhelmed the drift's power structures, driving her out in wave after wave of pure energy. He shone as brightly as an entire galaxy of stars, expanding outward in a detonation of elements and sound and light.

How dare you, she gasped. *How dare you!*

You can't push me out this time.

No! she screamed at him, sending a shockwave of sickness, but Ren batted it away.

Then she fled. She raced to life support and cut the systems and Ren repaired them in a blink. She sabotaged the grav and went for the air locks. Ren chased her from system to system, from circuit to circuit, from wire to wire. He chased her until he was stretched from the top of the drift to the bottom, from the docks to the lifts, from the locks to the comms. He swamped every available nook, welled and inundated, battered every system with power, until he controlled everything, and she curled into a small ball of dim light.

Ren wrapped tighter around her, squeezed and squeezed, focused on overwhelming her until she was a speck. And while he choked her, caged her within his supernova, he also expanded, filtered into the ships in the docking bay, and out beyond the confines of the drift into the smattering of satellites caught in the gravitational pull, and farther, into the ships on the outskirts—Phoenix Corps—and into space debris drifting by. He bloomed outward, soundless in the void of space, a shock of reds, blues, purples, and colors undetectable by humans.

She squirmed away, snapping his attention back to her pathetic squiggle of light, and then… she smiled.

Look what you've done.

Ren was a collapsing star. He was darkness and light, a supernova, scattering across the cluster in a tumult of creation. He was a concussive force of energy, elements, and color streaking across the night sky. He was the birth of a nebula and the terrifying swirl of a black hole.

He was shaking apart.

Warning alarms blared, and claxons flashed as the drift shuddered and threatened to break. Pieces of the structure snapped off. Cracks appeared in the bulkhead. Wires overloaded, burned, then blackened and twisted. The gravity threatened to fail. Life support sputtered.

"Ren! Ren, you have to stop. You're going to pull this place apart!"

Disconnected from his body, Ren faintly registered Asher's hands on his shoulders. He attempted to contain himself, but he was unable to shrink back. He was tearing himself apart, down to his constituent atoms, and he'd take the drift with him. His family would not survive.

He opened his human eyes, his vision filled with a blurred image of Asher's concerned face. Ren gritted his teeth. "Liam," he rasped, voice scorched from yelling. He blindly reached out for him and grabbed his wrist where he had his fingers wrapped in Ren's jacket. "Pull us in."

"What?"

"Pull us in. Pull us in. Pull us in!"

Liam lunged for Millicent, yanking Ren from Asher's grasp, and locked a hand around her ankle. Liam's eyes glowed green.

Ren blinked and fell.

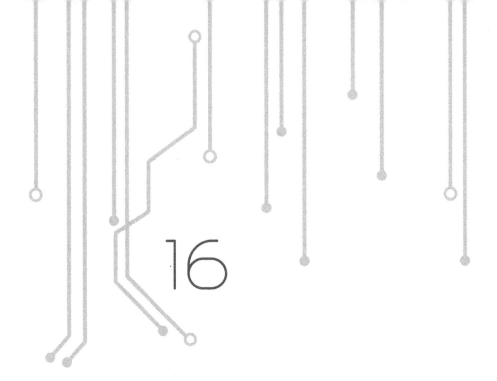

16

Gasping, Ren woke to blinding white. He raised a hand and shielded his eyes as he sat up. He was in a barren cube, surrounded by white walls. He wore a white shirt and white pants and Asher's jacket. And he wasn't alone.

Millicent lay prone, dark hair splayed over her. Her white dress blended into the floor creating an illusion that she was only arms and legs.

Ren shuddered and tugged on the collar of Asher's jacket.

"Hey," Liam said. He leaned against the wall. "Quick thinking."

Ren shook his head and ran a hand through his hair, pushing the long strands away from his face. He stood, though he was wobbly, and Liam steadied him with a hand to his arm.

"What happened?"

"I don't really know," Liam said, arms crossed. "Your eyes went black, and you shook like a leaf in a storm. Then all of a sudden, the drift began to…" Liam made a motion with his hand. "…break apart. Asher grabbed you and yelled a question, and you snapped out of it long enough for this to happen." Liam swept his hand to encompass the room.

"Not very decorative," Ren said, conjuring a smile.

Liam smirked. "I didn't have much time to create anything. This was the best I could do."

"What do you think is going on… outside?"

"Oh, we're asleep, on the deck. And hopefully you'll have stopped destroying everything."

Ren jutted his chin toward Millicent's body. "She's in here with me, which means she can't pull me into the systems like she did on the *Star Stream*. I think you stopped me and her."

"I hope so. That was terrifying. If I hadn't been so worried about you I would have fled with her guards when they ran."

"They ran?"

"Oh yeah, as soon as she fell to the floor and curled into a ball. Then the whole place began to quake when you went…" Liam mimed an explosion. "… supernova."

Millicent groaned, then stretched. She pushed up on her elbows then snapped her head up, palms flat on the slick, white floor. She flailed, then brushed her wild hair back. Her eyes narrowed on Ren, and she moved to a crouch.

"What have you done?" Finding her feet, she swayed, then thrust out her hand. "Why can't I… where is it?" She patted her hands over her body. "Where is it? I can't feel it." She clenched her hands in her hair. "I can't feel it!"

"Your power doesn't work here," Liam said, lazily. "Only mine."

"Give it back!"

Liam shrugged. "That's not how it works."

"You," She pointed at Ren. "You have ruined everything! Why couldn't you stay dead? Or stayed away? I wasn't hurting you. I didn't want you or your Phoenix or your crew."

"You endangered us all," Ren bit out. "Do you think they would leave me alone if you were running rampant, scaring people, venting them, taking over their homes?"

"I did what you wouldn't." She crept forward, features twisted in disgust. "The Corps would never leave us alone anyway. And Vos wanted to make us weapons. I broke away when you couldn't. I took control.

"You killed people."

"I did what I had to. I escaped Crei. I deceived you. I overthrew Vos. I won." She laughed. "I won!"

Ren rubbed his brow. "At what cost? You're alone. You have no crew. You have no family."

"I am free."

Ren shrugged. "You're really not."

She sniffed. "I have an army."

"You have zealots who are in awe of you and who ran off the minute you were defeated."

She cocked her head, gaze flitting between Ren and Liam. "You've found your brother. You have your Phoenix. You have what you wanted. Let me go."

Ren shook his head. "I can't do that."

"The Corps is evil. You know that. Let me destroy them. Let me finish what I've started! Get out of my way!"

Ren sighed. He couldn't reason with her. She was dead set in her beliefs, immovable as stone, and nothing he could show or prove or say would sway her. She was dangerous—not just in her power, but in her inability to look beyond her own desires. "No."

She cursed and stepped forward. Her face was a storm cloud. "Then I'll move you!" She rushed him, hands outstretched, voice caught in a scream.

The dream winked out.

⊣⊢

Groaning, Ren rolled on the drift floor. His whole body ached. His throat felt like dust, and his fingers were numb. His eyelids fluttered, and he squinted in the dim drift lighting.

"Ash?" He worked moisture into his mouth. "Liam?"

With a tortured sigh, Ren squirmed, and found he couldn't move his arms. Rope dug into his wrists, and his shoulders were taut from being bound behind him. Using his elbow for leverage, he got to his knees and wobbled.

A barrage of clicks sounded.

"Stay where you are."

Blinking blearily, the shapes around him sharpened into view. Millicent was to his left, similarly bound, but not moving. Liam sprawled next to him. He had electronic clamps around his wrists and his eyes were slits, but he was awake. A regiment of Phoenix Corps surrounded them. They didn't hold tech weapons—no pulse guns or electric batons. Instead, Ren stared down the barrels of ancient projectile weapons, like the one Zag had used on Crei.

Fear choked him. His heart beat a rabbit's rhythm. "What's going on?"

"You're under arrest."

Ren shook his head. "No, that's not right. My brother and I have an agreement with General VanMeerten." Ren couldn't see beyond the corporal's visor, but his hand holding the weapon shook.

"The general ordered us to detain you and prepare you for processing. She gave the orders to use the rope and the pistols."

Betrayal was a knife between his ribs, a wound in his side, and, despite the outcome being something Ren expected from someone like VanMeerten, it still burned.

"Where's my family? What have you done with them?"

"They were ordered back to their ship."

There was a commotion behind Ren, and he craned his neck. He couldn't see beyond the circle of Corpsmen surrounding him, but he could hear voices. Asher's and… was that Darby? And Rowan? They were alive? They were safe?

"Let him go!" Rowan commanded.

Ren watched in dazed awe as the group parted when she approached. Her strides were long and purposeful; her blond braid was swinging behind her. Asher marched at one shoulder and Darby at the other. Ren's gaze settled on Darby. He was startled to see the explosive device in her gloved hand. She saw him and winked.

"Yeah, you heard her. Out of our way and let our friends go, or I might just use this contraption." She shook it, and the group took a collective breath. She smiled, cheekily. "Oh, so you do know what this is."

"Release the brothers," Rowan commanded, stance wide, hands on her hips. She had a bruise on her cheek and a smear of blood along her jawline, but otherwise she was an avenging angel as beautiful as she had been when Ren first saw her on Nineveh.

"Our orders—"

"Your orders are what I tell you," Rowan snapped, pointing at the corporal. "Understand? No? Ren, show them."

Ren wrinkled his brow, confused, until he saw the recording device Asher held in his hand—Lucas's recording of the conversation with VanMeerten and Councilor Morgan.

Oh, he could kiss Lucas. He really could.

Focusing, Ren drew out a tendril of power, directed it at the recording, and fed it into the flashing signage above them. The image of the general and the councilor appeared, and the conversation played. VanMeerten's voice was loud and clear.

"An honorable discharge for Asher. Credits for Rowan. And a pardon for the technopath and his brother. Warrants and files deleted."

Ren rewound it and set it on a loop.

"As you can see," Rowan said, tenting her fingers, "we had a verbal agreement. I intend to see that honored." She gestured to Darby. "I'd prefer without bloodshed, but I could go either way at this point."

Darby's smile went sharp. "I know which way I'd prefer."

"This is… unorthodox." The corporal shifted.

Rowan raised an eyebrow. "I understand. I'd hate to be in your shoes, choosing between releasing a few prisoners or being blown to bits." She stepped forward. "I'll sweeten the deal. Let them go. I won't tell my little friend here to blast us all back to our fundamental elements, and we promise to stick around until your boss gets here. How does that sound?"

"Stand down," the leader said, raising a hand. "Holster weapons. Release the technopath and the dreamer."

None too gently, a pair of soldiers jerked Ren to his feet and cut his bonds. Ren released Liam before the soldiers could touch him; the electronic cuffs fell at his feet. Ren rubbed his wrists and unsteadily walked through the crowd of Corpsmen, who eyed him like the danger he was, until he and Liam were quickly enfolded by Asher, Rowan, and Darby and tucked behind them.

"And the girl?" the corporal asked.

Rowan wrinkled her nose. "She's of no concern to us." She raised her finger. "But I'd make sure to keep her bound and sedated."

She turned away and looped her arm through Liam's while Asher took Ren's hand. Darby walked backward, hefting the explosive device in her palm until they turned a corner and were out of sight. Then Darby tossed it into a trash receptacle.

"Fake," she said with a shrug. "All pretty blinking lights and no substance, if you get my drift."

Ren half-smiled, nodding slowly. Even with Asher's hand snugly in his, even with Liam at his side, even with Rowan smirking, and with Millicent behind them, captured, and Ren's freedom bargained for, he didn't think it was over. It didn't feel as though he was finished.

"Why the promise to stick around?" Liam asked. "I'd thought we'd teleport out of here as soon as possible."

Rowan's expression became more frigid than Ren would have thought possible. "Because I want to look VanMeerten in the eye when I confront her about going back on our bargain."

Ren shivered.

"Are you okay?" Asher asked.

Ren raised his hand in front of his eyes. "I'm a little disconnected." And maybe that was what was wrong. He was still in the drift. His power was bleeding out of him with each step he took, emanating from the soles of his feet into the deck plating and into the walls and circuits and systems, stretching out and up and down, repairing his mistakes, rerouting power, fixing, and searching, and—

Asher nudged Ren's shoulder and tightened his grip on Ren's hand. "Hey," he said softly, "come back to me."

The softness of the touch and the physical response—the blush rising in his cheeks, the stutter of his heart, the warmth in his belly—brought him back to his corporeal form. Yes, yes, this was real. Asher was real, and Ren slotted into his body, his tethers to the drift snapped, and he centered into himself, alive and whole and human.

He smiled. "I'm right here."

⊣⊢

Back on the ship, there were hugs all around, then medical exams by Penelope. Ollie suffered bruises and a strained back from fighting a squad of troops. Darby had a sprained ankle from when she dove into a trash chute to evade capture. Rowan had a painful graze on her leg, and Lucas showed off a black eye from resisting when Millicent's force broke into the ship. Otherwise, everyone was fine.

Liam pitched onto the couch in the common room and fell asleep. His snores were an ambient sound when the rest of them gathered around the worn table. Ren traced a scratch with the tip of his finger while he absently ran diagnostics on the ship.

"We'll send Jakob and Sorcha a message and let them know that Vos plans on returning to Erden to reclaim his fife," Asher said, sipping a cup of water, one hand firmly clasped in Ren's. "Maybe we can ask Liam to do it in a dream."

Darby snacked on an apple. "Who are they?"

"Friends of ours." Ren smiled softly. "They'll be able to stop him, I'm sure."

"Good. He sounds like a cog."

Ren's lips twitched into a smile. "He is."

"And VanMeerten? What are we going to do about her?" Lucas asked. He had his goggles on his head; the skin around his eye was puffed and darkening. "Frankly, I want our credits. We survived all this, and I want to spend some time on a resort drift."

Liam rolled over. "There are resort drifts?" he asked sleepily. "I wanna go." Then he snored.

"I'm with him," Darby jerked her finger over her shoulder.

"Does that mean you're staying with us?" Rowan asked. "Now that we're free to drop you off at any drift you'd like."

Darby tilted her head. "Is that an invitation, Captain?"

"Take it as you will."

Darby drummed her fingers on the table. "I'll stay. For now. I don't know what to say. I like this crew, even the marks and the bunnies."

"Well, add my vote for resort drift," Ollie said with a nod. "That's four."

Rowan smiled. "As badly as I need a spa day, we still have one last meeting, and I am looking forward to rubbing our success in her smug face."

"VanMeerten?"

Rowan scoffed. "No, my mother's."

"Oh," Darby said around a bite of apple. "You people still confuse me, but I'm good. There are plenty of places I still need to explore on this drift."

Penelope raised her finger. "No stealing, please."

Darby sighed and rolled her eyes. "Fine. No stealing. This time."

The chatter continued well into the late hours of drift's time, but as soon as there was a pause, Ren and Asher stole away.

They stumbled into their room, weary with exhaustion. Ren's hands shook from the adrenaline drop as his body finally was catching up with the day's events. Asher pushed Ren against the wall and clenched his fingers into Ren's hips. His breaths hot on Ren's neck. Ren trembled.

"Are you okay?" Asher asked, voice pitched low.

"I can't stop shaking." Ren laughed. "I'm good though. We won. I won and I'm here. What about you?"

Asher huffed, his cheek rasped against Ren's, and his voice was breathy in Ren's ear. "All I could think was that we'd be separated again. That you'd break apart in some effort to stop her. Or you'd be taken away or worse and I'd not be able to stop it. I don't know what we'd have done if Rowan's ruse hadn't… if that soldier hadn't…"

Ren frowned. He patted the back of Asher's head. "It worked. It worked, and we're on the ship, and Millicent is captured, and we're okay."

"For now. VanMeerten tried to go back on our bargain already. What if she tries again? What if Rowan can't stop her?" Asher shook in Ren's arms; his grip on Ren bordered on painful. "The Corps only takes. They take and take with no regard to anyone and—" Asher choked on air.

Asher's visceral panic pierced Ren to his core, and he clutched Asher closer. He wrapped his arms tight around his shoulders. "Hey, it's okay, Ash. It's okay. We're together and we're safe. And our family is safe. Breathe with me."

Several long minutes later, Asher's ragged breathing evened out, and he sagged into Ren's embrace.

Ren allowed his head to thunk against the wall.

"I think," Asher said, his voice breaking the silence, "that some time on a resort drift is a good idea."

The knot in Ren's chest slowly eased. "Understatement." He sighed. "Ash?"

"I'm fine." Asher sniffled. "Residual adrenaline and, well, unresolved resentment toward the Corps, but I'm good for now."

Ren raised an eyebrow, but acquiesced. "Later." He ran his fingers through Asher's hair. "We'll talk later and we'll address it together."

Asher nodded. "Together."

"Until then, how about a shower and a nap?"

Asher gave Ren a weary smile, but one that was genuine and bright. "Sounds perfect."

⊣⊢

True to Rowan's prediction, General VanMeerten and Councilor Morgan arrived two days later looking harried and uncomfortable. Called into VanMeerten's office, the entire crew faced her as she stood behind her desk. Asher's and Rowan's mother stood at her side.

She eyed them as if eyeing bugs under glass. Her lip was curled into a sneer; her gray was hair pulled back. She seemed to have aged since the last time Ren saw her; wrinkles were deeper around her eyes and mouth, and her scar was etched down the side of her face. Councilor Morgan was her opposite: impeccably put together, blond-gray hair in an elaborate twist, wearing flowing dove-gray robes.

Rowan stood across from her, decked out in drifter gear with a weapon strapped to her side and at her shoulder and her hair in one long glorious braid.

"You reneged." Rowan crossed her arms. "At least, you tried to. It didn't go so well for you."

VanMeerten's gaze cut sharply to Ren. He waved, a wiggle of his fingers, and the taut line of her mouth turned down.

"Reports were that my soldiers neutralized the threat, not you, and therefore the deal was off."

"Your reports were wrong. We," Rowan said, gesturing to the crew, "neutralized her. Your soldiers swooped in once Millicent was passed out on the deck from our efforts."

"Sadly, there is no video evidence supporting your claims. All of it was disrupted in some way." She narrowed her eyes at Ren. "I had to go by my trusted soldiers' reports."

"They lied," Asher said.

"Were they lying when they said the drift went into shutdown and the entire populace almost died. That you yourselves almost died."

"I fixed it," Ren said. "And as you can see, the drift is still intact and running without a single hitch."

"See? We've performed more than one service here." Rowan smirked. "Give us what you owe us."

Councilor Morgan sighed; her shoulders drooped. "Rowan, Asher, we can work something out, I'm sure. We'll compromise. Credits are doable, beyond that—"

"No." Rowan's glare turned icy. "We want an honorable discharge for Asher and we want Ren and Liam's files expunged with a promise that the Corps will leave them alone. Those are nonnegotiable."

"And credits," Darby coughed into her fist. "Don't forget the credits."

"You'll get credits!" VanMeerten's chest heaved.

Rowan stalked forward and braced her hands on the edge of the large desk, bending until her face was mere inches from VanMeerten's.

"Now you listen to me, you hag," she said, tone full of venom. "I know what you did to my brother. I know the things you put him through as one of your soldiers, leaving him behind, and then sentencing him to a dirt existence when he didn't fit your mold. And then, you killed our friend, murdered him because you didn't want to deal with the fact that there are people the Corps cannot control. You couldn't stop Millicent, despite your assertions, and you couldn't stop Vos, a measly planetary baron. You're weak. We know it. And it's only a matter of time before everyone knows it, unless you give us what we want, which isn't much in comparison to what you've done."

"Are you blackmailing me, Morgan?" She looked at the councilor. "Are you going to allow your daughter to do this?"

The councilor shrugged. "I have no control over Rowan or Asher. I never did."

"Ren can tell the cluster, you know. One transmission to every drift and every planet. I don't need to remind you that we're trusted in several different locales. One word from us and you'll have trouble all over."

That was a lie, but there weren't enough credits in the world for Ren to point it out. Rowan was fury incarnate, barely contained, and a sight to behold as her glare flayed the recipients to the bone.

"Credits," VanMeerten ground out. "Honorable discharge. The brothers freed. Records deleted. And we'll stay off the planets unless called." She pulled away from Rowan and raised a finger. "But don't test me, understand? You better fly clean and clear from this point forward."

Rowan smiled. "You won't need to worry about us, General. But, just in case," she pointed to Ren.

On cue, Ren's eyes glowed blue then darkened to purple. "I'll be watching."

"We'll be watching," Rowan amended, gesturing to the group of them. "As will the friends we've made planet-side and on the other drifts. And don't think for a second we'll allow the Corps any leeway whatsoever."

Asher crossed his arms. "None."

VanMeerten sneered. "I'll keep that in mind, Captain."

"See that you do, General."

VanMeerten leveled her gaze at Ren. "I hope this was worth it. I hope you got what you wanted."

Ren smiled. He had Asher at his side and Rowan and the crew at his back and his brother returned to him. Warmth and joy suffused him and nudged aside the fear and panic which had resided in his middle since the outset of his adventure.

"I did."

She nodded. "Have a good life, star host. I hope to never see you again."

"The feeling is mutual."

Rowan snapped her fingers and turned on her heel, ending the meeting. The rest of them followed. Ren cast one last look over his shoulder, then turned away, squared his shoulders, and put the Corps firmly behind him.

Asher followed suit. "It's done," he said, voice pitched low as they crossed the threshold out of the Corps offices. He blew out a breath, and his body relaxed. "It's done," he said again.

"It is," Ren agreed, taking Asher's hand, lacing their fingers. "And now we have credits, a pardon, and an honorable discharge to celebrate."

Asher smiled brightly; the worry that had creased his brow eased away. "That we do."

Ren laughed and, as they passed a viewing alcove, he paused in front of it, allowing the others to walk ahead, leaving him and Asher alone. Ren looked out at the darkness of space and the bright pinpricks of light stretching across the cluster. He pulled Asher close and kissed him, fervent and happy and free. Asher laughed into his mouth, and they kissed again and clung to each other. Filled with joy and relief, they celebrated in the darkened alcove with the stars their only witnesses.

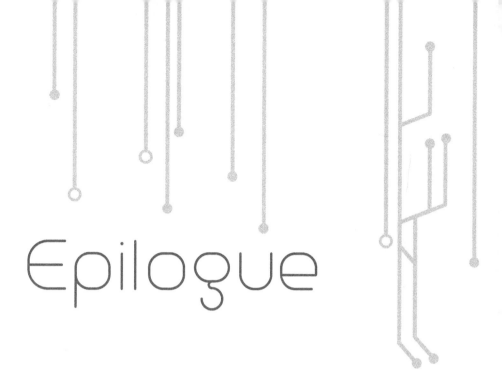

Epilogue

In the last six months, Ren had perfected the intricate dance of moving about on the drift during the rush times. He no longer bumped into anyone or allowed them to bump into him—Darby had laughed loud and long the first time Ren's credit chip had been stolen, but then spent a day teaching him how to be on the lookout for "people like her." He knew his way without getting lost or needing to bleed into the systems and find a map to his and Asher's home. He'd settled in here, in his environment and in his skin, and only had the occasional hiccup.

Ren slid between a couple arguing and ducked into the lit storefront for the best mechanic and tech support on the entire floor, maybe even the entire drift—him. Asher looked up from a vid screen where he argued with Rowan.

"Is that Ren?" Rowan's voice came over the screen. "Ask him. He'll settle it."

"I'm not asking Ren." Asher pouted. He tapped the toe of his boot and put his hands on his hips. "I'm right."

"You're not!" Lucas's voice sing-songed from off-screen. "Ask him. He's a duster after all."

Rowan raised an eyebrow.

Asher pinched the bridge of his nose. Ren furrowed his brow, stepped behind the counter, and nudged into the frame. His arm was flush against Asher's.

"What do you need to ask?"

Rowan tapped her mouth with her fingertips. "The tomato—fruit or vegetable? We picked a few up when we dropped off the cargo on Erden—Sorcha says hi by the way—and Penelope is on this kick about all of us consuming better nutrients, especially since she and Lucas have settled on this baby idea and…" Rowan trailed off. "You look unimpressed."

Ren laughed. "Are you serious? This is what you're arguing about?" He walked away, waving over his shoulder. "Tell Ollie I'll have those power sources ready for him next time you're docked."

"They're a vegetable," Rowan said in a fierce aside.

"Fruit," Asher said, arms crossed. "And you're a cog. I have to go."

"Fine. We'll be docking at your drift in a few days to pick up our next load. We'll discuss this more then."

"Fine." Asher switched off the screen.

Their place was merely a counter where Asher coordinated shipments for the *Star Stream* and Ren took orders for repairs. Their back room had a place for Ren to tinker and a set of steps to an upper level which housed their shared apartment. Asher kept his Phoenix Corps uniform in the closet, behind everything, and Ren kept a few trinkets—a shell from the beach by the lake and Liam's comic book—on the table by the bed. It wasn't much—a place to eat and sleep and the old couch from the ship with the spring that dug into Ren's back just so, but it was home.

"Hey," Asher said, following Ren into the back, "how'd it go?"

Ren sat in his chair, picked up a relay that had seen better days, and passed it back and forth between his hands. "Better. I like her, I think. Much more than the last one who didn't even believe people like me existed. She gave me some calming exercises that I hadn't tried before, and we talked."

"About?"

Ren shrugged. "Panic attacks. Nightmares. Millicent."

After the confrontation on the drift, Millicent disappeared. Liam tried to reach her once in a dream, with Ren present, but he couldn't find her. They didn't know what that meant, but guilt plagued Ren over the outcome of her defeat and capture. It was the way Darby had said, if the Corps wanted someone gone, they were gone.

He cleared his throat. "She'd like to meet my support system next time."

"Yeah?"

Ren nodded. "Yeah." And if Asher liked her, maybe he'd start seeing someone too, but one step at a time.

"Okay. I'm glad." Asher's mouth ticked up in a smile. "Sorcha says hi in case you didn't hear."

"Did Rowan say anything else? Did she see Liam?"

Asher walked all the way into the room and leaned against the wall. He was casual and well-rested and gorgeous. He'd let his hair grow and he'd taken to going on runs in the early morning hours while Ren stayed under the covers. "Sorcha is still leading all the villages. She has some new official title—I didn't really hear what it was—and Jakob works at her side. She saw Liam, said he helped unload the cargo. He looked good. Happy."

"Good."

When Vos returned to Erden, Sorcha was waiting for him, and he was arrested within minutes of his ship touching down, as was Abiathar. His army was given a choice, and to date, most of them have either left Erden or assimilated into the villages.

"The wedding is still on. We're expected, you know."

Ren tensed. "I know."

"You wouldn't miss Jakob's wedding, would you?"

Ren snorted.

"And it would be good for you to see Liam for yourself."

"I talk to Liam once a week, you know that." Liam's ability to visit in Ren's dreams had come in handy more than once, and Ren cherished the relationship they've developed. He hasn't been this close to his brother since they were small, before Ren's aspirations to leave the planet drove a wedge between them. "You're often there."

"Seeing him in dreams is different from seeing him in person."

"I know." Ren had a few hang-ups about going back to Erden: bad memories and bad feelings. Liam had gone home after their week-long stay on the resort drift and tugged Darby along with him. Darby didn't stay—too much dirt—and soon was back in the stars floating in and out of their lives as she pleased—sometimes assisting Rowan, sometimes helping Ren and Asher, but always looking for her next thrill. After she'd find it, she'd return to the family that had accepted her, either the *Star Stream* or to the drift and the small room she rented on the same floor as their shop. "I'll think about it. Let's see what the new therapist says. It's not for a few more months, right?"

Asher nodded. "Surprisingly adult of you."

That startled a laugh out of Ren and Asher's smile grew into a real one. "You were the one who was arguing with his sister about tomatoes. I don't want to hear anything about maturity from you."

Asher chuckled. "Point taken." He uncrossed his arms and nodded toward the mess on Ren's work desk. "By the way, you have a few new jobs. A ship that just docked is having trouble with its air recycler, and a restaurant needs something repaired in the kitchen."

"Is that your subtle way of telling me to get to work?"

Asher rolled his eyes. "That's my subtle way of reminding you that you're doing well here. Your business is steady. You have a caring and handsome boyfriend and a family of oddballs who love you. I know how your thoughts get after appointments sometimes, and you need reminders."

Ren smiled softly. "You have a handsome and caring boyfriend, too, you know. And he is very happy about where he is and how everything turned out."

"He better be," Asher said, abandoning all pretense and stalking across the small distance between them. He tilted Ren's face up and kissed him softly.

Ren pressed his smile to Asher's lips. Yes, he still had nightmares and panic attacks. Asher's shoulder ached on bad days. They fought about silly things and serious things, but always made an effort to make up. Their place was cramped, and their shower didn't always work, and there were days it was difficult for Ren to get out of bed and days when Asher stared at the uniform in the back of their closet.

But this—right here—Asher and him living together on a drift with their family safe and happy on ships and planets—that's what Ren always wanted.

And he finally had it.

Everything else was stardust.

Acknowledgments

WHEN I WROTE *THE STAR Host* back in 2015, I didn't have a plan other than to finish it and hopefully find it a publishing home. Fast forward three years later, and I've somehow managed to complete a trilogy. *Zenith Dream* is the culmination of years of hard work and countless hours of writing, rewriting, procrastinating, and editing. It's something I didn't know I could achieve and it's certainly a journey that I didn't take alone.

I would like to thank my husband, Keith, for all his support. Without him, I wouldn't have the ability to travel to conventions or have the time to create stories. He is my rock and the reason I'd survive a zombie apocalypse.

I'd like to thank my brother, Rob, who is my biggest fan. He buys copies of my books to give to friends and to his son's teachers. He is the first to congratulate me on my writing successes. He and my sister-in-law, Chris, are responsible for at least half of my sales.

I'd like to thank Carrie Pack, CB Lee, Michelle Osgood, Taylor Brooke, and Killian Brewer for being a great supportive team. They are the best group to experience a convention with and excellent writers. They're ready with advice and assistance especially when I need motivation or a brainstorming session.

I'd like to thank the organizers and authors of the Asheville Writer's Coffeehouse specifically Beth Revis, Jake Bible, Brian Rathbone, and Jamie Mason who are so kind and free with their knowledge and their advice. Also, Malaprop's bookstore is an amazing local resource and they've always been kind to me when scheduling author events.

Before I was a published author, I found a group of friends within the realm of fandom. I'd like to thank those friends who have stuck with me and still follow me on Twitter, specifically Kristinn for the cheerleading, and MJ for the help with naming characters. There are many more and I'd love to list them all, but I'm scared I'd miss someone, but please know, fandom friends, that your encouragement in my early writing days is one of the reasons I'm where I am today. I'd also like to acknowledge the College of William and Mary Science-Fiction & Fantasy club (Skiffy) that was a staple of my undergraduate life and introduced me to many different and wonderful aspects of the genre I love.

Lastly, this trilogy would not exist without Interlude Press and the team there who had faith in my work and the commitment to bring diverse stories to life. I'm asked a lot about why I choose to write stories with LGBTQ+ main characters—on panels, at conventions, by my family and friends—and I always have the same answer. Because I believe that everyone should have the opportunity to see themselves represented in fiction. I remember growing up and reading science-fiction and fantasy novels and reading comic books and loving Douglas Adams, and Robert Aspirin, and Robert Jordan, and Brian Jacques. But it wasn't until my brother gave me Mercedes Lackey's *Arrows of the Queen* that I read a fantasy novel with a female protagonist. I'll never forget that feeling of realizing that women could and did have a place in sci-fi and fantasy stories. My hope is that my stories can give that same feeling to a teen or young adult who is searching for a representation of themselves in the stories they love.

About the Author

F.T. LUKENS IS AN AWARD-WINNING author of Young Adult fiction who got her start by placing second out of ten thousand entries in a fan-community writing contest. A sci-fi enthusiast, F.T. is a longtime member of her college's science-fiction club. She holds degrees in Psychology and English Literature and has a love of cheesy television shows, superhero movies, and writing. F.T. lives in North Carolina with her husband, three kids, and three cats.

Her novel, *The Rules and Regulations for Mediating Myths & Magic*, won many awards, including the 2017 Foreword INDIES Gold Award for Young Adult Fiction and the 2017 IBPA Benjamin Franklin Gold Award for Best Teen Fiction.

Zenith Dream is the final installment to her Broken Moon series, which also includes *The Star Host* (2016) and *Ghosts & Ashes* (2017).

an imprint of interlude**press**

@duet**books**

Twitter | Tumblr

*For a reader's guide to **Zenith Dream** and book club prompts, please visit duetbooks.com.*

also by **F.T. Lukens**

The Star Host

Broken Moon, Book 1

Ren grew up listening to his mother tell stories about the Star Hosts—mythical people possessed by the power of the stars. Captured by a nefarious Baron, Ren discovers he may be something out of his mother's stories. He befriends Asher, a member of the Phoenix Corps. Together, they must master Ren's growing power and try to save their friends while navigating the growing attraction between them.

ISBN (print) 978-1-941530-72-6 | (eBook) 978-1-941530-73-3

Ghosts & Ashes

Broken Moon, Book 2

Three months after the events of *The Star Host*, Ren is living under the watchful eyes of the Phoenix Corps, fearing he's traded one captor for another. His relationship with Asher fractures, and Ren must return to his home planet if he has any hope of regaining humanity. There, he discovers knowledge that puts everyone's allegiance to the test.

ISBN (print) 978-1-945053-18-4 | (eBook) 978-1-945053-31-3

The Rules and Regulations for Mediating Myths & Magic

IPBA Benjamin Franklin Gold Award Winner

When Bridger Whitt learns his eccentric employer is actually an intermediary between the human world and its myths, he finds himself in the center of chaos: The myth realm is growing unstable, and now he's responsible for helping his boss keep the real world from ever finding out.

ISBN (print) 978-1-945053-24-5 | (eBook) 978-1-945053-38-2